UNDENIABLE

UNDENIABLE

Writers Respond to Climate Change

VARIOUS AUTHORS

Selected by
Leah Angstman, Laura Brzyski, S. E. Carson,
Anthony Clemons, Jen Corrigan, Summer Kurtz,
Steph Post, Eric Shonkwiler, and Jennifer Young

Curated and Edited by
Leah Angstman

Alternating Current Press
Boulder, Colorado

Undeniable
Writers Respond to Climate Change
Various Authors
©2020 Alternating Current Press

Alternating Current
Boulder, Colorado
alternatingcurrentarts.com

ISBN: 978-1-946580-15-3
First Edition: March 2020

*"We do not inherit the earth from our ancestors;
we borrow it from our children."*
—North American Indian Proverb

TABLE
of Contents

Poetry

LETTER

In the Alternating Current office, we joked that we'd have to give people a warning not to read this book all in one sitting because it's too depressing. We mused about how much the shipping would cost if we sent a copy to every member of the U.S. House and Senate. We joked about hoping the book would be obsolete and outdated in a couple years, when we finally had a new administration to effect change—how we'd look back on this anthology as a relic of how close we came to the apocalypse.

But they aren't jokes—not really. Don't read this book in one sitting, or you'll suffer from climate trauma; Congress are the people who need to read this anthology the most; and this book won't become obsolete, even if we get a change of administration, because it's too late for that. Dark humor is our way of dealing with the grief, confronting the truth, and accepting that the U.S. government won't do enough to help, so we have to pull more than our own weight, do more than our fair share, tell our stories over and over again in the face of corporate, lobbying, ignorant, and misinformed adversity, while bracing ourselves for the worst to come.

Within these pages, you'll find a lot of dark humor—a very valid response—and you'll even find some sparks of utter optimism among the grief, but mostly you'll find the horror, the shock, the devastation, the sadness you'd expect from such a heavy topic. There are the reoccurring subjects: fossil fuel overuse, wasted water, sinking backyards, disappearing whales, food shortages, new bacteria, carbon, pipelines, drought, the disproportionately affected based on race, religion, ideology, wealth disparity, circumstances of birth and location. Women talk about not wanting to have kids born into this dying world; immigrants talk about the refugee crises to follow; and everyone rages against the corporations taking advantage of the land's vulnerability in order to turn a profit. There are the horrifying ladies you know by name: Sandy, Katrina, Irene—and there are the obscurities and anomalies that are slicing us open by a thousand slow cuts. What will surprise you, though, is how much this devastation has caused people to pause and reflect on the absolute beauty of this world, even in its darkest hurricanes of chaos.

Featuring 65 pieces of nonfiction, fiction, hybrid, and poetry by 52 authors, this anthology is a document of our times—from the anger and righteousness of those left behind, to the fear for the bleak world we're leaving in the hands of those still to come. It is our hope that this anthology becomes obsolete, but it is our knowledge of a greedy and careless humanity that knows, with sorrow and certainty, that these pieces will remain timeless.

NEW TROPICAL PATTERN

Michael Garrigan

I was born on a ridge that now fills with water
a few times each summer. Grass
would turn brown, tight with thirst
but now stays lush with drink.   Mushrooms grow.

We gather at bridges to feel the spray
of water crashing into cement
        and to be close to the torrent
        of a new tropical pattern.

Handfuls of good soil
        pushed
                down
                        into the Chesapeake
soon farms will be riverbeds, oxbows of grain silos, and rotting barns.

It's not that I have to worry about the sump pump
        always running. The hoses leak. I duct tape.
It's that the forests have become muddy. Trees shorter. Water deeper.
        I do not know where to go.

NOT TO GO THE WAY OF THE LOWEST OF THE SOLOMON ISLANDS

Kelly R. Samuels

Latitude 1.352083,
Longitude 103.8198360000001,
Elevation 58m

Purchase the far-off forested parcel, acres in need
of clearing. Lay your claim now, dreaming of it broken
into segments. This, yours. That, mine.

Your grandfather said, *Only land matters.* Bought fields
to the north and to the west, even the dip
where the groundwater swelled and lay fetid. Even some
of the marsh, where you thought no road could go.
Little money in the bank, but this.

So, yes, he would approve
of the floating structure, too, like the suspended raft
in the one of many lakes that summer, the one
you would not swim out to.

And of the hollowed-out land, dug even below
what threatens. The cave that others
only nominally related to you were scared of.

Of reclamation. Of sand
from the sea bottom, the rock and rubble,
the blasted concrete, crushed granite. All you now stand on:
some sort of invention. What was not, now is.

Yes, he would sanction.
Say, *It's ours for the taking*
and reshaping.

PLANETARIUM

Stephanie Devine

They are born on the edge of winter, when it is still cold, biting, but the icicles on the trees are dripping, wet. We wrap them in scraps of our wedding clothes—the girl in white silk, the boy in black wool. We'd worried there might be two, when, despite everything, her belly grew big. But it's one thing to worry and another to face it. When she won't take the second, the boy, I carry them both to the cracked window to watch water slip from the leaves in heavy drops, and I tell them their first story about the way we used to be. About two-foot-tall cake, orbs of red fruit floating past on plates of silver, people screaming in song. Outside, the piles of brown snow are thawing, and all the sky is a single cloud.

We are always careful with what we tell them. That's the deal we have. When we first realized she was with child, my wife waded into the river and lowered her head beneath the gray surface. I returned from a trap and found her there, dragged her out, legs only just kicking. I told her, maybe it was time for children again. Maybe this was God's way of saying it's time. She didn't speak for three weeks, maybe four, who's to say anymore. When she finally did, she said, *Only if we do it right.*

So when they are out hunting and spot, for the first time, high above the cracked pavement, posters of giant tomatoes, the color of blood, and they run home to tell us, we tell them the story of the fat farmer and his rows and rows of plants, each exactly—perilously—the same. We tell them how the fat farmer was greedy and vile and sent his clones to everybody in the land.

What's a clone? they ask. Were they bad for you?

Yes, we say. Poisoned.

And later when, digging through a pile of trash, they pull out an old advertisement for beer, we point out the people of the old time and say look how strange and smooth their skin is. Rusted orange sliced with luminous, painful white. These people never worked, we say. They only wasted. The children nod their heads in agreement.

At night, after they go to sleep, we lie with dirt lining our fingernails and tell each other different stories.

Microwave popcorn, my wife whispers. Butter and salt.

Sushi, I say, with fluffy, sticky rice.

With salmon, she whispers back. Pink and slick.

One day when the boy, almost a teenager, pitches a bone off his plate and onto the sinking floor, we retell them the story of the selfish woman who tossed her mug out the window after each drink.

And what happened to her, I ask the boy?

The pile of mugs got so big it collapsed, he sighs.

By now they know the stories by heart.

Yeah, says the girl, smiling. And it buried her alive.

That night my wife and I play a darker game, and each word seems to fall from space.

The girl? she asks.

Maybe a politician, I say.

Yes, she says. Or a lawyer.

Same thing, I say. Or was.

What about the boy? I ask, and she turns to me, rustling dust out of the blanket.

She whispers, almost nothing: You.

Sometimes my wife gets very tired, and sometimes she coughs up red, and it's those nights I lead the children up to the hilltop and teach them what I know about stars. I point out the Big Dipper, the Little, Orion, Leo. I make up new stories to go with them. The humble hunter, the quiet beast. Did you do this with your dad? they want to know. We have not taught them the word grandfather.

I tell them that, in the old days, our atmosphere was so saturated with light, the burning bulbs of our architecture blotted out the stars. They mouth this new term—architecture—with uncertain lips. I say we had to invent theaters with screens that mimicked the sky, just so we could remember what it looked like. That's how I learned the world, I say. In a theater.

Never like this? they ask, bodies sinking into the wet grass.

No, I say, never.

When they are fourteen, their mother passes in the night. I roll over to reach, and her arm is ice beneath my fingertips. Minutes later, I am running, panting into the dark.

I'll go back, eventually, because I must. But on this night, I splash into the river, which has passed from gray to olive, knees jumping high, until I slap onto my back. Lifting my eyes to the black sky, I see that we have not prepared them. We have taught them to survive, not to be as we were. But we've not prepared them for what they'll become. We've not addressed the instincts that scream from behind cell walls, the voices in each of us that breathe: *Even the stars belong to you.* I can make out Gemini, barely. Stellar bodies glowing against a shrinking perimeter.

I want to answer every question they have. Confess to my constellation of lies. Tell them that, of course, I am the fat farmer, and their mother the selfish woman, and what's worse, I wish we could be again. That while our bellies howled, and we learned the shapes of our stomachs in their emptiness, their mother and I whispered food to each other to sing ourselves to sleep. That it was we who destroyed the world, and we would give anything for another shot at it.

And maybe I will tell them someday, when it's my turn to descend into this shimmering, uninterrupted sky, under millions of unspoiled lights, that what I miss most of all is breathing in the seventy-one-degree, recycled air of the planetarium, leaning back in the seats, and staring up into an impossibly large universe.

WHAT MY MARCH CRABAPPLE DOESN'T KNOW

Leah Angstman

The world my window sees might be all there is to come,
to tell my crabapple it's too early for these buds:
not yet, not yet, please wait a bit. Ice will find you peeking.

But to teach patience when I have none is illusory.
I might as well teach the moon to swing low into
horizons and peter there, her light to cease between fences.
We none of us know patience enough to tell this.

We're careless with future selves, like we'll be here
to change our minds that day, to take it back
when we've decided who won,
words tossed at a younger sibling.

I can't look to a winter-springing tree without sorrow; she's too soon.
They say autumn is the time for dying,
when strength grows hollow and drops her leaves,
eyes pale to gray while color trails from them,

but I say it is the spring now:
when the early birth tattles of deaths to follow,
all coming springs too dry too brown
for this one too soon too green.

EXTINCT

Stacey Forrester

Ex·tinct
ikˈstiNG(k)t/
adjective
adjective: extinct
1.   (of a species, family, or other larger group) having no living members.

Part One: Thriving

Since I have been alive, at least 23 species have gone extinct. We got self-ish, and we stopped caring, and in a blink of a geologic eye, they disappeared. I read that in the 1980s, there was this bird that was native to just one of the Hawaiian Islands, the Kauaʻi ʻōʻō (*Moho braccatus*). The article I read had a picture of the Kauaʻi ʻōʻō, and I remember it clearly, its shape bright and sharp. A year after you were born, a male of these birds was recorded singing a mating call, and by the next year, it was never heard or seen again. "At least we had captured his last love song," they say. The Southern Resident Orcas are teetering on extinction. "Endangered," they say. No Resident Orcas were born the year I was born, nor the year you were born, in case you were curious. I know you are probably not, but knowing these things and mapping them out is how I place myself and the things I love beside markers in this life.

I have felt the Orcas inside me since I was very young, decades before I met you, back when the population was healthy. When I was small, I would mimic how they roll and how they play while I swam in the water at my grandparents' beach house. I would draw myself beside them in my journals, page after page, my mom says. I have lived this long and have never seen one with my eyes, which you used to say was almost funny considering I grew up on an island surrounded by the Salish Sea. I have never seen one, yet know them in the way that you know others with whom you live in the same home.

Part Two: At Risk

The Southern Residents are not like other Orcas. They do not hunt mammals. They are more playful than the Transients. I read once that it was this playfulness made them targets for humans who wanted to pen them like property back in the 80s. We don't do that now because we know that animals are better left wild, and if I learned anything from my time with you, it would be that this sentiment applies to humans, as well. We keep them wild, but we poison their natural homes with oil and noise. The Orcas just want to be free and protected in waters of the Pacific Northwest, the only home they know, and that is just one of the parallels I share with them. If you and I were out for dinner, and you happened to ask who my favorite Resident Orca was, my eyes would get that sudden intense sparkle that they get when I talk about things I love, and I would gesture with my hands a little more than I had been five minutes prior, and probably spill some of my drink while telling you that it would be a tie between Scarlett (R.I.P.) and Oreo. This dinner and that sparkle won't happen, though, at least not between us.

Part Three: Endangered

The world is burning, and it hurts to breathe in summer, and we are choking the life out of all that we have been given. For these reasons and a half dozen others, I knew as soon as the pink lines showed up that I couldn't, in good faith, accept the parting gift left on the doorstep of our former home. Feminism has taught me that no one benefits from using metaphor when you mean biology, even when poetry wants you to, so all this to say that somewhere toward the end of our timeline, I was pregnant and then wasn't. We were at risk for a while, and then suddenly neither of us was capable of loving or protecting the other, and so we crossed a line we could not come back from. I found out once you were already halfway out the door, so I made the Choice on my own. It was going to be a secret, between the whales and me, but I was always the worst at hiding from you, so then it wasn't a secret anymore. Seven days before my appointment, I sunk from the toilet to the cold tile floor, and I inspected the grout. I noticed an old razor of yours that had slipped under the vanity, and I held it close like I had found treasure. I lay on the floor of the silent house listening to the last love song recorded deep inside my cells, sharp.

Part Four: Extinct

In the rare moments when I ponder my passing on the role of mother, I think about the Orcas. I think hard and acknowledge that I can't imagine raising a daughter to whom I would have to tell bedtime stories about things I love in the past tense. I would use my maps and point out landmarks, and I would say "used to" when I spoke of you and when I spoke of the whales. Her eyes would not know to light up when someone asked her about the whales, or her parents' love, and she would probably not list her two or three favorite Resident Orcas because there would be no more to name.

I read that the rules of biology state that extinction is the absolute end of an organism or of a group of organisms, most often an entire species. The moment of extinction is generally considered to be the "official" death of the last individual of the species, but as often happens, the capacity to breed and recover was likely lost before this point. I don't know if I need to explain it, but a Resident Orca could never be replaced with, say, a Transient Orca, and for sure not a Humpback. A whale is a whale, yes, like a boy is a boy, but he is not you, and biology doesn't work like that. Months have passed, and I saw your new love, her face close enough to mine to make it familiar, and that fact is positioned bright and sharp inside of me. The same but different, either way, not replaced.

Part Five: The Aftermath

This summer, a mama Orca from our own endangered pod balanced her dead calf on her head for three weeks before letting it sink to the bottom of the ocean. I am not going to attempt to appropriate her profound loss in any way, and I am trying to avoid words like death and life in relation to what is ultimately my capital -C- Choice, but I can say with great certainty that had I seen her grief before becoming aware of my own tiny stowaway, I would be a little less fazed by her display. I was glued to the CBC for days and weeks, following her tour obsessively and feeling her loss in my belly the same way I had felt life there. The summer came and went, full of moments where I would almost let your memory drown, but then something would happen, like me stumbling upon a single sock of yours when moving a piece of furniture, or finding two other versions of the last birthday poem I wrote you in the corner of my hard drive. I would then pick the memories back up for another kilometer of the journey.

Epilogue: Rebirth

The mourning will last for eleven months. The spark, my own cells, and their entanglement to yours takes time to pass, much how it took time to be. When I grieve, it will look like this: me showing a tiny girl how to float in the saltwater at my grandparents', the way I was taught. I will teach her to stick her little round belly to the sky while I float close by. In this grief, we are touching heads while we float, my inky hair tangling with her strawberry-blond, the dark water cradling her. I will miss this moment that did not happen, even though I know that, at this rate, the waters will likely get too toxic to safely hold anything I love. Sometimes, in this same dark place, I will feel careless and I will feel selfish and I will be all too aware that I will one day have no living members in my own lineage.

I will wade through this part, and I will swim out of this mess and be just fine because I have a lot of obscure skills, like being able to hold my breath for a long time. I will wake up halfway into the twelfth month and take a boat to my childhood home. The boat will not be allowed to leave the port because three Resident Orcas will block the way. My insides and the ship's engine will slowly rattle to life as the sun is setting, and I will see that the littlest whale of the three is familiar in the way I know myself. The whales will swim beside us until we reach the open sea, and this will be enough time for the littlest to show me that she is loved and free, spending her days rolling her round belly to the sky and her nights floating and sleeping in the arms of the ocean we both get to call home.

RECONNAISSANCE

Wendi White

At times I glimpse their shadows shifting
between the trees shorn of leaves.
Befeathered, bemused, they wait
and watch. Four hundred years later
in the half light of solstice, they waver
on the shores of the James, the Lafayette,
the Elizabeth to see if *tassantassas*[1] still squat
upon the land, if the intruders have enough corn
to last one more winter, if they will survive until the dogwoods
sugar the forest with white and pink.

Chickahominy, Nansemond, Mattaponi, Keoghatan,
ghosts conquered but not cowed by coal trains
that carve their fields, cars that clog rude highways,
landfills that leach into the tidewater.

At each new moon, ever-present though erased,
rivers rise higher, and manicured lawns erode
by inches. Perfectly pruned boxwoods shrivel
at the touch of creeping brine. Waterfront property
plummets while Virginia's gentlemen pour their last
rounds of fine whiskey only plunder could afford.

The scouts appraise the strangers' waning strength.
They report to Powhatan whose imperial dreams
lacked the English King's scope, but nonetheless
were granted some acreage in history. "Take heart,
Great Chief. Here the strangers first made land,
but here they sink in the mudflats; they fall back to the sea."

---

1. *Algonquian word for "strangers," used to describe the Jamestown settlers.*

WHALE FALL

Dionne Custer Edwards

We take for granted bloat. The keeping of things.
Gas strangles spare bad air in the jaws.

Whales offer a strange and precious work.
Swell with carbon until they fall,
so we might breathe without distraction.

The ease of breathing is well-fed.
Few consequences thrive in pretending.

A ship drifts. Turns its bow into a dagger.
Shortens the life of a balloon.

Denizens on the seafloor feast,
or scatter pieces of bone
and flesh. Those that float and scavenge

find sanctuary before end times. A cold seep
pooling toxins and small living things.

While the rest of us wait.
Stare from the sidelines as curious or critic.

Wealth disparity looks like whale against barge,
a metal and skin wreckage, an ocean.

CHEZ MAGNIFIQUE

Matt Tompkins

Tucked down an alley in Proctor City's once-stately Old Quarter, the small café Chez Magnifique operated business-as-usual right through the Great Drought. It never shut down, never seemed to run out of anything, and never raised its prices. Customers could still get a large slice of carrot cake for $4.25 and a latte for $3.50. The service was fast and courteous, and the patrons were unfailingly civil.

"Delightful," said Mr. James, sipping from a chipped china cup.

"Marvelous," said Ms. White, dabbing orange-colored crumbs from the folds at the corners of her mouth.

"Delectable," said Mr. Vellum, gesticulating with his fork.

"Magnifique!" said Mrs. Gallow, who added a theatrical wink.

All four chuckled voluminously at the small, well-worn joke until their laughs resolved into thick, raspy wheezes. They were dressed formally—the men wore threadbare, three-piece tweed suits, and the women wore faded satin gowns. The customers, like their clothing, appeared advanced in age, balding and blotchy, but meticulously cared for.

At the next table a small boy sat with his mother. Theirs were unfamiliar faces in a café peopled solely by regulars, and their manners and mode of dress were casual by comparison.

"What's the matter, Jeffy? Don't you like your cookie?"

The boy's face was squashed like a rotted pumpkin. He raked his tongue with a napkin. The mother looked puzzled. A peanut butter cookie missing only one child-sized bite sat on a stoneware plate in front of the boy.

"If you don't eat your cookie, I will," said the mother.

She picked up the cookie and held it in front of her mouth. The boy did not react. The mother took a small bite from the edge of the cookie; her mouth distorted involuntarily, and her throat convulsed. She spat the bit of cookie into a napkin and waved to the waiter, who stood behind the counter.

"Excuse me!" the mother called.

"Yes?" The waiter turned to face the mother but didn't move from behind the counter. "Is something the matter, ma'am?"

"Yes," said the mother. "Something's wrong with this cookie. I think it's gone bad."

"I don't see how," said the waiter. "It was baked fresh this morning."

"Still," said the mother. "There's something off. See for yourself."

The waiter moved reluctantly from behind the counter to the table. He placed the fingertips of his right hand lightly on the tattered tablecloth and stared down at the cookie on its plate. "It looks fine," he said.

"Try it," the mother urged. She pushed the plate toward the waiter.

"After you've eaten from it?" the waiter said. "Honestly, ma'am, I have no idea what sorts of sicknesses you and your child might be carrying." He raised an eyebrow. "No offense," he added.

"Then try another from the same batch. Or break a piece from an edge where we didn't bite. For heaven's sake, you don't want to be serving bad cookies, do you?"

The waiter spoke between pursed lips. "Very well," he said. He broke a crumb-sized morsel from an unbitten edge of the cookie and placed it in his mouth. As he bit down and chewed, an expression of concentration crossed his face. There was a grinding sound from between the waiter's teeth. "It tastes fine to me," he said. His eyes squinted, but the rest of his face was neutral, impassive.

"It's not fine," the woman said. "We'd like something else instead."

"Are you sure?" the waiter asked. "If you don't like this perfectly good cookie, maybe this place just doesn't suit you. Perhaps you would be more content elsewhere."

"Excuse me?" she said. "We're paying customers here. Have I done something wrong? Are we unwelcome?"

"I'm just trying to be helpful."

"Let us have a slice of that cheesecake, would you?" The woman pointed to a glass pastry case at the end of the service counter.

"Certainly," the waiter said.

Behind the counter, he pulled a plate from the top of a tall stack and took a tarnished pie server from a bin of utensils by the small sink. He reached into the case through an open space where a pane was missing. He placed the cheesecake delicately, ceremoniously, on a plate, then walked back to the woman and dropped the plate on the table. He plunked a fork down, so it bounced slightly before settling.

"Thank you," said the woman.

"Certainly," said the waiter.

The woman lifted the fork and perforated the cheesecake. It gave a gritty resistance that reminded her of the cookie. She raised the fork to her mouth and closed her lips around it. Again, the grimace. Again, the convulsion. Again, she spit the clump of grainy pulp into a napkin.

The woman looked at the waiter. He was staring back at her, waiting.

"This is bad, too," said the woman. "Just like the cookie."

"I don't know what to tell you," said the waiter. "The other customers seem to be satisfied. Maybe it's just you."

"Okay," said the woman. "I can take a hint. We're leaving."

"Have a pleasant day," said the waiter, tonelessly.

The woman took her son's hand, and they walked out together, the woman shaking her head, the boy still grimacing, his lip curled tightly up under his nose. The waiter stood behind the counter wiping his hands on a dishtowel. He watched their backs as they left.

Mrs. Gallow, still seated with her friends, turned in her chair and addressed the waiter. "Why, whatever was the matter with them, dear?"

"Seems they didn't like the food."

"Didn't like it? Why, that's preposterous. Unheard of. Un—"

Mrs. Gallow's remark was interrupted by a stifled gagging sound, followed by a coughing fit. It was a wet, hacking cough. The waiter looked on blandly and waited for it to subside. When it did, she continued speaking as if nothing had happened.

"After all, Marcel, everyone knows that since, well, since the rains stopped, this is the only place in town where the food is any good at all. Anyone with a functioning tastebud agrees."

Mrs. Gallow's tablemates nodded in agreement, releasing little puffs of white, powdery makeup from their collars.

"Thank you, Mrs. Gallow," said the waiter. "You know just how to nurse my ego back to health."

Mrs. Gallow and the waiter shared a smile that almost broke into laughter, but didn't quite make it.

"I should have known better," the woman said. She had led her son by the hand out the door and then out of the dim alleyway, back into the late-afternoon sun. "I just should have known better," she repeated. "Should have known it was too good to be true."

The woman's name was Dolores Blunt. She was thirty-two, a single mother of her single son, Jeffrey, who was five. Dolores had spotted the inconspicuous signboard for Chez Magnifique as Jeffrey and she walked through the Old Capital, a part of the city unfamiliar to them. Jeffrey had just been immunized at an improvised clinic set up in an abandoned storefront, and Dolores had wanted to buy him a treat for his patience and bravery. She felt robbed, duped, by the disappointing experience. Typically, no one promised her anything. She'd learned to expect nothing, to be content with what she received. But this—the raising and dashing of her hopes, however small, however low the stakes—felt like an unfathomable betrayal.

Dolores and Jeffrey had taken a convoluted, two-hour, four-transfer bus ride to get there, and it would take them as long, on the same set of buses, to get back.

"Come on, Jeffy, we need to get home."

"But I'm hungry."

"I know, sweetie. We'll have dinner when we get there."

They walked three more blocks to the station, arriving just in time to climb onto a departing bus. Through the windows they watched the city lurch into motion and slink slowly by. More than half of the storefronts were vacant or showed signs of distress—cracked panes, faded going-out-of-business signs, steel bars, chain-link, padlocks. There wasn't much, and what there was, was tenaciously protected.

Dolores and Jeffrey sat close together watching the scenery. Often, Jeffrey would reach over, tug the frayed hem of Dolores' sweater, and say, "Mommy, look!" Dolores would reply, "Look at what, Jeffy?" even when it was obvious what the boy was pointing at. This was her way of urging him to describe, to develop his language, to make his own sense of what he saw. After a while Jeffrey dozed against Dolores' arm. She continued to watch the buildings and people trickle by. Each time they reached a transfer, Dolores lifted Jeffrey from his seat. Finally, the last bus pulled into the station near their home.

"Wake up, baby," she said. "It's our stop."

They stepped off the bus and quickly walked the three blocks home. Dolores was anxious and tugged at Jeffrey's hand. When they reached their building, Dolores keyed into the exterior door. She had her keys out ahead of time, so the two could duck in quickly, spending as little time as possible standing still on the street. When the building door clicked shut behind them, Dolores relaxed some. They walked down the long hallway to their apartment where Dolores keyed in again and then shut, latched, and bolted the door behind them. Her shoulders dropped, and she took, without realizing it, her first deep breath in hours.

"I'm still hungry," said Jeffrey.

"I know, sweetie," said Dolores. "I'll make us dinner."

Dolores went to the cupboard and pulled out two foil packets, each the size and shape of a slice of bread. She took down two bowls, ripped open the packets, and dumped out the contents: gray powder that looked like household dust. A synthetic macronutrient blend—more nourishing than dust, but not much tastier, and the only thing in the house. From the refrigerator, Dolores took a small jug of water. She measured a few spoonsful into each of the bowls and stirred until the dust was moistened into a pasty muck. All the while, she shook her head, trying to dislodge the memory of the café. She wondered whether she had imagined it, whether the whole thing had been a sort of urban mirage, summoned by a cocktail of austerity, nostalgia, and desire. But, no: the anger, tying knots in her gut, was very real.

"Dinner, Jeffy."

She set the two bowls and two clean spoons on the folding table where two plastic chairs sat waiting. Jeffrey came in from the living room, his coat and shoes still on. They sat down, picked up their spoons, and ate together in silence.

In the small commercial kitchen, through the velvet-curtained doorway behind the counter of Chez Magnifique, Marcel, the waiter, stood surveying his work in the glow of a single bare lightbulb. He stood over a stainless-steel table scattered with cookie cutters, pie plates, cake tins, loaf pans, gelatin molds, icing bags, and other baking implements. The table was pushed against a bare cinderblock wall. On the wall above the table, there was a shelf, and on the shelf were tubs, each one filled with a thick, heavy, grainy paste. Using an ice cream scoop, Marcel spooned out the pastes and packed them into the various molds, squeezed them through the piping bags. He shaped them to resemble cookies, cakes, pies, and other pastries.

Marcel made the paste himself. He made it from sand, with a minimal amount of water added. Not the precious, potable water that was government-rationed, but the murky wash water, which was less closely guarded, and came at less of a premium. He got the sand from farmers whose desertified land was good for nothing else and had not produced crops for several seasons. They parted with the sandy soil for free, or nearly free— *dirt cheap*, Marcel sometimes joked, generally receiving a dry and lifeless response from the farmers. The only stipulation was that Marcel had to go and pick it up himself, which he did once a week with a borrowed cart that he pulled behind his careworn bicycle, riding beyond the city to the desolate rural outlands.

At the café, Marcel had a small but devoted clientele. For the most part, they either had been, or now claimed they had been, members of the socio-economic elite—former aristocrats of the city. Now, they folded themselves into his chairs every day to tell each other grandiose, meandering anecdotes and eat cakes made of sand.

When Marcel had finished shaping and arranging, he covered his creations with damp towels and placed steel storage tubs upside-down over top to seal in the moisture and keep them fresh. This kind of effort seemed almost perverse, but his livelihood depended upon people buying into his illusions, and even people who ate dirt wanted to eat the best-looking dirt they could get.

When Marcel's preparations were complete, he pulled a chain to douse the light. Then he stepped out into the back-alley darkness and swung the door shut and locked behind him. The city no longer supplied electricity to the lampposts, so even on the sidewalks, the night was dense with deep, shadowy pockets. At irregular intervals, coffee-can lanterns burned in shop windows, the only visible signs of life.

Marcel walked two blocks and ducked into one of the firelit storefronts. The proprietress was ancient, and she handled the money and goods with veiny, arthritic claws. Her eyes shone from deep-sunk caves. Marcel assumed a son or grandson must have been waiting in the back room—surely a woman in her condition could not be tending the place alone; she would be too tempting a target for thieves.

Using money from the day's sales, money drastically devalued but not quite worthless yet, Marcel bought a small paper packet of cornmeal and a thumb-sized, waxy nugget of lard. Where such scarce commodities as grain and lard came from, even in such tiny quantities, Marcel did not know, did not ask, tried not even to think about, and suspected his ignorance might be for the best.

As he walked along, he heard faint wails and banging echoes in the distance. Finally, he arrived at a dilapidated apartment block, where he turned a key to unlock two deadbolts and then the doorknob itself, but the door only opened two inches; it was chained from within.

"Pssst!" said Marcel.

"Who is it?" said a small, high-pitched voice from inside the door.

"It's me, your papa!" said Marcel. "Who else?"

"My papa who?" said the little voice.

"Your papa, Marcel!"

"My papa Marcel who?" The little voice giggled. It was a game Marcel's young son, Michel, played often.

"Okay, little one, open up," said Marcel. "Papa is tired."

The door closed to a crack, then swung open to reveal little Michel standing in patched red pajamas in the darkened room, grinning. As Marcel entered and shut the door behind him, Michel wrapped his arms around his father's knees and squeezed tight.

"Where's your nana?" asked Marcel.

There was a soft glow from down the apartment's central hallway. "Snoring in her chair."

Marcel made a game of walking around with his son latched to his legs. He waddled like a penguin to the kitchen where he set down the packets of cornmeal and shortening and lit a burner on a small, portable, propane stove. He took a pan from a hook on the wall and put the small hunk of lard in the pan. While the fat melted, he scooped out the cornmeal, added a small amount of clean water, and kneaded it together. Marcel formed the meal-mush into patties and dropped them, one at a time, into the larded pan. When the cakes had browned, Marcel took a towel from a shelf nearby. He folded it twice, set it on the counter and set the pan, still hot from the burner, onto the towel. He picked Michel up and sat the boy on the counter next to the pan of corncakes. Marcel took one of the cakes, blew across it, and handed it to Michel, who received it eagerly with both hands. Marcel took a cake for himself and chewed it slowly while the boy devoured the first one, then two more, before looking suddenly sleepy.

Marcel carried his son down the hall and put him to bed, then returned to the kitchen to wrap up the last of the corncakes, which sat cold in the pan.

"Gout," said Mr. James. "It must be. I'm convinced of it."

"Do you think?" asked Ms. White. She pursed her lips. "I'm certainly not a doctor," she said. "I suppose I'll take your word for it."

Mrs. Gallow had not shown up at Chez Magnifique that morning. Her friends sat around their usual table, speculating about her absence.

"I must agree," said Mr. Vellum, nibbling at a slice of cake. "What else would she be suffering from but gout? It's obvious: too much rich, decadent food!"

"Indeed!" said Mr. James. His face twitched into a strained smile. He looked over at Marcel, who was working quietly behind the counter. "Isn't that right, Marcel? Too much rich food around here?"

Marcel nodded and reflected Mr. James' uneasy smile. Mr. James coughed into his handkerchief—a brown, grainy clump appeared alongside a fresh, wet spot of red. He drew the cloth away and stuffed it in his vest pocket. Marcel nodded, his forehead tight, and then he turned away, wiping his hands on a dishtowel.

Just then, the café door swung wide and slammed against the wall. Dolores stood silhouetted in the doorway. Marcel looked up. At first, he didn't recognize her.

"Good morning. Welcome to Chez— Oh," he said. "Welcome back. I'm surprised to see you again."

"What's good today?" she said.

"I— everything is good," he said. "I made it myself, fresh this morning."

"Well, then, I'll take one of those, and one of those, and one of those," Dolores said, pointing at three of the trays in the display case.

Marcel hesitated, then nodded and bowed slightly. "Very good," he said.

He kept his eyes on Dolores as he plated the pastries and handed them to her on a dented, tarnished metal tray. She took them to a corner table and sat facing the wall, away from the counter and the group of regulars. She surveyed the collection in front of her: a slice of orangish carrot cake, a square of dark fudge, and a tan-and-brown éclair—all perfectly formed in their palette of earth tones. Dolores reached out and pressed a forefinger into the carrot cake. Its point crumbled like an arid cliffside. She poked the cake again and again, until the whole slice had eroded away, revealing not the sponginess of cake, but the granularity of sand. She picked up the fudge square, palmed it, and closed her hand around it, making a fist. She watched the corners ooze between her fingers. She rubbed the pads of her thumb and forefinger together and felt the grit, heard the substance grinding against itself. The éclair she laid flat on one hand and then pressed and slid the other hand over top of it, crumbling it apart, causing bits to rain down onto the plates and the tray in front of her. She took a moment to gaze at the ruins before she picked up the tray and returned to the counter. Marcel was facing the sink, his back to her.

"I'm finished," she said.

Marcel turned and looked at Dolores, then down at the tray. He frowned. "And, how was everything?"

"A little dry," said Dolores. "Suppose I could get something to wash it down?"

Marcel searched Dolores' face. "Of course," he said. "What would you like?"

"A latte."

"Very good," he said. "Go ahead to your table, and I'll bring it out."

"No thanks," she said. "I'd like to watch you pour it."

Marcel stared at Dolores for a long moment, at a loss: She was challenging him. He leaned forward and motioned her closer to the counter. "Would you like a tour of the kitchen?" he said. "I can show you where I make everything. Since you seem so interested."

Dolores had the instant, horrifying vision of being bludgeoned with a rolling pin. But he was a slight man and she was still strong; she could manage him. She walked around the end of the counter and followed Marcel behind the curtain and into the kitchen.

"As you can see, this is a café. Nothing more, nothing less," he said quietly, when they were both behind the curtain.

"A café that sells pastries made of dirt? How do you keep your customers?"

"My customers," he began, then paused to consider. "My *regular* customers get what they've come for."

Dolores snorted and glanced around the small kitchen. She paced across to the prep table where Marcel made his pastries. She lifted the lid from one of the bins and stuck her hand into the sand, pulled out a fistful and sifted it through her fingers. She reached into another bin, grabbed a handful, and dusted it onto the table. There was a bucket of brown water nearby, and she reached into this, too, cupping her hand and drawing out a palmful. She mixed the water with the sand and made a paste. She formed the paste into a small ball, and then flattened it into the shape of a cookie. A pasty puck. She lifted the grainy lump to her mouth, took a bite, and swallowed hard. Her jaw tensed and she retched, convulsed, and spit it onto the floor. She flung the paste-cookie against the wall where it splattered into a spray of particles that fell like fireworks.

"It makes them happy," said Marcel.

"It's a lie!" said Dolores.

Marcel gave an almost-imperceptible shrug.

Dolores clutched the metal prep table, with its row of inset bins full of dirt and water. She tugged at the table's beveled edge and tried to topple it, wanted desperately to see it all splattered across the floor. But the table was bolted to the wall and didn't budge. She tried again, leaned into it, applied all the weight and leverage she could muster. Veins bulged at her temples and wrists, until finally her arms went limp and fell at her sides.

Dolores cried. Marcel touched her on the shoulder, but she swatted his hand away and then swung wildly, hitting the side of his face hard with a half-open fist. Marcel reached up to touch the budding welt below his eye, and Dolores ran out of the kitchen, through the café, into the alley. Outside, she spat dirt and bile. She wiped her eyes to better see through her tears. She exited the alley onto the sidewalk, and by the time she got to the bus stop, she had finished crying and was ready for the long ride home.

In the dining room of Chez Magnifique, Mr. James was coughing loudly. He held his handkerchief to his mouth. The center of it, which had been a dingy gray, was now soaked a deep red. Ms. White fanned herself with a napkin from the table. Mr. Vellum leaned over and patted Mr. James gently on the back.

"Hey there, old boy, are you all right?"

Mr. James said nothing. His eyelids fluttered, and he collapsed onto the table. He twitched once, twice, and a patch of blood bloomed across the white linen of the tablecloth, crawling toward his companions, seeping under their plates and cups and saucers.

"Heavens," said Ms. White. Her powdered face became even paler.

"Dear boy," said Mr. Vellum. "Well, I think ... rather ... shall we? Is it that time?"

"Oh, yes, I'd say so," said Ms. White.

Mr. Vellum got up, pushed in his chair, and pulled out Ms. White's chair as she stood. He offered his elbow, and the two of them walked out of the café together, acting for all the world like nothing had happened. Acting like Mr. James was only napping after eating a bit too much sugar.

Marcel stood behind the counter and stared at Mr. James. He opened his mouth, but there were no words. For a few moments, he stood there, wringing a dishtowel between his hands. Then he turned toward the doorway that led into the kitchen. Just beyond the curtain, he could see a mop and bucket leaning together conspiratorially.

Outside the café, all over the city, a red-brown rain began to fall, smearing and spattering the parched, dusty buildings and the thirsty ground. It was the first time in years anything had fallen from the sky, and at first it seemed it must be a hallucination. As Dolores rode toward home, she noticed the tinted liquid hitting the bus windows and running down in rivulets. She slid her window open and reached a hand out to feel the dampness on her skin. She thought she should probably feel excited, or relieved, or maybe even scared—the color was wrong, not like the rain she remembered. But the truth was, aside from the cool moisture of the droplets, aside from the swaying lull of the rolling bus, she didn't feel much of anything at all.

A NURSE IN APPALACHIA

Donnie Welch

for my mother

Last week a kid died of boredom,
racing a train because there's nothing
better to do. He was fifteen.
When the family came to identify the body,
it was the sister who told the coroner
the mangled torso, both shoulders out of socket,
face caved in like a pit mine,
was definitely her brother.
The parents waited outside.

Only God and coal companies move mountains.
The old man who ran out of money for meds
threatened to come back with a gun
like he always does. He hasn't been the same
since his only son died in an accident.
There was an investigation, of course,
but the mine wasn't found at fault—
accidents happen, after all.
I went home and prayed for the guy.
What else is there to do?

Tonight, I worked a birth.
The mother was sixteen, and her husband
was on shift when she went into labor.
She was a trooper, didn't want Stadol
and only screamed toward the very end.
Once that child, a daughter, was born,
the mother's eyes were diamonds.
But off in the distance, an explosion,
a new mine being opened, and soot
came in clouds through the valley.

THE PONTIAC PLAN: PHASE ONE

Joumana Altallal

for Pontiac, Michigan

The Architect stands suited
over t(his) Space Age City

his weight tabled
against a blueprint crowded

with the knuckled skin of new rises
t(his) penciled labor that hums

him to life.

Like its Chief, the City is a calculated
afterlife someone has left unburied.

The Architect orders the clean-up
of t(his) american catastrophe

every rendition
in which the City is not asphalt, phoenix,

high school football must be piped,
unremembered. He draws:

the river as it clots
mouthless into a womb of tar,

mistakes its hunger
for contagion, names it

a kind of sickness
that seeps

and seeps and must be
hemmed shut.

If the proper decisions are made now the city will have a future the people will call it their own the city is sick there is a need this development will not be a giant jewel box sitting in the middle of a ghetto it will not be wiped off the american map rebuilding is necessary it will make a profit it will not be sick rebuilding is necessary there is a future here it will not be black

---

The italicized portion is borrowed from several news clippings citing architect C. Don Davidson's vision for the Pontiac Plan.

AND IN BARROW, ROSES WILL BLOOM

L. N. Lewis

For an unknowable period of time, 93952^8 rode a 26.7-degree Celsius, 96% humidity vortex of air in a shower stall of Housing Module 18 at Axion Oil & Gas Corporation's site 5211B in ANWAR, the Arctic National Wildlife Refuge on Alaska's North Slope.

93952^8, a 0.1-micrometer drop of jelly enclosed in a plasma membrane, knew none of that. It could not realize it shared the shower stall with Tim Pierson, a 41-year-old drilling engineer from Oklahoma City. It did not understand that Tim Pierson was about to catch a Cessna to Fairbanks. It did not care that Tim Pierson would then fly on to join his wife at a gymnastics meet in Ann Arbor, Michigan, where their 14-year-old daughter, Audrey, was competing. Moreover, 93952^8 did not appreciate the consequences of a warm updraft of air sweeping it into Tim Pierson's right nostril.

93952^8 had two eons of experience with enervating cold, far less with these levels of humidity and heat. Hardiness and adaptability were about to be put to the test as it tumbled past epithelial cells that lined the nasal passage like microscopic brickwork flailing lethal, whip-like cilia that 93952^8 barely evaded. Internally, a chemical alarm went off. Immobilizing goo sprayed from a dozen directions, and 93952^8 fired back with its own munitions. Hundreds of Tim Pierson's protective phagocytes exploded. 93952^8 snuggled against one of the dead cells and then penetrated it, devouring it from inside. As 93952^8 ate, it swelled. At the point where it seemed it, too, would explode, a dark line bisected its jelly. 93952^8 split into two. Four. Eight. ...

Sent: 7:27 a.m.

10 horas 27 minutos 45 segundos

Loco!

Dulce topped off Akil's coffee.

"What time does he get in?"

"Eleven-fifteen. I teach a dance class, come home, get some sleep, then meet him at Newark. We'll take the train, then catch a Lyft uptown."

"Give him a hug from me."

Dulce moved between the tables of Mike's Rincón like the 22-year-old dancer she was, springing from the balls of her feet, suppressing the urge to break into some bachata. She didn't skimp at her job as she oversaw that Rogelio's mangú was topped by an egg overeasy, that Lili Cruz got Half-and-Half with her Constant Comment, and that the batata with Mr. Jerry's bacalao was fried crispy. But today, three time zones away, Mateo was pulling her focus. Mateo and Danh would have shut down their restaurant by midnight, and then Mateo would have sped home, slept, and headed to Sea-Tac in pre-dawn darkness. Now at cruising altitude in a middle seat, he would be sipping coffee and thinking about her. And she was dreaming about wrapping around him like a passiflora, about being spoonfed tres leches in bed at the Saint Nicholas Inn.

"¿Y qué clase de locura es ese?" asked Lili, looking up at CNN.

"—*the oil and gas giant was performing tests inside Alaska's Arctic National Wildlife Refuge, a cause of much controversy and protest. Axion's headquarters in Houston, Texas, reports they received emergency phone calls from the Alaska test site at around 3 a.m. Central Time describing a mysterious illness striking the approximately 80-person exploratory team—*"

"I heard half 'em dead," said Mr. Jerry.

"Horrible," said Dulce, taking his plate.

The kitchen was crowded now. Tommy and Elena had arrived, and Raf and Mike were at the stoves. Mike's huge bulk bent over a cast-iron skillet of frying plantains. He flashed Dulce a grin. "¿Te vas a escuela?"

Dulce hung up her apron. "Claro. Tengo una clase de modern dance."

"Muy bien. Tengan cuidado, ¿me oyes?"

"Sí, jefe."

Mike leaned down so his daughter could give him a kiss. Swinging her jacket, Dulce stepped out of the back door of Mike's Rincón into the October morning.

Mateo sat between a sleeping businessman and a Seattleite who had actually eaten at Ho Chi Migo.

"Those crepes. Those crepes were amazing," the woman said, eyes wide behind steel cat-eye frames.

"Oh, the banh xeo. We put our own little spin on them with the shrimp-chili-mango filling."

"So good I wrote you guys a Yelp."

"Thank you! You look kind of familiar. Maybe I saw you from the kitchen."

His phone chirped a text notification:

```
Sent: 5:31 a.m.

AT
TA
CG
CG
    TA
    CG
    CG
    CG
GC
CG
CG
AT
```

He deleted it and texted Dulce:

```
Sent: 5:35 a.m.

Are you sending me código secreto?
```

```
Received: 5:37 a.m.

No, k dice?
```

```
Sent: 5:39 a.m.

Alfabeto: QCKTISLZLE

Where y@?
```

```
Received: 5:45 a.m.

On the train on my way to class.

I can't wait I can't wait I can't wait!
```

The businessman groaned and fidgeted in his sleep, and Cat Eyes was busy with her phone, so he took out a pencil and opened his cuaderno to a self-portrait as a winged dragon with a scraggly goatee and John Lennon glasses mounted by a bikini-clad woman holding aloft a fiery sword.

"That's interesting," said Cat Eyes.

"If it bothers you, I'll work on something else. You don't have to call the TSA."

"You're good. Jessica."

"Mateo."

From icebound dormancy to full function at 40 degrees Celsius, 93952^8 and its descendants adapted with remarkable speed. Tim Pierson's lumbering 37.2 trillion-cell organism couldn't match the challenge. Shock troops blasted a brew of cytotoxins and invasins, withering Pierson's olfactory nerves, dissolving his gleaming, white connective tissue barricade, the dura mater—almost instantly consuming the delicate arachnoid and pia maters that sheathed his brain. Pierson fought back, his defensive microglia pumping cytokines, chemokines, and nitrous oxide, but gradually he was laid open to the invaders who divided, divided again, and then settled down to eat.

The wing's fore glowed, lit by the rising sun. Mateo and Jessica reclined in their seats, gazing past the businessman through the small window at the violet and gold clouds.

Text notification cheeped.

```
Received: 6:11 a.m.

CG
CG
CG
CG
    AT
    CG
    TA
    GC
AT
AT
CG
GC
```

He held out his phone to Jessica. "Look at that. I keep getting that."

"What is it?"

"I don't know." Mateo turned back to the window. The businessman's head was turned toward him, face waxen, eyes transfixed, the pupil of one gray iris dilated. Mateo softly asked him, "Excuse me, are you—"

Mateo's glasses flew off as some hectic force collided with his face. The narrow, three-seat row turned pink and red. His nose was a geyser of rich, dark claret, and the businessman was flailing in his seat, his bobbing head wearing a full beard of strawberry milkshake-colored foam. Jessica stood, screamed, and stumbled into the aisle as flight attendants hurried from both ends of the plane.

All four walls and the ceiling of Dulce's tiny bedroom were covered with worn-out dance shoes, music video stills, programs, posters, postcards from the Dominican Republic, and photos of school, dance, family, and Mateo. Dulce and Mateo mugging, goofing, smirking, locked in an embrace.

She packed her bag and then spent over an hour trying to decide what to wear. She wasn't sure if they would just cuddle for the night at the hotel or go to dinner and a club. And the weather was so weird, warm, sticky, more like August than October. She put on a short, sleeveless, black lace dress with black gladiator sandals. Checking her phone again, the scary "Alaska Outbreak" story appeared in the headlines. Half-listening, she sorted through her makeup case until she found the right shade of lipstick, *Bloodlust*.

Now the furrowed brow was Travis Chang's as he listened to "*Dr. Peter Harmon, CDC epidemi—*"

"*—believe we have found the organism involved, but we haven't identified it. These bacteria are un—*"

"*Some new bacteria can just appear out of thin—?*"

"*—permafrost thaws in vast areas of the Arctic. Bacteria, fungi, and viruses that have been locked in ice for thousands, even millions— Some organisms may only have been dormant, and in warming temperatures could be—*"

Dulce finger-combed her hair into a wild fro and then opted to wear it up.

"*—perfect segue— Rhonda Norton, former Axion employee— huge animal carcass— reburied—*"

Spraying *Les étoiles* on her pulse points, putting on the antique crystal earrings Mateo had given her three birthdays ago, and tossing her phone in her purse, she missed the footage of endless mud, black rivers, and gray skies; the aerial shots of Axion's lifeless housing modules, rigs, and trailers; the narration stating that 86 Axion employees were confirmed dead; and the chyron repeating that the hunt was on to locate an unidentified Axion employee last sighted onboard a Cessna eight-seater to Seattle.

93952^47 and all descendants of 93952^8 shared the characteristics of life: cellular organization, reproduction, metabolism, homeostasis, heredity, response to stimuli; growth and change; and evolution. Their only intention, insofar as they had intentions, was survival. Killing was incidental. There had been no aim to kill the mastodon on that windswept Arctic plateau; the gigantic herbivore's solitary death was the outcome of the microbes' need for food overriding their need for shelter. Twelve thousand, three hundred, fifty-seven years later, the same faulty processes would lethally impact Tim Pierson. By excessive exploitation of him as a food source, the germs destroyed him as their host. Tim Pierson was a husk slumped in the seat of Compass Airlines Flight 2677, his remaining brain matter oozing from his nose. 93952^47 could have perished with Tim Pierson. Instead, an evolutionarily more advantageous path was taken, and the progeny left Tim Pierson the same way their ancestor had entered him. By air.

Mateo lay on a cot at the rear of the plane holding Jessica's hand. He wasn't sure which was worse, the maddening pain in his face or the shouts and screams from the other passengers.

"I'm calling out and calling out, and none of my calls are going through," said Jessica, her face wet with sweat and tears. "We are landed. Why the fuck can't I call out?"

"Keep texting. Dulce is answering my texts." His voice, adenoid and muffled, boomed in his head, amplifying the pneumatic drill inside his skull. He shifted, froze a moment, and then reached inside a pants pocket. "Look. What do you think?" He held a small velvet box up to her, and she opened it. The ring gleamed in the dark.

"Oh, Mateo, she's going to love it."

"Yeah. Do me a favor." He laid the ring on his chest. "Take a picture of it."

Sent: 7:22 p.m.

te ammmmo y simpre t he
amddo desde primera vista n Georg walsh Elementry, fith grade.

cuano t vea, vo a besarte p un mes entero.

ten fe

Received: 7:23 p.m.

No te preocupes Corazon. Nos vemos bien pronto. Y tu sabes k te amo te amo te amo te amo

The line snaking to the ticket counter through belt barriers felt like no air-port line Dulce had ever experienced. A dozen security officers and Com-pass officials stood at the margins. A man behind her in line who began yelling, "You KNOW what's happening!" was quickly led away. Everyone else focused on their phones, following newsfeeds reporting that Compass Flight 2677 was being held on the tarmac at O'Hare Airport.

Dulce turned to a woman with a left half-sleeve tiger tattoo and *Brunswick* delicately etched on her right wrist. "Who are you waiting for?"

"My wife." She glanced at Dulce's little black dress. "You had other plans for tonight. Didn't we all. Who are you waiting for?"

"My boyfriend."

The woman winced. "Any of his family with you?"

"No, just me. My family is his family."

At the counter, Dulce faced another woman, a Compass employee wearing a blazer, a pin, and a slight smile that was pleasant yet impenetrable, conveying absolutely nothing.

"Your name, please?"

"Dulce Renee Valdez."

"Ms. Valdez, who are you here to meet?"

"My ... husband, Mateo Sotomayor."

Three minutes later, Dulce was walking down a long, windowless, fluorescent-lit corridor. She heard footsteps running to catch up to her. Arm-in-arm, Dulce and Brunswick entered the auditorium.

Received: 10:41 p.m.

CG
CG
GC
AT
  TA
  CG
  CG
  AT
GC
GC
CG
CG

He was alone now. He didn't know where Dulce had gone, but he was surrounded by an odor that summoned a vision: his mother. He was standing on tiptoes to reach her crimson smile and her *Butterfly* cologne. Then he was at the port in Veracruz, walking hand-in-hand with his grandfather, assailed by diesel and fresh and rotting fish. Now at his mother's bedside at University Hospital, inhaling the odor of sweat, ammonia, and disinfectant. Mike Valdez holding him tightly as he breathed his odor of chiclé and Newports. Pork and yucca, cebolla y plátanos tantalizing him at the table of the Valdez family, but being too grief-stricken to eat. Skateboarding in an abandoned parking lot with Dulce Valdez and her aroma of Bubblicious and baby powder. Chopping fresh coconut in the kitchen of Mike's Rincón. And then, a presence that highjacked all of his senses. Five tons of flesh caged in ice for 12,357 years corrupting in warm, humid air. Fermentation and rot, liquefaction, putrefaction. A dizzying descent into darkness. And then: nothing.

Sent: 11:10 p.m.

Mateo I am calling you over and over please pick up *contestame*

Received: 11:11 p.m.

GC
GC
AT
GC
   GC
   TA
   CG
   GC
CG
GC
GC
TA

The room felt like a January day. A blue-clad attendant at the door handed her a clipboard with forms, a pen and marker, and a sheet of cardstock where she was instructed to write Mateo's name. Past that attendant and along the wall stood more airline employees dressed in blue, holding clipboards and boxes of Kleenex. Beyond them, there was a white cloth-covered table with pitchers of water and a coffee and tea station. Finally, there was an area enclosed by blue partitions. The carpet was a blue houndstooth, and blue draperies hanging from the high ceiling rustled with the blasting air conditioning. Goosebumps rose on Dulce's bare arms.

Rows of chairs spaced two yards apart faced a podium. Families, couples, and individuals distributed themselves evenly around the room. When the auditorium filled, the double doors shut, and a Compass employee with a maternal air took the podium. The woman gently explained that Compass Flight 2677 from Seattle to Newark International remained in lockdown on the tarmac of Chicago's O'Hare Airport due to an infectious illness onboard. Health professionals had boarded the plane, and everything possible was being done to care for their loved ones. The Compass staff here in this room had information on their family members, and these staff would sit down and share all known information with them.

It began like a slow detonation. Sometimes a long exhalation. Sometimes a sharp intake of breath. Then the screams. A man shouting "NO" over and over. A woman keening. An entire family erupting in sobs. Calls for EMTs who hurried from behind the partitions to Brunswick, who had hit the floor in a dead faint.

Now a Compass employee sat down beside Dulce, a white man close to retirement age with tired blue eyes. Without even hearing his slow, careful exegesis, she knew. The ice broke under her chair. She was falling. Freezing black water rushed up to meet her.

The temperature at Axion site 5211B was strikingly similar to that of Newark International Airport Conference Room 26: 17.6 degrees Celsius versus 17.3 degrees Celsius. 5211B did have far higher humidity at 68%, which was only logical.

5211B was active again, now with pathologists, forensic scientists, epidemiologists, and lab technicians sweating in HAZMAT suits as they slogged in the mud between Quonset Huts. It was far safer to analyze bodies and specimens onsite than to transport them back to the CDC.

The mud again revealed the mastodon carcass that Axion employees had attempted to hide. Pathologists sought usable tissue samples in the rotting hulk, and then construction workers with a backhoe tried to bury it a third time, but two meters down struck black water. The remains were covered with quicklime and giant sheets of white plastic to limit exposure to the balmy, mosquito-laden air. Quicklime and tarps, however, would not purge the microorganisms inhabiting the housing, air, and soil of 5211B and embedding the upholstery and carpeting of Compass Flight 2677, which still sat on the tarmac at O'Hare.

Staphylococci anwarellia, the newly named progeny of 93952^8, had survived the mastodon, the ancient horse, and the giant short-faced bear; had outflanked and outmaneuvered extinction; and now were swarming in the mud splattering satellite phones, safety goggles, and landing gear.

The collective lives of every species must one day end. The only question is duration: years, centuries, millennia, eons? There was no way of knowing how much time *anwarellia* would have for their second chance. The bacteria had no understanding of the interplay between vanished glaciers, warming mud, heating skies, boots, earthmovers, and airplanes in their reemergence, but they ventured blindly on, driven by happenstance and hunger, by a mesh of genetic material in the cytoplasm of each of them, by the will to survive.

THE KNACKERS AT WORK

W L S

It is their duty to go. To dress in waders, fluorescent
orange vests for safety, disposable respirators to filter
small particulates, caps cinched tight over their ears,
long sleeves to fight the sun. It is their job. They drive
to the manmade river where the suburb's runoff gathers.
To where Canada geese feed on stiff, bacterized turf grasses.
One goose has succumbed to grief. Her bloated belly stuffed
with bottle caps in every shade they can think. Why she was
compelled to assemble such a collection they can't gather. They fish
the jumble of bone and feather into a black plastic trash bag
while her mate honks, flapping wildly in their direction. One lobs
the bag into the back of the truck with the others. *She's just some
goose. No one special.* There's no ceremony for this. If there
once was a ritual, it was long-ago lost. The Knackers
settle to call her Becky and they chant her name over the sluggish
water, slick with swirls of oil that stink in the sun. They say
Goodnight Becky. Goodnight Becky. Goodnight, goodnight, goodnight.

THE KNACKERS & THE MIGRATORY
BIRD TREATY ACT OF 1918

W L S

It is illegal to shoot a Canada goose outside the designated season.
To cull the flock, when permitted, when the nest can be found—
on an elevated surface near a swift-moving body of water—
when the life-bonded pair (*the goose-parents*) are out
jerking blades of grass with their beaks or dredging silt,
a certified wildlife management professional wearing nitrile gloves
may dip the egg in corn oil to deprive the embryo of oxygen.
If, not knowing, the mother continues to roost, this is called
a wind-egg. Nothing to hatch but a gust, a waft. But, there
are other ways to addle an egg, their coworker once told them.
The spade could simply slip while turning soil in a tired field.
Was it a nest? Or a tangle of withered hay. Was it an egg?

ROUND BLACK GRAINS

Kevin Doyle

At the wake we talked about the time Justin nearly died, in the Glen trying to save the sand martins. Really, what was he thinking? The colony of birds had been living in the urban wilderness for as long as anyone could remember, their nests long tunnels burrowed into the sandy deposits left behind when the glaciers receded. A consortium, Skellig Developments, planned to build houses beside the ancient abode but had discovered that the birds enjoyed protection under some obscure bylaw. They hatched a plan, a compromise it was called, to build the sand martins a new home, a short distance from where they had always lived. These units, concrete towers bristling with hollow plastic pipes, were superior to sand dunes apparently—studies had shown. They didn't suffer from the damp, they were durable, and they could even be painted to merge with the surrounding terrain.

The city council was thrilled. Finding itself mired in an ethical dilemma of stupendous proportions—could progress run roughshod over these ancient dwellers?—they finally saw a way out. Voting to lift the injunction, they accepted the generous offer from Skellig, and a few days later, the new towers were hauled into position.

That night a strange contraption also appeared, blocking access to the site. It had three spindly legs intersecting four meters above the ground. Hanging from the apex of the structure was a tiny capsule not unlike a chair-o-plane seat. Sitting in this was Justin.

A garda explained that he had seen the structure before—a tripod it was called—at an anti-Shell Oil protest in Mayo. It was designed to interdict the movement of ground vehicles along narrow lanes and roadways. It couldn't easily be moved; in fact, assistance would have to be summoned.

This arrived shortly. From a van marked *Garda Specialist Unit*, three police officers dressed in black alighted and filmed the scene. Their peaked baseball caps read *G.S.U.*, and they had with them a dune buggy that they took around for a while, mostly up and down the narrow track obstructed by the tripod. They examined the obstacle, took pictures with telescopic lenses, and rattled its spindly legs. They ascertained through a combination of measurements and stress tests that Justin's abode was structurally sound. A cherry picker was sent for and duly arrived—rented, it later emerged, from a subsidiary of Skellig's called Skellig Equipment. We jeered and sang songs, held away as we were at a distance from the standoff by a robust chain-link fence.

The strange thing was the sand martins. We could see them, too, in the distance. In the beginning, they had fluttered about in squalls—there was quite a population of them. But as the day progressed, as the onlooking crowd grew in size, the colony took up a stationary position on the cliff face and watched in silence.

The garda unit were serious men. Two went into the cherry picker cabin, while a third videoed proceedings. The picker rose like a serpent's head and drew level with the capsule. Some time was spent talking to Justin, reasoning with him, but apparently—we read this later in the newspaper, the one that described us as a rent-a-mob—that he couldn't be reasoned with. So eventually, battle was joined and pepper spray was used. It was a sight: seeing the tripod rock from side to side, Justin swinging wildly in the capsule.

He was finally extricated and brought down, escorted to a position near the building huts and offered tea. He was informed that he wouldn't be arrested. Apparently Skellig Developments had endured enough adverse publicity.

A bulldozer moved forward and smashed the tripod, now divested of its human inhabitant, into the ground. Earthmovers followed quickly, trundling up the narrow road to the dunes. We saw a JCB's claw rise up into the air and swipe wildly at the tallest dune. The sand martins scattered into the air as a wedge of sand separated from the cliff face and fell down.

In the hiatus that followed, knowing that our cause was lost, Justin broke free again. Dodging gardaí and a variety of Skellig goons, he ran forward and dived into a collapsing heap of sand. It seemed to take forever before it was understood what had happened. Gardaí and Skellig employees ran to help. Anger followed panic. Shouts of *madman* and *who does he think he is* could be heard. The JCB driver was livid and the first to claw at the mound. There were fears of another collapse, but that stopped nobody. Within a few minutes, Justin's head of black hair was located. A vent space to his mouth was cleared next, and after that his shoulders were released. It was only a matter of time then. They excavated quickly, uncovering a figure contorted around his own cupped hands. He shouted, spluttering the words as they pulled him to safety, "Gentle please, gentle, mind the birds."

There's a photo of the moment on *Indymedia*. A collection of men in orange hi-vis vests and white helmets are gathered around Justin. In his lap, nestled for protection, is a collection of sand martin chicks. The fledglings had withdrawn their heads so far into their bodies that their necks had vanished. They looked scared, their eyes only round black grains.

CARBON

Marc Beaulin

Driving late night through the pass
with narcoleptic mountains pressing in
from either side & Coltrane struggling
through the static of the radio while

whitebark pines are dead & dying right
outside my window & pelicans & sea
turtles are dead & dying, still, in
the black waters of the Gulf & Éliane

Parenteau, age 93, Alyssa Charest Bégnoche,
age 4, & 45 others dead along the
tracks in Lac-Mégantic but then the radio
clears & a horn sounds out pure as fire

For a moment any future is possible

Until I realize the passenger door is
ajar & the noise & smell of the wind
writhing through the breach become a
presence seated next to me & when, by

degrees this presence becomes palpable
enough to see from the corner of my
eye I speed up & say,
"I knew you'd have dark hair."

POST-KATRINA MARDI GRAS

Cynthia Gallaher

Katrina, huffy hurricane, howler, homewrecker,
how could New Orleans celebrate after the likes of you?
was it not your winds, but rains that broke the levees?
left homes lopsided, lost lives, misplaced identities
in wake of this August flood.

Lakes Pontchartrain and Borgne swelled and
spewed mighty waters as if from Neptune's mouth,
south across the Ninth Ward, Arabi, Chalmette,
that God of the Sea was the one in our living rooms,
if he didn't climb all the way to the roof,
he at least was knocking at our door.

"but not having Mardi Gras in New Orleans
would be like not having Christmas," some say,
while carnival floats awaiting next year's celebration
were "floating" in streets after levees gave way.
"Fat Tuesday" had grown so slim,
you could count its bones.

could New Orleans ever gain back
what Katrina had stolen?
somehow trumpets sounded, drums pounded,
whistles blew, maracas shook in anticipation,
and NOLA pushed Mardi Gras plans ahead,
taking pride in its annual February vacation,

exuberant, gaudy and giddy as it seemed
to forget past troubles, take new time to dream,
could it happen between building and tearing down,
between devastation and renovation?
could it happen among those on their way back,
and those who still had a long way to go?

it happened.

down St. Charles Avenue and Canal Street,
but with fewer krewe members on floats,
those lost to Katrina,
crowds still wildly reached for "throws"
of beaded necklaces, flashy doubloons
that showered down,

cheered marching bands
from flooded-out high schools,
caught up as ever in the annual whirlwind
of lavish masks, hats, and costumes,
profuse confetti, striped umbrellas
up and down noise-filled streets,

while other streets stood silent
amidst collapsed roofs, overturned cars,
roadways strewn with muddy shoes,
furniture and stuffed toys,
a watery Ash Wednesday come early,
with much disappeared, much washed away.

LINKEDIN THOUGHT YOU MIGHT BE INTERESTED IN THIS POST-CLIMATE IMPACT JOB: ENVIRONMENTAL MIGRANT MANAGEMENT AND SOIL-FREE SOLUTIONS

Ashley Shelby

In June 2024, due to the nationalization of the Post-Climate Impact agriculture sector, LivingSystems, Inc., and Aeroponic Farm Cooperatives merged, creating a new company with a global presence. Hydroponic Nutrient Solutions (HNS) is now drawing a combined $2 billion in revenue and boasts more than 13,000 employees. Over the next year, we'll be working to make HNS the industry leader in vertical farming and soil-free solutions. In addition to its commercial activities supplying vertically farmed produce to Non-Impacted American citizens, HNS deploys all over the world to assist in climate events and to ensure that environmental migrants receive necessary nutrition during migrations.

Sound exciting? HNS is currently able to offer job candidates a wide array of employment opportunities and benefits that are among the most competitive in the Post-Climate Impact Agriculture and Refugee Management industries. We are currently seeking to fill the following position:

Position: Director of Disaster Resilience and Refugee Feeding Programs

Reports to:
Vice President of Climate-Impact Strategics

FLSA Status
Salaried (Exempt)

Position Summary
Director of Disaster Resilience and Refugee Feeding Programs is responsible for managing the performance of all matters related to agronomic stockpiling and government-regulated refugee nutrition programs (per the Nutrition Standards for Environmental Migrants Act of 2023). Director will also serve as an agronomic project consultant on all implemented Disaster Resilience projects, as well as on an as-needed basis during Large-Scale Refugee Events (LSRE). Director will also be expected to deliver a TED Talk.

Minimum Requirements—Education and Experience
- 5+ years of Climate-Impact Agriculture industry experience
- Familiarity with pre-Impact agricultural and social conventions
- Master's degree in related technical area (e.g., agronomy, crisis management, migrant services, etc.); PhD preferred
- Strong knowledge of:
  - Implementation of risk solution strategies in high-pressure environments, often prior to or during Climate Events
  - Financial Analysis related to operational support and government regulation, particularly in balancing compulsory international aid and commercial activities
  - Management of Environmental Migrant Nutrition Disbursement during Climate Events
  - Fluency with diverse modalities of emergency and development aid
  - Firearms training

Key Accountabilities:
Regulatory Compliance
- Provide support and guidance on all assigned activities governed by the U.S. Agriculture Nationalization Act of 2022
- Ensure all stockpiling operations and storage procedures adhere to local and federal regulations

Environmental Migrant Program Design and Execution
- Ensure HNS' Environmental Migrant Program (EMP) modality in all assigned regions is up-to-date and geared toward industry and government best practices
- Monitor Nutrient Disbursement during Climate Events and ensure execution is carried out at high level of quality and cost-effectiveness
- Work closely with the technical team and operational leadership to ensure complete compliance with federal Environmental Migrant Nutrition programs, while also boosting HNS' commercial capacity to support company's fiscal health
- Occasionally meet with leaders of hostile Impacted areas for coffee/tea/culturally appropriate libation

Disaster Resilience Planning
- Perform in the capacity of subject matter expert and authority on all agronomic and emergency management in assigned regions, including severely impacted areas, such as Philippines, Saudi Arabia, Yemen, and Los Angeles
- Develop short- and long-term climate resiliency plans for HNS

that take into account a rapidly changing environmental context and quickly evolving Client Needs
- Leverage existing plans for hydroponic and aeroponic inventories, including commercial stock and Refugee stock, to reach maximum output
- Work closely with horticulture and soil teams to analyze forecasts, anticipate industry shortages, and develop larger yields in order to keep pace with ballooning demand since the collapse of California's agriculture industry
- Be adept at operating in a calm, neutral mode

Desired Attributes:
General
- Good at "real-time" problem solving
- A stable residence, survival retreat preferred, if access to satellite communication is reliable, and adequate personal emergency preparedness resources on hand
- No active or pending tax liens or penalties (e.g. Federal Obesity Tax, Conspicuous Consumption Fine, Obsolete or Inefficient Vehicle Penalty, etc.)
- Emotional intelligence in situations involving catastrophic human impacts
- Familiarity with the work of Norman Vincent Peale
- Willingness to travel to Florida

Teamwork
- Collaborate with all agencies operating within the U.S. Department of Displaced Citizens (DDC), as well as relevant federal emergency response teams, including Environmental Migrant Rapid Response (EMRR), California Wildfire Tactical Corps, and others
- Interface with heads of foreign governments, particularly in Impact areas, and work with global aid organizations to disburse Refugee Nutrition
- Commit to eliminating entrenched organizational and governmental barriers while maintaining necessary synergy and employee morale
- Be a "team player" and take part in office events, such as birthdays, retirement parties, and flu shot clinics

Physical Demands and Work Environment
Due to the unprecedented nature of current and future Post-Climate Impact weather events, travel needs will be unpredictable but constant. Below is an incomplete aggregation of physical requirements:
- Work outside in variable weather conditions including heat (wildfire and drought), rain (typically torrential), and wind (up

to hurricane-force)
- Travel throughout assigned regions (50-60%), often in areas where critical infrastructure has been heavily damaged or destroyed
- Travel for team meetings, trainings, etc. (2-3 times/year)
- Willingness to participate in mandatory therapy sessions once a week with your assigned psychologist

Benefits:
Hydroponic Nutrient Solutions offers a competitive benefits package that strives to meet the needs of its employees in a challenging post-currency economy. All HNS employees, exempt and non-exempt alike, receive a baseline salary of 25/lbs of mixed HNS produce$_1$ a week, which can be consumed or bartered, depending on the employee's needs. Salary bands 8A through 10C receive additional poundage, determined by job title, as well as seeds for use or bartering. Exempt employees receive an additional 30/lbs of mixed produce a week, as well as biannual allotments of hard red wheat.

In addition to a competitive salary, HNS offers its employees an array of world-class benefits, including:
- State-of-the-Art Hygiene Facilities and Private Shower Pods with generous weekly water ration
- Individually assigned mental health therapist
- Share of HNS Carbon Credits awarded based on yearly performance
- Daily shuttle services
- Generous yearly cloth allotment
- Access to HNS' large archive of Sheltering-in-Place supplies, and discounts on company-owned generators, quicklime, siphon pumps, and other emergency goods
- Tuition reimbursement for basic skills training, including welding, carpentry, applied foraging, and post-media technologies
- Pre-tax personal stockpiling program, with company match

Hydroponic Nutrient Solutions is an Equal Opportunity Employer.

---

1. *Excludes Tier 1 produce, such as apples, grapes, almonds, pistachios, all citrus excluding kumquats, and all berries*

WHALESONG: THE QUIET AFTER

Kim Harvey

Another whale washed up dead
on the beach today, belly swollen
with trash, bag after bag after bag
pulled from the young whale's gut,
calcified plastic the size of basketballs,
dregs and grit, the suck of death.

That island of floating garbage in the Pacific
is now three times the size of France. Our
recycling is shipped to China—boatsful of
Amazon boxes, to-go bowls and lids, plastic
milk jugs, Starbucks cups. We're all complicit.

Fish swim through crevices we don't see. Our trash
has reached the ocean's deepest hidden trenches.
Mauna Kea is the highest mountain on Earth
from base to peak, higher than Everest by 4,000 feet.
So much is submerged under the sea.

Our bodies are 60% water. Vibration sense
is buried close to the spinal cord. Beethoven
composed three symphonies after he went deaf
by sawing the legs of his grand piano and lying on
the floor, so he could feel the vibrations
through the bone conduction of his skull.

I read somewhere that researchers played different
styles of music on a nonstop loop to cheese wheels
to see how soundwaves affect the flavor. The ones
exposed to Mozart and Zeppelin were mellow, but the
hip-hop cheese came out on top in a blind taste test.

Music changes things on a molecular level.
I saw T-Pain being interviewed on a talk show.
The T stands for Tallahassee, where he comes
from. *And where does the pain come from*,
they asked him. The mother of all questions.

The missing fragments of Sappho's fourth poem
were found in the rubbish dumps of an Egyptian
town. A poem about an aging body reaching back
for the kind of love it once knew in youth, written
on a folded postcard-sized scroll of papyrus found
with the casing of a mummy. There are no accidents.

Leonard Cohen said that *Dance Me to the End
of Love* was inspired by the story of a string quartet
forced to play outside the crematorium while
their fellow prisoners were killed and burned,
knowing they would be next.

Every workday I pass a mural in West Oakland.
Huge sunflowers with blue, red, and goldenrod human
faces in their centers. Harvesting the heads with a clean cut
will not kill the plant, only the flower itself. Like any plant
that flowers, it will eventually grow more heads. We hold
what cannot be said. We are all spiraling toward death.

Some days the world is so heavy, I barely have
the strength to move. Then I feel my dog's
soft fur pressed against my leg, her wet tongue
licking my hand, begging for food.

While the *Titanic* was sinking, the musicians
stood on the deck and played their violins
until the very end when the ocean
swallowed them whole. What I'm trying to say is
we have to do something.

What I mean is I need to find a way to love
the world again with this breath

    and with this breath,

        and with this one.

RESILIENCE THEORY

Vivian Faith Prescott

We know how to die in our ruins, how to embrace
      regret inhabiting the deep chambers

of our island. Like the diffused sun, flickering
      its passing, we're sure

we have done this before. But yet we have no
memory of it; nothing

is scratched on the bathroom walls.

There are no symbols for this theory on our drums.
Our newspapers are crumpled in the corner.

We no longer remember how to create fire
      or how to trace starlight with our stories.

We are unsure of our capacity to absorb
      these disturbances.

They talk about undergoing change,
how to reorganize our beliefs, to forget

the snowbridge over the river,
and the old snow dug up by a reindeer.

We used to speak quiet around glaciers.
      We could name ice in a thousand ways.

Who has seen us delight in our superstitions recently?

We didn't listen
to council—we walked over our tracks

without looking down. Based on the results
of this study, the future will be spent searching

for ground drift, hard frost, and loose snow—
words and senses melting in the spring. No foothold.

WASTING WATER

Marilyn J. Evans

In a few minutes, I'll take a damp washcloth to my mom, so she can wipe her face. It's two weeks before my birthday, so she cried in her sleep last night—she calls it wasting water—because my dad died six years ago today. She cries on this day every year, but that's the only time she ever does. She's strong and calm most times. I want to be like her when I'm older. I won't be as pretty because I look too much like my dad, but maybe I'll be okay.

The damp cloth will be enough for now. It's Saturday, so we'll have a real bath tonight after all the chores are done. A whole gallon each for a bath, that's the rule. It may seem really wasteful, but we use the water again afterward for cleaning the house and watering the garden. Water has to work at least two times, Mom says. We can even wash our hair since we both have it cut short. I have an old picture of my mom when her hair was long. It was really beautiful, kind of a shiny red-brown.

"Mom." I knock softly on her bedroom door, in case she's not awake yet. The sun has been up for a little while, long enough that I got the morning chores done, but it's still early.

"I'm awake, Livie," I hear her say. I come into the room as she stretches. She doesn't sleep late ever, so it's nice she looks rested. I hand her the damp cloth, and she smiles then rubs it across her face. The tear tracks disappear.

"It's Saturday," I say, sitting on the daddy side of the bed. She still sleeps close to the wall as though he might come back someday.

"Bath night. And water for Mr. Wilkins today," she says.

"I checked the tanks and the pumps' pressures," I count off on my fingers, "turned out the chickens, milked the goats, mucked out Ruby and Ruben's stalls and fed them, and made you some breakfast."

"So, if I sleep late every morning will you do all my chores?" she says, laughing, and grabs me and hugs me. I don't protest or struggle. We don't snuggle as much as we used to, and I'm afraid if I squeal and giggle too much, she'll stop.

We're quiet a minute while she holds me. I lay my head on her shoulder. I finally move because I think she might start to cry again.

"I started a new batch of yogurt yesterday," I tell her while she climbs out of bed and pulls on her canvas overalls, just like mine. She wrinkles her nose. I like yogurt, but she doesn't so much because she says the goat's milk isn't as good as cow's milk. I don't remember what cow's milk tastes like. The cows went away the third year of the drought. Even the Brangus and African-cross cattle used too much water, she says. We had sheep for a while, but they were kind of stupid, and the wild dogs and coyotes picked them off pretty easily. The goats are smarter. The old buck is mean and smells bad, but we keep him in a yard by himself away from the does except during breeding time.

We eat our yogurt with sunflower seeds and apples. Because Daddy built catchments on the downhill side of the trees to give them as much water as possible, the old apple and pear trees never let us down. Well, except that one year when the frost came late and killed the blossoms. But the persimmon trees still had some fruit that year, so it worked out. Besides, we had dried and canned apples to tide us over to the next year. I remember when we had strawberries, but that was long ago now. We preserve as much as possible when we have a good harvest, even if we have lots of fruit left over from the years before. That's the rule. Rules are what keep us alive, Mom says.

After breakfast, we fill two five-gallon jugs with water for Mr. Wilkins. He trades us our water for his firewood and smoked fish. I don't know how he gets his fish. It's kind of a mystery. Mom says fish have essential nutrients. I looked fish up on the Internet—we still get a connection three hours a day when the satellite is in range—and I learned about omega-3 fats. The Internet is my school. I think chemistry is my favorite thing to study. Of course, everyone studies the weather, but that gets tedious—I like that word, "tedious"—when it's all anyone ever talks about, and it never changes much.

"Do you want to try riding Ruben today?" Mom asks me while we clean our bowls in the sink. The little bit of wash water catches in the bucket below to use later for the garden.

"Really?" I ask, and she nods. Ruben is still awfully green for riding, but he's been steady every time I've ridden him around the farm to check the electric fences.

"Wear your helmet and vest," she adds.

I hate the safety vest because it's hot, but there's a nice breeze today, so I don't argue. I put it on over my long-sleeved shirt and overalls. Since I'm wearing a helmet instead of a hat, Mom greases me up with sunscreen and makes me wear sunglasses and gloves. All that can make you really hot, but sunburn is a lot more uncomfortable and lasts a lot longer.

After we're dressed, we get the horses tacked up. Ruby still has her English saddle and a nice bridle. She was a show horse once. Mom told me she couldn't stand to part with Ruby, and Daddy agreed the horse could stay if she earned her keep. Even though we don't have a car or truck or tractor, we've done pretty well, thanks to that horse. She's getting older now, and having a younger horse to help her has been good, although they drink an awful lot of water when they're working. Tractors don't need water, but they need fuel, and refineries need a lot of water. There's no "lot of water" anyplace, so there's no tractor fuel, at least not around here. In the end, keeping Ruby turned out to be a pretty good thing.

Ruben was an accident, kind of like me, I think, although I don't ever let on to Mom that I think that about myself. The horses that were released by people who couldn't feed them in the early days mostly died because they didn't know how to be wild. Some survived and formed herds that trampled fences and raided what few crops grew during the droughts. People ate a lot of horse meat in those days, so the herds learned to avoid people. Horses are smart and remember a long time, but the bachelor herds, young males that the lead stallion runs off from the group, are a little braver or more stupid. Anyway, one of them got to Ruby, and some months later Ruben was born. He's four now and mostly broke to the harness as long as Ruby is hitched with him. Our harness is cobbled together, but it works for most things we need.

Ruben isn't as big as Ruby and fits me better. Besides, we get along because we sort of grew up together. We don't have a saddle to fit him, so I always ride with a bareback pad. I like it better than a saddle because I can feel all his muscles moving when he walks. He stands still and is pretty good while I put it on him. His bridle is a halter with an old snaffle bit tied into it and some rope for reins, not fancy leather like Mom's, but it gets the job done—that is, once you get it on the horse. He's a little less good when I put it on him, acting ornery, raising his head up higher than is easy for me to reach. We manage after a little discussion.

Mom and I load the water into the panniers on Ruby. My mom is pretty light, so Ruby can carry her and the water without much trouble. We always go slowly when we take the water because we're also checking our fields and the perimeter. Mom says Daddy plowed up the road in the early days so no one would wander onto our land during the crazy times. You have to be pretty close to our house and barns to know we're here or that the place is not just another abandoned farm.

We ride across the dry grassland—what used to be grassland, anyway—and over the dead area, that is our firebreak. There haven't been many wildfires in the past three or four years. Maybe what could burn has burned, or there are fewer people to throw cigarettes around or light fires. Maybe there are so few rainstorms even lightning strikes don't start so many fires. We used to see the smoke and smell it on the wind, but our firebreak has never been breached.

Mr. Wilkins lives near the bluffs where a river used to run. His property is next to ours, but it's still pretty far away. He's the only neighbor left that we know of. Mom says a lot of folks tried to hold on for a long time, but by the end of the fourth year of drought, they were mostly gone. I don't remember too many of them, although there was one family that visited us to say goodbye on their way to somewhere. I remember a boy about my age at the time who kissed my cheek and cried. I think he might have been my cousin, but I'm not sure. Someday I'll ask Mom about it when she's not as sad as she is today and can talk about older times without danger of wasting water.

We ride up to Mr. Wilkins' farmhouse near the bluff. It was a grand house once, bigger than ours, with a wide front porch and leaded glass in the windows, upstairs and down. We don't see any signs of life in or around the house. That's not too surprising since the dog died three years ago. Mr. Wilkins thought it got in a fight with a cougar or coyotes. We hoped he was wrong because that would be very bad for the livestock. No cougars or coyotes ever showed up, so maybe he was wrong.

"Mr. Wilkins," my mom calls to the house. "We're here with your water."

We wait a little. Mr. Wilkins isn't as jumpy as he was in times past when he was likely to fire a warning shot before you got in shouting range. This is unusual, though. Most times he's out of the house by now and helping Mom down from her saddle. He's a sort of mannerly old man if he knows you. I jump down from Ruben and take off my helmet and vest to get cooler. The day has warmed up fast.

Mom gets off Ruby and looks at me. I shrug, and Mom hands me her reins. She walks to the front door and knocks hard.

"Mr. Wilkins. You home? We brought your water."

No answer again. Mom opens the front door slowly. She doesn't want to get shot, but she does want to see what's going on. She looks at me again, and I shake my head. I don't know what's going on, either, but I feel nervous.

She goes in the house and comes right back out. "Put the horses in that pen over there around the side of the house, and come in quick." The pen is old and kind of rickety, but our horses don't have anyplace much to go, so it's okay to leave them there.

I do as she says and hurry into the house. Mr. Wilkins is on the floor in his living room. He is cursing even more than usual. He's using words I've never heard or read before, and I read a lot.

"Broke my damned hip, didn't I? Thought you'd never get here. No, it's no use. Happened two days ago. Yes, thanks." My mom is giving him sips of water to rehydrate him. His skin is gray, and he looks real bad. I remember when Daddy died, and I'm thinking Mr. Wilkins is pretty close to dead. He won't let Mom try to move him or help him except to give him water. He does let her give him some of the painkillers she keeps in the backpack she always has with her.

"Now you listen, Missus Robertson, and listen close. I don't have long, and there's a lot to say," Mr. Wilkins says. "There are notebooks here, and you're going to need them. There are lots of books explaining it all. I got no one to leave it to, and you might be able to use it. You know how to maintain solar panels. I know you have one windmill. It might not be like mine, so there are directions on that shelf." He points to a bookcase.

I like books. We have lots, but he has more than we do, shelves and shelves.

"I wrote a little bit of a will, but I don't think anyone will challenge you. The most important thing is you've got to maintain the farm."

Mom looks out the window at the barren scrubby waste that surrounds the house.

"Not that one, woman," Mr. Wilkins says impatiently. "The fish farm."

Well, that's just crazy talk. I laugh, and he gives me a dirty look and starts cursing again. When he winds down from that, he takes a deep breath and speaks to my mom again.

"There's a shed right up against the bluff. That's the entrance. The key's hanging by the kitchen door. You'll need to take the water you brought and add it to the tanks. You should do that now. Then look around and see if there are any questions you have right away. You'll need to check the balance of chemicals, the nutrients and pH and so forth, but not right away. It's mostly stable and self-sustaining. Pick some vegetables if you want. Then come back here, and I'll explain as much as I can before I. ..."

He stops talking and lies back, then sighs and closes his eyes. Mom and I look at each other again. She sets a water bottle by Mr. Wilkins and goes through to the kitchen. I follow her. I've never been in Mr. Wilkins' kitchen before. It's full of strange things like big glass bottles with spirals of tubing in them and lines leading to some kind of power source. After looking around for a minute, we see a wall rack with keys hanging on it by the back door. One of the keys is labeled "Farm Shed," so Mom takes it from its hook. We go out by the back door and to the pen where the horses are waiting. They nicker at us, asking what's going on. I wonder myself as we take the water jugs out of the panniers. The rule is work smart, not hard, so we find an old broom to run through the jug handles to carry each one between us around to the back of the house.

Right up against the bluff covered with dried-out weeds and tangled vines, we see the shed looking kind of ragged and abandoned but with a strong lock on the rickety door. That door is deceiving. When we unlock it and swing it open, we find it has steel plate behind the old weather-stained wood. The next surprise is how cool and moist the air behind the door feels. I have trouble breathing for a minute. The shed leads into a cave, but it's a funny kind of cave.

"This was a limestone quarry," my mom says. "I had no idea this was here."

The walls are lined with a kind of insulation, which reflects the light from the lamps over the trays that float on big square tanks of water. The trays are full of vegetables, all kinds, including cool-weather vegetables we only grow in the early spring or late fall. In the tanks are fish, swimming against a gentle current. I've seen videos of fish, but never alive in real life, at least not that I remember. They're beautiful and quiet, like a dream. So, this is where Mr. Wilkins' fish come from.

"This is aquaponics," my mom says to herself. She looks at a gauge labeled "Water Level" on the side of the nearest tank. The level is a little below the mark. She pours in water from one of our jugs, then she checks the other tanks. There are four. It takes nearly all the water we brought. We pick some of the vegetables. They're different from the ones that grow in our beds and hoop houses. The tomatoes are soft and really red. The lettuce is tender and juicy feeling. We pick what seems ripest that looks like it can't go much longer without going to waste. There seems to be a lot.

"What does he drink?" I ask as we pick. If all the water we bring is for the fish, what has Mr. Wilkins been drinking all these years?

"He must have some kind of water source. Must be a well or a cistern somewhere," Mom answers.

We lock the shed door behind us and go back to the house, putting the vegetables in the kitchen. Mom sends me out to look after the horses. We don't know how long we're going to be here, so I unsaddle Ruby and take off Ruben's pad, then look around for something for them to eat and maybe something to drink. In another rough-looking shed, I find a blue tarp over some really old hay. I break a bale apart and smell it. No mold, so that's good. This was the best kind of hay once, a long time ago. There still might be some good in it. At least it will give the horses something to do. I leave them nibbling while I figure out what Mr. Wilkins drinks. Hopefully, he won't mind if I give some water to the horses. If he really is dying, he won't need it, and the horses are always thirsty.

I find a standpipe hidden in one corner of the hay shed. I look around until I find a bucket on the back porch of the house. The water comes out of the standpipe fast, so the source is strong. The problem is I can smell the iron in it. You could drink this water for a while, but you might get sick if you had to drink it every day. Before I give it to the horses, I better ask Mr. Wilkins if it's safe.

I go in the house, and he's talking a mile a minute. "The wind turbines on the bluff supplement the solar panels. There are four marine batteries that store the electricity." He stops and looks at me. "What is it, girl?"

"The water from the standpipe in the shed. Is it safe for the horses to drink?"

"If you can get them to drink it, it won't hurt them. It's pretty nasty, but short-term it can't harm them. It would kill the fish. I filter it before I drink it, but my filters are getting old. I've got an electric still, but it takes too long and uses too much energy. My solar still works, but it's slow. You see why your water has been a blessing to me," he says, looking at my mom.

I've never seen stills, but I've seen pictures. I'm guessing that apparatus in the kitchen is the electric still. I wonder where he keeps his solar still. I'd like to see one.

I go out to water the horses. They sniff and snort a little at the water, but finally they drink it. It takes me several trips with the bucket to give them their fill. By now the day is getting on, and I'm hungry. Breakfast seems a long time ago. I'm also getting worried about the chores. I don't like leaving the chickens and goats alone too long. There's no telling what sort of critters might be on the prowl, even if we haven't seen coyotes in a long time. It's not so bad in the day, but near dusk it might be dangerous for our animals.

Mom meets me on my way back into the house. She's thinking the same as me.

"We'll have some lunch, then you'll head back. I don't think Ruben is so buddy-sour that he won't go back home without Ruby. I'd best stay here with Mr. Wilkins. I doubt he'll make it through the night, and I don't want him to die alone. Will you be all right taking care of the chores?" She smiles. "I hate to ask since you already did more than your share today."

"I'll be okay. We can't leave the goats and chickens by themselves," I say, agreeing with her, but I don't feel confident. I've never spent a night without my mom.

"All right," she says. "Let's have some fish and salad." We brought goat cheese and dried fruit with us, so it's a feast we share with Mr. Wilkins on the floor. He doesn't eat much, but he seems to like the company. At least, he isn't cursing like he usually does.

After we finish, I get Ruben ready. I leave the pannier and empty water jugs with Mom because I don't know how Ruben will handle them. We start for home, and I turn to wave goodbye to my mom, but she's already gone into the house. The ride back seems really long, across the dry, scrubby fields that haven't grown crops in years. All my senses are alert. The wind has picked up, and Ruben doesn't like it. He realizes he's leaving his mother, but he knows he's going home. I can see him deciding which is the most dangerous. Neither of us has been away from our mothers before, so I can understand.

"It's okay, Ruben. I won't let any tigers eat you," I tell him. I try not to think about hungry cougars and coyotes.

He seems to be calming down a little as we walk along, but he's sort of dancing, almost trotting in place. I nudge him with my heels and encourage him. Since I don't have stirrups, it's hard to post his trot, and I'm getting tired and jarred around. When we get to the firebreak, a dust devil whirls up, making him spook, shying fast to the left and leaving me in the air with no horse under me. I land hard enough to knock the wind out of me, spooking him even more. Now he's whirling around trying to decide whether to run back to his mom or back to his home. That gives me time to get off my butt and grab his reins. I don't cuss him out because I'm not feeling all that brave myself. It's a struggle to get back up on him because my tailbone hurts, but I'm not walking home, and I don't want him to think he can throw me off any time he feels like it.

By the time we get near the house, Ruben has settled since he's on familiar ground, but the wind is still strong. The sky has turned a dark and ugly kind of greenish color. It does that sometimes this time of year, but it never brings rain.

Rain only comes in the spring and fall. In the winter, a little snow falls. That's what serves for water these days, and we catch what we can in the cisterns. The water from the two wells comes from closed and open aquifers that we use carefully. They aren't always reliable because they have to recharge—the open aquifers from the rainfall, such as it is, and the closed aquifers from seepage throughout the closed system. There's no way to know who else is using that closed aquifer water, so we don't know how long it will last. During the ten-year drought it's lasted this long, but that could end any day. It's fossil water, and there's no replacing it. We only use it when we absolutely have to.

I put Ruben in his stall, brush him off, and make sure he has food and water. He turns up his nose at the rough stuff in his manger.

"Don't go expecting nice hay all the time, mister," I warn him. He seems to like the water fine, though, since it's not full of iron.

I'm in no hurry to get the chickens into the coop, but the dark sky has encouraged them to retire early, so I go ahead and shut them in for the night. I stay a minute listening to their soft clucking and crooning. It calms me some. As for the goats, we leave the kids with their mommas and only milk once a day, so there's nothing much to do with them but check and see they didn't get into any mischief while I was gone. They always come back from browsing, so they can get their water. We control when they drink; otherwise they might wander off anywhere. The electric fences serve as a warning, but if they were determined, they could get through them. Goats are like that. I toss them some goodies from the garden and give a good ear scratch to Judy, my favorite. They're looking a little thin, so it's probably time to move them into the next pen in the rotation so they have more to eat. I'll have to remember to water the ground poles for the electric fence tomorrow, so the electricity will conduct.

After I turn on the garden's drip line, I look around for any eggs laid in funny places. Seems like it's about time to put one of those broody hens on a clutch, I think. I'll talk with Mom about that. That's when I remember Mom isn't here.

Suddenly, I'm really scared. I don't know why. There's no good reason, but that's how people are, I guess, when they're alone and not used to it. I wonder how Mr. Wilkins stands it with no one to talk to, and I wonder if he's ever scared. He doesn't have any animals except fish. Since his dog died, he has no one. I feel a terrible sadness come over me for that lonely old man, making me feel glad my mom is with him during his last. All this reminds me of Daddy, and that makes my eyes burn. I don't want to waste water, so I think about other things like stills and how to power them. That makes me feel less sad.

Finally, I'm out of things to do, so I have to go in the house. It seems too quiet and so dark by now with twilight and clouds that I think I might put on a light. We have some LEDs that are bright enough to read by and don't use much power. And with the wind that's been blowing all afternoon, the turbine will have charged the batteries. The rule is no lights when the sun is up, but I can't see to do anything, so I think maybe that rule can be bent a little. Besides, I'm still a little scared. I know it's silly, but I can't help it.

I don't know what to do with myself. After the big lunch, I'm not hungry, so I pick up the last book I was reading, but the words don't make sense. I sit looking at the pages for a while without thinking much of anything.

The thunderclap makes me scream. I didn't expect it, and it nearly scares me out of my wits. I laugh at myself. Then the rain starts. It's a hard rain, and those always pass quickly. Still, you have to catch all you can, so I wind up a flashlight and hurry outside into the near dark. The wind nearly knocks me off my feet as I run around the house and the outbuildings, checking the downspouts to make sure they lead into the cistern channels. The lightning flashes again and again with thunder so loud I think I'm going to be deaf.

After I finish checking the downspouts, I realize I might as well turn off the drip line to the garden until I know how much rain we are going to get. When I'm done, I go back in the house and take off my wet clothes. In my underwear, I sit in my chair in the living room and listen to the wind howling like an animal until it settles down, the lightning and thunder passing on, but the rain still pounding on the roof, in the yard, all over the farm.

I get up out of my chair, uneasy, to look outside again. It's not like any rain I've seen before. Now that the lightning has stopped, I step off the porch and let the rain fall all over me. That's when I remember it's Saturday, and with all the things that have happened, I forgot to take my bath.

I run back inside, laughing, and get the soap and my dirty clothes and point the light out the front window so I can see. Then I run back out just off the edge of the porch and strip off my underwear, lather up first myself, then what I've been wearing all day, and let the rain wash my clothes and me clean.

By the time I'm back in the house hanging my things in the kitchen and drying off, I'm kind of chilled. I wrap myself in a blanket, then eat a hardboiled egg on a bed of fresh greens I brought from Mr. Wilkins' place and drink some milk. The rain still hasn't stopped. I'm getting a little worried. I put my wet clothes back on, wind up the flashlight again, and go to the barn. The horse and goats are snug and quiet. The chickens in their coop are the same. But as I'm going between the buildings, I'm walking through the beginnings of mud. I take off my recently clean clothes and my moccasins when I get back to the house. Never in my life have I had to clean mud off my shoes in the summertime.

I want to stay up as long as it's raining, but now I'm really tired and cold. The sky is wasting water, and that makes me afraid all over again. It doesn't rain in the summer, not like this. I want my mom, but she's helping an old man die. I crawl into her bed, so I can fall asleep on the mommy side against the wall.

In the morning, the sun is shining, and the air is heavy with moisture, almost like the fish cave. I've slept late, and the goats and chickens need tending. By the time I finish my chores, I'm hungry and muddy. There won't be any need for the drip lines this evening. The ground is soaked.

I'm not sure what to put in my backpack to take to my mom. I decide on hardboiled eggs, cheese, and dried fruit. I also fill two water bottles with fresh, sweet rainwater—even though the amount of it is unnatural.

Ruben doesn't much want to leave the farm on his own, but I convince him. The firebreak is muddy, and he reluctantly picks his way through it. There are no dust devils to spook him today. The sun is high by the time I get to Mr. Wilkins' house. Out of habit I call out when I'm close. My mom comes out, her face sad and tired. When I jump down from Ruben, she hugs me a long time. I'm so glad to see her I want to cry, but I don't.

Ruben and Ruby have a lot to say to each other when I put him in the pen and take off his gear. Ruby has rolled in the mud and is a disgusting mess. She looks proud of herself. I'm afraid Ruben is going to copy her bad behavior.

On the floor in the living room, Mom has laid Mr. Wilkins out straight and covered him with a sheet, so I know he's dead.

"He said he was going to dig a grave for himself but decided he'd rather be exposed."

"What's that?" I ask.

"That's when you put someone up on a platform, so the animals can eat them. Some people call it sky burial. It's not done much these days, but it's what he wanted. He says he owes the world something. I don't know what he means by that, but it was his last wish, so I guess we need to do it."

For such a skinny old man, Mr. Wilkins weighs a ton. The horses are scared of the smell of death, so we don't try to use them to carry his body. Instead, with Mom at his head and me at his feet, we carry him all the way to the top of the bluff. The path he uses to get up to his turbines is steep, narrow, and scrubby, but it has a rock base, so at least it's not muddy. By the time we're done and have said words over him, we've missed lunch and are hot and dirty.

Mr. Wilkins' place doesn't have any rain barrels. That seems stupid to me. Mom and I use some of the iron water to wash off. I got to wash in the rain last night, but Mom still hasn't had a good bath. I'll make sure she gets one when we get home.

After we eat, it's time to go home. The rain and being without Mom had made me eager to get back to normal life. Things haven't been the way they're supposed to be, but as we ride, Mom tells me things aren't going to be quite like before.

"If we're going to keep the fish farm going, I'll have to be over here at least twice a week. We'll have a lot more food."

"But we don't need more food."

"Well, you'll still want fish, won't you?"

"I guess," I say, but I'm not convinced.

During the next week, we spend more time at Mr. Wilkins' place. I learn about the stills and study the chemistry of fish farming. I don't want to enjoy it because it's not what I'm used to, but I can't resist the chemistry of the whole process. I spend a lot of time in the evenings studying the books I bring back home. Chores are a little easier because Mr. Wilkins' old hay and new vegetables mean we can spend less time finding forage for the horses, and there's more food for the chickens and goats.

Mr. Wilkins' aquaponic farm produces a lot of food, and we aren't sure what he was doing with it. Surely he didn't eat it all, him being so skinny. Eventually we find his compost pile. It's deep and wide and rich enough to grow anything. I'm outraged that he threw away so much food. It seems evil. He should have been drying or canning or something to keep it against hard times. As far as I can tell, all he ever preserved was the fish he smoked. I think the smoker is interesting and decide to make a study of it for possibly preserving our chickens and goats.

The next time it rains, Mom is home with me. This is the second storm in ten days. We sit together on the porch and watch it fall, splashing on the ground, making mud.

"This is how it should be," Mom says, smiling and rocking in her chair.

She's wrong. It's not supposed to rain in the summer, I'm thinking, but I don't argue.

On my birthday, my mom makes me a pie. We only have pies at Yule, but she says it's a special birthday. "Olivia, you're fifteen today, nearly a grown woman," she says as she lights a little candle stuck in the pie.

I blow out the candle after I make my wish that things could get back to normal. For my birthday present, Mom gives me a green silk nightgown made over from a housecoat she found at Mr. Wilkins' place. It's the softest thing I've ever felt, cool and buttery, fine-woven and slick.

"You should have pretty things now," my mom says. Why now, I wonder. Because of my fifteenth birthday? Because we have the things Mr. Wilkins willed to us? Because of the rain? She doesn't say, and I don't ask, but the pie is good.

That wasn't the last of the rain. When grass grows in the firebreak, I know things aren't ever going to be the same and not just because of the fish farm. The horses stop and drop their heads to eat as often as we'll let them. They won't touch the rough hay in their mangers at night. We have to watch them closely, so they don't get sick from too much green grass. Stranger still, the riverbed near Mr. Wilkins' house where all the trees grow and where we get firewood has got a trickle of a stream running through it. Brush is sprouting up all over the farm. I have to move fences so the goats can eat it to keep things from being lost under the foliage. I never knew vegetation could be so aggressive. It shows up everywhere no matter how hard you try to stop it. It's a struggle to keep the path to Mr. Wilkins' wind turbines open. I'm thinking of bringing some goats with me to eat the trail down. Everyone but Mom and me is getting fat. Even the goatmilk tastes different. Mom likes it better, so it must be more like cow's milk.

The summer is over, and still the rain is coming every week or so. We've got fields full of haystacks and have harvested more vegetables and fruit than we can put by. We're running out of material to cut canning membranes, even with the supplies we found at Mr. Wilkins' place. The dry spells of weather between the wet give us time to dry fish and vegetables and fruit. We tried our hand at smoking fish and chickens and are having pretty good success. We've been killing some of the young roosters. There were too many eggs to eat, so the hens have been sitting on them and turning them into chicks and those turn into chickens. We can't bring ourselves to waste anything, but I don't know what we're going to do with all this food.

It was cold this morning and getting out of bed was a hard time. Fortunately, we have plenty of firewood for the stove. All the rain caused water to collect in low places, like the old riverbed and old ponds where trees have grown. Now those trees are dying from too much water. Seeing this prompted us to make drainage gaps in the catchments for the fruit trees. It nearly broke my heart to do that because my daddy built those catchments, but now they are killing rather than helping the trees. We may end up with a pond in time. Mom says the sound I keep hearing is frogs. I sort of remember frog songs, but it's been a long time.

"Livie, how much rope do we have?" Mom asks after the fire is going and we are eating breakfast.

"In use or free or all together?"

"Free."

"Must be close to a hundred meters, I think, but that's just a guess. Why?"

"We need to run a strong line between the house and the barn. If the precipitation keeps up through the winter, we might have some bad blizzards," she explains.

I don't understand what she means. After breakfast, we find rope and run a line between the house and the outbuildings. It looks pretty silly. We spend the rest of the day putting up more hay and sowing winter wheat.

It's the day before Yule, and now I know why we have a strong line between the house and the barn. The sky is white, the ground is white, and I can't see a meter in front of me. But the animals still need tending. Mom warms water to replace what will have frozen in the night. I pull on my warmest clothes, and I'm grateful for Mr. Wilkins' little feet. Without his old winter boots, I'd be in trouble. My goatskin moccasins work for most things, but not today.

Carrying a jug of warm water in one hand, I pull myself along the rope, realizing without that line I would be completely lost in a few steps. By the end of the second trip back and forth, my fingers are so stiff they barely bend, and my eyes burn from the white. My nose is a lump of ice. Mom takes her turn for the next two trips, bundled in my dad's old winter coat and as many layers as I had on during my turn. By the time we finish, we know we won't be able to check the fish farm until the blizzard stops. Even then, it might be difficult to get there. Nothing outside looks familiar around our farm. I understand now why Mom has been using the compass on the past few trips to the Wilkins' place.

Since we're pretty much snowed in for Yule, we decide to take it easy. The chickens aren't laying now that it's dark for so much of the day, and the goats have been bred so they don't need milking. The horses are happy to run around in the snow for a little bit acting crazy, then they are just as happy to get back in their stalls. We spend the rest of the day preparing the only male goat born last season. By the end of the day that lonely young bachelor will be in a better place—our stomachs.

While supper cooks, pie and roast goat with root vegetables, Mom spends our computer-connection time checking the weather. She's been doing that a lot these past few months. I sew and read and, while she's not looking, wrap her present in a bit of nice cloth tied up with a ribbon. We're both dressed in our pajamas—me in my silk from my birthday and Mom in a pretty nightgown she always keeps for days off—but we have warm sweaters over them. A few candles that we save just for Yule we put in some pretty glass holders and place on the dinner table. Last thing before we eat, as the sun sets and darkness falls, is exchanging our gifts.

"Livie, it's beautiful!" My mom genuinely seems to like the fancy hair toy I've carved from some applewood. I saw a picture of one and tried to copy it. Now that she's growing her hair, I thought she might like one. "Here," she says, lifting her hair up and turning her back to me, "help me put it in place." We struggle around for a few minutes then get it figured out.

"That's real pretty, Mom." I take one of the candles into her room to get the hand mirror on her dresser and bring it to her. She smiles and admires her reflection. She looks beautiful.

"This is for you," she says, handing me a wrapped lump.

I can't tell what it is from the shape, but it's bigger than the hair toy. I unwrap it, and I can't breathe for excitement. They're real metal stirrups with old leathers that have been oiled.

"They're certainly not new, and I had to do a lot of oiling and messing around with the leather, but they seem pretty sound. We'll attach them to the bareback pad tomorrow."

"Thank you, Mom. They're wonderful." Gripping the stirrups tight in my hand, I kiss her cheek.

"You know," she says, "Mr. Wilkins has a lot of odd bits and pieces around his farm. We might yet find a saddle for you among all that stuff in his sheds." The weather and fish farm have kept us so busy that we haven't had time to go through all the things he left us.

"Mom, could we set a place at the table for Mr. Wilkins?"

She looks surprised. "Why, yes, I think that would be a good idea."

We eat our feast and afterward, all warm and full, toast Mr. Wilkins with our apple cider. I'm happy in spite of the snow.

The early spring is a nightmare of mud. The snow stopped falling every week or so only when the rain started. It is cold, bone-chilling rain that leaves mud so deep the horses lose their joy. The only time I ever seem to be warm these days is when I am scrambling up the bluff at Mr. Wilkins' farm, checking the turbines. I'm up there today, finally warm and breathing hard from the climb, cursing under my breath, when I see the scariest thing I've seen in years. I run all the way down the trail as fast as I can without breaking my neck, shouting.

"Mom, smoke! I saw smoke!"

She looks at me like she doesn't know what I'm saying. Then she asks, "A brushfire? It's too wet to worry about that."

"No, it's like a," I can't find the words, "like a humanmade fire. Like a," it finally comes to me, "like smoke from a campfire."

She understands now. "Which direction?"

I point downriver.

"I'll get Mr. Wilkins' gun," she says. "You go get the horses ready. We'd best be at our own home if they're coming this way."

We have stopped always carrying guns since the predators stopped coming around in daylight. When the game animals migrated out or died off, the cougars and coyotes left the area. We had to make the livestock not worth the trouble so the hunters would follow their natural prey. The theoretical cougar that killed Mr. Wilkins' dog was the last we heard of anything being in the area, and that was three years ago. With the rain returning, the game might return, too, and that would mean predators would return. As we ride quickly back to our own farm, I'm thinking we might be smart to carry guns again.

That night, after doing our chores and having dinner, Mom is at the desk. She's constantly looking for information now. "Here," she says, and turns the screen so I can see it. "It's a land rush."

I read the article. Land is being given to anyone who will farm it. If they leave the coasts and go farm the land, they can claim it.

"But that land belongs to someone," I say.

"It used to. It may not now. I don't know. I have to find out," she says as the Internet connection drops. The satellite has gone out of range.

We wait and watch, but nothing comes of the smoke from the river. Within the next weeks, though, we see campfire smoke every few days, always along the river over the ridge. No fires ever come all the way up the branch that runs by Mr. Wilkins' house—the branch that now has water in it all the time and grows each day—but we figure it's only a matter of time.

Finally, it's time. A party of two flat-bottom boats that can be heard long before they can be seen are putting their way up the branch that has become a modest but consistent stream. There are two men per boat, one at each end and between them, large humps covered by canvas tarps. Mom is ready for them.

"Hello," they call cheerily to her where she's standing on the bank. They kill the little motors that have been struggling to push their boats upstream. They start to drift backward.

"You can turn around and go back the way you came now," Mom says to them, her voice level but firm. She's got the rifle resting easily on her arm, pointing down to the ground.

"We don't want any trouble, ma'am. We just came to claim what's ours," the man in the lead boat says. He has a kind of slick and greasy look, like he eats too many things that haven't been stored properly.

"There's nothing here that's yours."

"Well, we have a land grant saying we can take this property," he says looking at Mr. Wilkins' fine house with hungry eyes, as though he wants to eat that, too. "This land was foreclosed for failure to pay the mortgage and back taxes."

Mom brings the gun up now and points it at the man who starts to sweat and look around him like a dog caught in the chicken house, mindful of its sins. "That will be a lie. There is a free-and-clear deed for this farm and tax receipts for the past ten years. Now get off this property, and don't come back."

My mom sounds really dangerous. I don't know if she'll shoot the man or not. I don't have any desire to carry his big hulk to the top of the ridge for the vultures to eat, that's for sure.

The man looks at the other men. I can't tell what they're thinking, but I see one of them in the hindmost boat reaching down for something. I step out from behind a bush where I've been watching all this and chamber a round in my own rifle. The sound makes the guilty-dog man's head snap around. The reaching man stops and holds very still. I'm not very big, but Daddy's gun is big enough to make it up.

"Sorry, ma'am," the dog man says, holding up his hands. "Honest mistake. The landscape has changed a lot, and it's sometimes hard to tell where we are."

"I can understand that," says my mom in a reasonable voice, lowering her rifle. "You gentlemen get your boats turned around, and you'll be fine."

The stream is so narrow it takes a bit of doing to get the boats pointed downriver. Mom never takes her eyes off the men. When they disappear around the ridge, she sits down hard on the ground, shaking and crying. I run to her and sit beside her.

She suddenly starts laughing. "I was so scared!"

"You didn't look scared. They were the ones who were scared."

"Livie, there were four of them. If they had guns and were ready for us, we'd be dead now, if that's the kind of men they are."

That never occurred to me. Now I'm scared. "What are we going to do?" I ask.

"I'm not sure. Mr. Wilkins kept good records, so I know their claims weren't legitimate. And we have records for our place. I've used your father's life insurance to keep up the tax payments on our land. I'm not sure how well the will Mr. Wilkins made is going to hold up if we claim his property, but that's for courts to decide, not river rats like that." Mom stands up and brushes the dirt off her overalls.

I've never thought about any of these things, taxes and mortgages, wills and deeds. I'm surprised my mom has. It's something I didn't know about her.

Mom heads for Mr. Wilkins' house. "The next people who come might not be deterred so easily," she says.

That night we make two signs. They say: "Private Property No Trespassing." The next day, we ride Ruben and Ruby down the branch and plant the signs on either bank. Mom has a hard time convincing Ruby to wade across the deepening river, but she manages. When she rejoins me on our side of the river, she looks around.

"We probably need to make enough signs to mark all the boundaries. People may not just come from the river."

The nearest road is a gravel track about a quarter mile from Mr. Wilkins' front door. We decide signs should go along it to mark the boundaries as well as along the open fields where our land ends. Always before, we tried to hide any sign of our existence, but now we'll mark our land to show where we are. It doesn't make sense that a piece of wood with words on it could deter a land grabber, but Mom says that's what gives us the right to shoot them if we must. I don't understand it, but I figure she knows more about it than I do.

That night Mom looks on the Internet some more. I'm reading an old law book I found at Mr. Wilkins' house.

"Even coming this early in the spring, how will they get the land ready and things planted in time to grow enough to survive the winter?" Mom is looking at the screen and not really talking to me.

Over the next few days, Mom starts changing how we do things. We have more to do than ever. Because of the fish farm and all the grass and brush growing up from the rain, we have more food than we could ever eat, but Mom has put the broody hens on more eggs. We're going to have an awful lot of chickens pretty soon. All but one of the kids born last year were females, and all those got bred and had their babies, so there's more milking than ever. That means more milk and yogurt than we could ever eat, so we're making a lot of cheese. Even with the fish farm and all it produces, Mom has added more beds to our garden. Every night we're falling into our own beds completely worn out.

Then Mom lets me in on her plan. "These people going upriver are going to need supplies. We can sell or trade our extra food to them."

I really hate this idea. It seems wasteful, somehow. It seems dangerous. "Why?" is all I can say.

"There are some things we need that we don't have. We can get those with the money we make."

"What do we need?" I can't think of anything.

"Salt blocks for the animals. We're down to two. Canning supplies. We're nearly out of membrane material. A real saddle for Ruben. New clothes."

"I don't need clothes."

She ignores me and goes on. "We could use a real harness, and we need fresh breeding stock, roosters and a buck goat."

"I suppose," I say reluctantly, knowing it's not good to inbreed our stock too much.

"We will be helping people. And we can maybe meet the new neighbors we're sure to get. We might even be able to pick our neighbors." This last part she's saying to herself, thoughtfully.

I don't have anything to say to this. I don't want to meet people. I don't want neighbors. I leave the house and go to the barn that has the rich smell of animals and fresh bedding. In his stall, Ruben is lying down. I sit next to him, laying my head on his warm side.

"We don't need clothes," I say to him. He nickers softly, and I feel tears run down my cheeks.

We set up our market on the big river over the ridge from Mr. Wilkins' place. It's slow at first, but as more people come, we sell more. We keep our guns close, and those who looked shifty get a warning. So far, we haven't had to kill anyone.

By late summer, we have a thriving business and a reputation. People know they can get fresh vegetables, milk, eggs, and sometimes fresh chickens and fish on their way to free land up the river. Now that more people are coming, it's more civilized along the river and less dangerous, but I hate the people. I'm still nervous all the time, and I've never been so tired in my life. I help Mom set up each day, then escape to the farms to do the chores, tending the fish and the gardens, the chickens and the goats. But Mom is happy and seems to have more energy every day, coming home in the evening, working long hours getting ready for the next day's market. She's letting her hair grow even longer. I keep mine short. She wears dresses sometimes instead of overalls all the time. I patch the knees of my overalls when they wear through and only take them off to sleep. She talks about the people she meets every day. I listen, pretending to care because I love her and want her to be happy.

On the anniversary of my daddy's death, two weeks before my birthday, my mother cries at night. I feel bad because I'm glad things are more like normal. For my birthday, I get a real saddle. I would rather have had our old life back where the sky isn't wasting water all the time.

Today, with the leaves on the hillside above the fish farm turning the color of flames, after I've adjusted the acidity in the fish tanks and am heading back to the house, I hear Mom calling for me. I grab my gun off the back porch and run toward the river, my heart pounding. There's Mom sitting on Ruby and talking with people in two flat-bottom boats just like the ones we saw earlier in the year. I take aim as I'm running, a really stupid thing to do, but I let the gun drop into the crook of my arm and slow down when I see that she is laughing. She jumps down from her horse.

"Tess, you always could sit a horse better than anyone I knew," the woman in the boat is saying.

"Livie! Come meet Rachel and her family," my mom calls to me.

I walk down to the boats that they are pulling up onto the bank. The woman is a little shorter than Mom, with blond hair pulled back from her face into braids. The two men stepping out of the boats look similar to one another, both tall, but one dark-haired and the other blond like the woman. The blond man has a mustache. My daddy had a mustache. The boy is about my age, halfway between the men and the woman in height, with hair the color of Ruben's, chestnut. All of the people have strangely pale skin like they have lived under rocks. They're wearing similar outfits, broad-brimmed hats and long-sleeved shirts, loose trousers and strong-looking boots. Just like the people before, the boats they are pulling onto the shore have canvas-covered humps in the middle. The woman and boy somehow look familiar.

"Rachel, you remember my daughter, Olivia. Livie, this is my best friend, Rachel Adams, and her husband, Ted," she points to the dark-haired man, "her brother, Luke Haywood," with the blond mustache, "and her son, Nathan."

I recognize the woman now. She was the one who came to visit that I thought might be an aunt. Just a friend, then. And the boy who kissed me on the cheek and cried was her son, not a cousin. I mumble hello, but I feel cautious and uncomfortable. I thought I was my mother's best friend. But, of course, she had friends once. Before the drought when everyone left their farms, before the crazy times and the empty land with no one for miles and miles.

"Come in. We'll fix something for lunch," my mother is saying.

We've all settled around Mr. Wilkins' dining table with smoked fish and chicken, vegetables, cheese, and a pitcher of sweet water flavored with sumac berries. Mom says it tastes like lemonade, but I don't know what lemonade tastes like.

"Rachel, why on earth would you try to come so late in the year? How do you hope to make it through the winter?" my mom asks, looking worried.

"We thought we could reclaim our old house, so we wouldn't have to worry about building a shelter," Ted answers for his wife.

I don't like that much. He wasn't the one asked.

"We think we can make it with the supplies we have and maybe trade with the river people that are starting to get more numerous," he says.

I think they're pretty stupid if they think they can get through a hard winter, especially one as hard as the one just past, with what they've got in those boats. Besides, if the snow is heavy and the rivers freeze, how are they going to manage to trade with anyone, them with boats and no horses?

Mom looks sad and shakes her head. "Oh, Rachel, I'm so sorry. Your place burned in one of the early brushfires. There's nothing left there at all."

Tears fill Rachel's eyes, and I feel bad for her. All four of the boat people are looking worried. That's the first sign of sense I've seen in them so far.

"What are the conditions you signed on for?" Mom asks Ted.

Instead his brother-in-law, Luke, answers. These people don't pay any mind to who's being addressed. Is that how people are downriver?

"We signed on for whatever abandoned property we could secure and maintain for one year with continuous occupation and some improvement. The improvement is pretty open-ended," Luke says, smiling at my mother.

"Luke's a lawyer," Rachel says. She's smiling now, too. That makes my mother smile, and now they all look like a bunch of fools all smiling at each other.

My mom looks thoughtful as we eat our lunch. The boy Nathan is looking at me like he's never seen a girl before. I ignore him. I'll be glad when all these people move on to whatever property they are going to claim and get out of my life.

"Luke, how valid would you consider a will that was never witnessed?" my mom asks.

He seems surprised at the question and thinks a minute, rubbing his mustache. "Well, in these times with people sort of thin in the interior and the likelihood that there would have been no one around to witness a document, I think it would depend on how contested it was. Why do you ask?"

"Well, Mr. Wilkins made a will leaving this place to Livie and me, so in theory we own it free and clear. But it could be claimed it's abandoned since he's dead."

I understand what my mother is thinking and start to open my mouth, but snap it shut again. She can't. She just can't.

"If you were to claim this place as abandoned, and we deeded it over to you, you'd have a double claim. It's in pretty good shape, but there are a lot of improvements you could make to it."

"Tess, that would be wonderful!" Rachel's eyes tear up again. She's crying for happiness this time.

Ted, her husband, is looking out the window at the scrubland around the house. "There's lots of land here we could make ready for late crops. We could buy food from you, Tess, if you'd sell it to us," he says. "We could pay you for the property when we got on our feet. ..." His voice trails off, and he looks uncomfortable. At least he has enough honor not to want something for nothing. I'm liking him better.

My mom laughs. "Oh, I think you'll do just fine." She pushes away from the table and holds out her hand to Rachel. "Come with me. I have something to show you."

The boat people are as surprised by the fish farm as we were when we first saw it. I don't feel comfortable with Mom telling them about it. It was a secret that Mr. Wilkins shared with us. Somehow, it seems like betraying him. But as they stand talking, I realize if we're free of the fish farm, we can spend more time with our own place. Some of our old life might be gotten back. It will be different, but maybe more like it was before.

As Mom leads us all back to the house, Nathan walks beside me and speaks to me for the first time. "Do you remember me?" he asks.

I don't look at him. Best to be honest to avoid regrets in accumulated lies, my dad used to say. "Yes, I remember," I tell him.

"Did you miss me?" he asks.

I stop walking and look at him, amazed. "Why would I miss you?"

Red creeps up from his neck to cover his face. He turns away and doesn't say anything else to me for a long time.

The boat people are a mixed blessing. All the roofs for all the buildings on both farms get patched and any chinks in the walls, doors, and windows closed up, making them snug and secure, but there are just too many people around our place all the time. We've acquired a new rooster and buck goat, so we don't have to worry about inbreeding anymore, but there are more of us eating things and will be all winter. Mom has decided to sell less down on the big river, even though she has help from Rachel running her market now.

Mr. Wilkins' place—I can't think of it as the Adamses' place—has garden beds all around it, putting that huge compost pile to good use, ready for planting seeds in the spring. The fish farm is continuing to thrive but isn't the sole source of vegetables anymore. It's not even the sole source of fish since some are in the rivers now. Beets and turnips and other autumn vegetables are already producing and get canned faster with more people helping, but we all get in one another's way until we get a routine down. I see Mom more often, but she has a lot on her mind and is more distant than before, like she's here and not here at the same time. And that Luke keeps finding reasons to come by. He has a bicycle and rides it across the fields to our house. He can be useful, but I get awfully tired of him underfoot all the time. Sometimes he brings Nathan, who has his own bicycle.

We have plenty of wood stored for the winter, but I'm worried we need to manage our trees to keep from overharvesting. I'm thinking about this, wondering if we need to figure out some alternative sources for heating, as I'm mucking out Ruben's stall.

"Hello, Livie."

It's Nathan. I think of him as the Adams boy, not my neighbor or Mom's friend's son. He's almost not a boy anymore. He's taller than me, and looks a little better now that he's not so pale and sickly like when he first came up the river.

"Hello," I say. No point in not being nice to him. His family has helped us out a lot. I'm not nearly so tired all the time as I was before they came. They aren't as objectionable as the river rats would have been as neighbors, so in all, I guess I should be glad. But I'm not very glad.

"Livie, I was wondering, do you think I could hire you to teach me how to ride a horse?"

I'm stunned into silence. My first question is, do you mean you can't ride? My second question is, what do you mean 'hire me'? There are a lot of other questions, but they're too jumbled to make it to the front of the line, and none of them get past each other to my mouth.

"Um, sure, I guess." I don't know what else to say.

He smiles, showing lots of teeth, and says, "That's great! Can we start tomorrow?"

"I guess."

"What time?"

I think a minute. Ruby is the calmer horse, so we should start him on her. It would be better if she were a little tired so she's less lively. "How about in the later afternoon?"

"Okay. I'll be here. How much do you want for the lessons?"

I have no idea what to ask. I'm not used to money. "I'm not sure. Maybe we can trade something," I say. I'm more comfortable with barter.

"Do you know how to swim?" he asks.

There was never any place to learn to swim. "No," I say.

"Fine. I'll teach you how to swim."

Before I can say I don't want to learn to swim, he's out the door and gone.

I can only say that Nathan Adams is not a natural horseman. I hope I will be a better swimmer than he is a rider. Working on the farms has increased his strength, and he rides his bicycle a lot, so his balance is at least passable, but he has a long way to go, and it's a hard road on that long way. Still, he is determined and seems not to mind how often he has to get up off the ground. I'm afraid he's going to break something, but the one thing he is good at is falling.

After the lesson, we're brushing Ruby and letting her eat some apple bits for a treat because she really didn't mean for him to have such a hard time.

"How do you get around downriver?" I ask Nathan. "Besides by bicycles, I mean?"

"Mostly we walk." He runs the stiff brush over Ruby's thickening winter coat. "But there are some public transports, like buses and trains if we have to go a long way. There are lots of sailboats along the coast and up the inlets. Now that there is water again, the refineries are back working, making gasoline for the boat motors and maybe even for cars and trucks soon. People say the electric powerplants will have enough water to start working again by spring if this winter is like the last. Everything is changing back the way it was before."

He's answered way more than I asked, never looking at me, chatting away as he brushes. By the time he leaves, my head hurts. I go to the computer to find out if what he has been saying is true. I can't believe a year and a half of rain can make everyone think it's all back the way it was before the years of drought. All the people downriver seem to be using water like it will never go away again.

In Mr. Wilkins' house, the Adamses call Yule 'Christmas.' I would rather be home eating our own meal, but they want to show their gratitude for all our help. They have gone to a lot of trouble to get a ham for the feast. It's so salty I can barely eat it, but I manage some to be polite. At least the vegetables, cheese, and pie are good. I am embarrassed because I didn't realize I was expected to give them presents. They give me a dress made of light cotton. I can't imagine where I would wear such a thing.

My mother gives me a pair of strong winter boots and a nice bridle for Ruben. They're perfect. I give my mother a new pillow filled with soft down from the many chickens we've killed over the year. I'm glad when we can finally make our goodbyes and escape home with our presents. I hang the dress in my closet and forget about it as I head out to the barn to tend the animals.

By spring, the mud is as bad as last year. Everything is growing as thickly as before, and everyone is getting fat but me. Mom is not so very skinny this spring. She looks younger than last year. She spends a lot of time over at the Wilkins' place or at the market on the river. Nathan still comes for his riding lessons, but everyone is really busy putting in crops. Ruby and Ruben are plowing fields for the additional grains we'll be growing. There was a lot of conversation this winter over the best crops to raise for a profit. We're not growing just what we want to eat or sell now. Apparently, we're going into agribusiness. There is even talk of cattle. Mom seems to want a milk cow, and Luke has promised her he'll find a way to get her one.

No one asks me what I think. All the changes worry me. We are heavy on the land. I worry about putting back what we take out, preserving what we have. I worry about wasting water.

It's two weeks before my birthday, so in a few minutes I'll take a damp washcloth to my mom. My dad died eight years ago today. Mom cries on this day every year, but today I open the door to her room and find she's already up and outside. I follow the sound of her laughter. Standing in the yard is Luke Haywood holding a lead rope with a cow on the other end and a calf by its side.

"Livie, come look! It's a Jersey." She puts her arms around Luke and gives him a kiss on the cheek. "Oh, Luke, she's so beautiful."

"I always keep my promises," he says and kisses her back, only on the mouth. Mom should push him away, but she doesn't. Her arms are around him as she leans into him admiring the cow.

"I'll make room for her in the barn," I say and hurry off. I'm stunned. I should have seen it coming, and now that I think back on the past several months, I know I'm stupid to be surprised. My eyes burn, and I swipe at them angrily. I won't waste water over the likes of him. But to have it happen on this day, the day my dad died. It's cruel. I feel a sob catch in my throat.

Everything is wrong. Every single thing in the world is wrong. Or maybe I'm the one who's wrong. They all seem happy. They understand the rain and the mud and the new crops and the different animals. I don't know this world anymore. I don't know where I am.

I sit in the barn a long time, thinking. Maybe I should try harder to adapt. That's what kept us alive so long. We adapted everything on the farm to our needs in hard times. Now times are different. Maybe I should adapt. By the time I finish making a nice place in the barn for the cow to rest, I've decided, if nothing else, I'll let Nathan teach me to swim.

For my birthday, though it was the last thing in the world I would ever ask for, my mother, Rachel, and Luke take me on a trip down the river to a little town that has sprung up a few miles below where Mom first set up her market. The journey will take two days, so we'll spend the night in the town while Nathan is tending our farm and Ted is tending the fish farm.

We take the two boats that the river people arrived in, powered by their little motors that have an easier time going downstream than up. I'm nervous because I still can't swim, though Nathan has done his best to teach me over the past two weeks. At least I can float, so I'll be able to drift like the logs that go along with us, maybe coming to shore someday if I kick like he keeps telling me. Brush is growing along the banks, its feet washed by the slow-moving water. In some places people have cleared landings to what look like farms lining this newly reliable water supply.

I say the town sprung up, but more it regrew with old buildings being occupied again, cleaned up, repaired, and returned to service as stores and places to eat and sleep. And to be married. The excuse for the trip was my birthday, but the real reason was so Mom could be married to Luke Haywood. I'm not caught off guard this time. I know there's nothing I can do to change her mind, so I don't try.

We buy new clothes and shoes and important supplies like canning membranes and salt blocks for the animals, then we go to the Justice of the Peace. It seems it doesn't take long to get married. Just some words and a kiss, and my world is destroyed forever.

We eat in a restaurant where the vegetables aren't as fresh as I have at home, then we go to a movie theater. I can't remember ever being in a movie theater before, but I've seen movies. I don't know what this movie is about. I can't concentrate sitting there in the dark. There are too many people too close to me, and I can't breathe. I try to be quiet as I stand up from my seat and slip out of the theater.

"It's not that great a movie. I've already seen it," Rachel says. She's followed me.

"It's not that," I say. I don't know why I should have to explain anything to her. "I just ... there are too many people here." Might as well be honest. "I'm not used to so many people."

She smiles and takes my hand. "I can understand that. You're always more comfortable with the animals than with the people," she says.

I'm surprised she's bothered to notice, but she's right. I prefer the company of animals.

"Livie, I know some of the changes that have been taking place are hard for you. Your mother is worried about you."

That's the first I've heard of it. Why hasn't she talked to me, I wonder.

"She doesn't know what to say to you," Rachel says, like she read my mind. "You've both been alone so long. I know your mom missed your daddy for a long time, but she's been lonely, even with you for company. She's missed having a husband." She doesn't say anything for a few minutes, then adds, "She still loves your father, you know. And she loves Luke, too. And she loves you."

My eyes fill, and I can't stop it from spilling out. I'm wasting water, but so is the whole world.

In the morning, as we're eating breakfast in the hotel dining room, my mother and her husband talk to me about the university further downriver.

"It shouldn't be anything to get you a GED," Luke says. I know what he's talking about, the General Educational Development exam that is a substitute for a high-school degree, which I would need to go to a university because I've never been to school. "You're one of the smartest kids I've ever met."

I smile, but I don't know how many kids he's ever met.

"There are grants and scholarships available to help with expenses," he goes on, "and I could probably set up some sort of law practice to help out our finances. Apparently, there are some land disputes that need sorting out, so I'd have my work cut out for me without having to go too far from home."

He means my home, but now he'll live there, too, sleeping on the daddy side of the bed. I feel my fists tightening under the table and make myself relax them.

My mother looks like she's lit from the inside, smiling and happy. "And the farms are going to make a really good profit," she says to me. "You can study anything you want—chemistry, law, even veterinary medicine. It might be a year or two before we could get it all together, but in the meantime, you could visit the school and find your way around and see how you like it."

"It sounds okay," I say. I'd never thought about leaving the farm. I'd never thought about a future. Now my future is being planned for me. It's not the first time Mom has talked about me going away to college, but it always seemed like something far distant and impossible. Now I feel rushed, like she and Luke would like me to go away and leave them to our farm.

We've been back home for a while, and I'm getting used to Luke being around. He works hard and keeps his promises, but he isn't my father. I'm back to my usual chores, and there isn't much more talk about college at the moment.

"Livie, come look what I got for my birthday!"

Nathan is hollering, scaring Judy while I'm milking her. I nearly lose hold of the pail.

"For Pete's sake, Nathan, calm down. You're scaring the goats."

"Oh, sorry," he whispers.

I finish up and put the milk out of harm's way, so I can see what Nathan is so excited about.

Tied to the hitching post near Ruben's and Ruby's paddock is a mean-looking gelding, sort of mud-colored with a rough coat and sorry, sad eyes. Still, he's standing quietly and seems to have pretty good manners, in spite of his appearance.

"That's a nice horse you have there, Nathan," I say. I pat the horse and lift his lip to look at his teeth, then pick up his feet one by one to check his hooves. He's sound all the way around. I put my head on his chest and hear a strong heart, no wheezing in his lungs and a nice gurgle of digestion.

"Get up, and let's see how he goes," I say.

Nathan grins. He unties the horse and slips his foot into the stirrup of the serviceable saddle that looks like it came with the sale. He turns the gelding away from the barn at a nice walk, then trots him back. It's a steady, easy gait that doesn't cause Nathan too much alarm. His riding has improved a fair bit over the months.

"Where did he come from?" I ask. It would have taken some doing to get him upriver by boat, and I don't know how far away the nearest farms with horses are these days. I never had any need to know or care where my nearest neighbors were or what resources they had, except for Mr. Wilkins.

"I'm not sure," Nathan says, jumping down and patting the horse. "I think Dad got him from the town downriver, and someone rode him here."

"Well, let's see if we can't improve on his grooming some," I say and lead Nathan to the barn to get him started on brushing the poor beast's coat. Even with grain and good grass and grooming, the horse isn't ever going to be a beauty, but he seems grateful for nothing much being asked of him except a calm walk and a slow trot. I imagine he'll canter if we asked him, but I can't think why we ever would. I suspect he's a used-up farm horse who lost his spirit and all hope and is happily surprised to be spared slaughter.

"What do you think you might call him?" I ask.

"Lazarus," says Nathan.

By Yule, my mother is showing. She'll have her baby before Rachel has hers. It's like every female everywhere is pregnant except Ruby and me. And all the males are awfully proud of themselves: Luke and Ted, the new buck goat who isn't as mean as the old one, that new rooster who struts and crows and acts like he's responsible for the creation of the whole world. Only Nathan and Ruben are fit to be around, neither of them pregnant nor proud. Lazarus, being a gelding, holds no opinions.

For a Yule present, Luke built Mom a sleigh that Ruby can pull to get us all from our place to the Adamses' farm, since he doesn't want Mom riding now that she's pregnant. He says he can put wheels on it in the spring. He hasn't gotten the hang much of riding, and bicycling isn't possible in all weather, so I think the sleigh cart is as much for him as for her. Still, it's a practical gift as long as the snow is on the ground. It has been so far this winter, though not as deep and dangerous as last year.

We take the sleigh to go to the Adamses' house to have Christmas dinner like we did last year. I'm finally coming to think of it as their farm rather than Mr. Wilkins' place, now that they've done so much to it. It's nothing like when Mr. Wilkins was here, for better or worse. They still maintain the windmills on the bluff, but they've completely abandoned the fish farm. I think that's a sad and terrible mistake. They figure with fish in the rivers and vegetables growing in the gardens, there's no need to keep it going. I think the loss of the fresh vegetables in winter is a tragedy. They've started a mushroom farm in the old quarry instead, and, while it seems silly to me, they say there's good profit in it.

We have roast beef for the feast, the meat provided by our farm from the Jersey cow's male calf. I'm glad we killed that beast who had no respect for fences and made us chase him all over creation. Eating him is fine revenge, even if the beef does give me a stomachache. In the end, I'd say he and I came to a draw.

This year, I'm ready for the gift exchange. With the hide from our retired buck goat, I made soft shoes for the coming babies and a few odds-and-ends for the rest, like wallets, since they're thinking about money all the time.

"This one is for you, Nathan," I say, handing him his package.

He looks pleased and surprised. "What is it?"

"Well, that's a stupid question. Open it and find out."

He looks embarrassed and opens the present. "Wow, Livie, thanks. And thanks from Lazarus, too."

I put together a grooming kit for his horse with a stiff brush, a hoof pick made from an old iron spike with a leather-wrapped handle, a curry comb made from reworked saw blades, and a wide-toothed wooden comb for the mane, all in a little box with a handle, so it's easy to carry. I wanted to include a pair of scissors if he wants to trim a place for the bridle path, but I ran out of time and materials. Lazarus looks less awful compared to the other horses now that they have their winter coats, too. With all the care Nathan has been giving him, he might actually look nice by spring when he sheds out. The horse's spirits are better now, though I think he's a little lonely except when he comes to visit Ruby and Ruben or when they visit him. I can see him and Ruby out the window now, standing nose to nose, breathing into each other's nostrils. It's a nice, calming sight.

After all the exchanging and eating and talking and even some singing, we hitch up Ruby and bundle back into the sleigh to head home before dark. The runners make a soft shushing sound going over the snow. The moon is already up, and the sunset is giving the snow a soft, reddish glow. As we cross the place where the firebreak used to be, I see movement out of the side of my eye.

"What was that?" I ask, turning my head fast.

Luke pulls Ruby to a stop. In the twilight we see three deer wandering parallel to us, headed back toward the river. They are the first deer we've seen in years. Ruby isn't bothered at all. That means she's used to them, but for some reason they make me uneasy. The thought gnaws at me; if the prey are back, the predators won't be far behind.

"We need to start carrying guns again," I say to Luke and Mom.

Luke looks at me. "Yes, it would be nice to have some venison," he says. Close enough, I think.

Luke is turning out to be pretty handy. He made a cradle for the baby and has a fair grasp of gardening. I leave all cow tending to him, but I went along when he had the cow bred at a farm downriver. I can almost stand the smell of the cow now, but the milk tastes like the cow smells. I stick to goatmilk.

By spring when all the kids and the calf are born and all the milking begins again, Mom is big as a barn and hardly any use at all, though she keeps trying.

"Was I this much trouble?" I ask her.

"My dear child, you were twice as much trouble," she says.

I believe her. It makes me laugh.

I never really understood that pregnant women are beautiful, but she and Rachel both seem different than they were before. Their skin has a sunrise brightness. They are calm, even when the goats have their kids breech and they have to be pulled at midnight, or the cow gets loose wandering around in a blizzard. Even when Luke and Ted have to be gone for three days at a time all the way downriver to fight a legal case. They have a serenity, a constancy, like the world will go on whatever happens. Animals don't do that so much. Only humans. Only human mothers.

With animals there's no telling what time of day they'll be born, but it seems like so many want to come in the middle of the night. This little baby is coming late in the afternoon. I don't know if that means anything, but I hadn't expected it. Rachel wanted to be here, but it's hard for her to travel with her being so pregnant, too. Luke is here, home from his traveling. Mom and I can handle it fine, but it's good to have an extra pair of hands, though Luke is nervous as a green horse in a windstorm. I keep him busy making hot water and getting towels ready. I've helped Ruben and a whole bunch of goats get born, so I figure I have a pretty good idea what to expect. Mom has some prior experience, but apparently there was a midwife in the area when I was born.

Luke has read up on childbirth on the Internet. He's timing the contractions. I'm not sure what he thinks that accomplishes, but it keeps him busy.

"I think it's time," Mom says. She's sweating and panting. She grips Luke's hand and grits her teeth, pushing down hard. Then she stops and pants some more. I can tell she's hurting Luke's hand, but he doesn't say a word. When she catches her breath, and her face tightens in pain, she pushes again. I'm ready, watching a little head all covered with red hair making its way to daylight.

The whole thing finishes up without much trouble. He's a boy, red-faced and screaming. Even before the afterbirth is delivered, they name him John, after Luke's father. With his umbilical cord all tied off, I hand him over to his momma who lifts him to her breast for his first meal of colostrum to make him strong and able to fight off disease.

"Livie?" It's Nathan at the door knocking.

"Come on in," I call.

"Mom sent me over to help with the chores," he says as he comes into the house.

"Well, that's pretty good timing," I laugh. "Come meet your new cousin, little John."

Nathan is following the sound of my voice to find us in Mom's bedroom. When he sees the baby, he stands still with his mouth open, all amazed.

"What's wrong?" I ask. "Never seen a baby before?"

"He's so tiny," Nathan whispers, then he congratulates everyone all around.

The childbirth mess is still here, so I clean it up while Nathan admires his cousin, but not long after all the fussing, he joins me in washing out the linens. He isn't at all squeamish about the fluids and stains, and I have to say I admire him for that.

After he helps me with the chores, Nathan and Lazarus head back home to spread the good news. I've come to think more highly of Nathan. In fact, I think he's going to be a fine horseman someday.

Almost a month to the day after John is born, Rachel starts her labor. Nathan came for me and Mom at dawn. We hurried over in the sleigh cart as quickly as we could. The labor has gone on all day. Nathan and his dad, Ted, went to our place a little while ago to help Luke take care of our animals. That was to get Ted out of the house as much as anything. He's nearly worried himself sick. Rachel is resting now. The worrisome thing about the labor is it comes and goes and doesn't seem to follow a sensible rhythm.

"Livie," my mom says to me quietly. "I'm afraid the baby may be a breech. I want you to try to feel for the head. Your hands are smaller than mine."

When a goat has its baby breech it's not such a dangerous thing. Sometimes you lose the doe or the kid or both, but not often. With humans, it's a little different.

"You think she might be breech?" Rachel asks us.

I swear that woman can read minds.

"We're going to find out," my mom says, trying not to sound worried.

I wash my hands carefully and reach into Rachel to feel for a head. Mom can tell by the look on my face that I feel feet instead.

"Rachel, we're going to try to turn the baby from the outside and see how that goes. Okay?" my mom says.

Rachel nods.

Mom does the maneuvering while Rachel bites down on a cloth. It takes three tries. Rachel bears it. There are a hundred things that can be going wrong right now, including getting the umbilical cord around the baby's neck and choking it.

"Livie, see if the shoulders are in the way or if the head is straight and tucked down. Do you think you can do that?"

"I'll try," I say.

We check, and this time I feel a smooth, round head. With the next contraction, Rachel bears down and cries out, then the contraction stops, and we look at each other, waiting. With the next contraction, out comes a baby girl just like Rachel has always said, but the baby is a strange color, not at all like when little John was born. She isn't moving or making a sound.

Mom quickly clears out the baby's mouth and nose, then swings her upside down. She slaps the baby girl on the behind. I've never seen my mother strike a human or an animal, but I guess there's a time and a place for everything. That baby gasps and lets out a scream, all indignant. She takes another breath and screams again and doesn't stop until she has a nipple in her mouth. Rachel has tears in her eyes, and my mom is laughing. Rachel finally falls asleep with her daughter still at her breast, all the pain lines leaving her face and making her look beautiful.

By the time everything is complete and tidied up, the baby is asleep, too. That being born must be hard work, or at least this time it was. I'm glad my mom was here, and I didn't have to do this on my own.

When the men come back, they're so noisy they wake Rachel, and the baby starts crying. We all celebrate, congratulating Ted and Rachel for such a pretty little girl. She looks mostly like a baby and not so very pretty, but parents don't know any better.

"What do you plan to call her?" my mom asks.

"We thought we might call her Teresa, after you," says Rachel.

My mom blushes. I've never seen her blush before.

When we get home that evening to close up the hen house and shut the goats in for the night, I can't find Judy, my favorite doe. It's not like her to stay out. I don't bother putting a saddle back on Ruben, just jump up on him and ride the fence line to see if maybe she got through someplace and is off having a feast in forbidden fields. I call to her, but she doesn't answer. That's not like her, either. She usually bleats to me when I call because she knows I'll scratch her ears and call her sweet, silly names.

By the time all the light has left the sky and the moon is up, I've found no trace of Judy and no breaks in the fence. When Ruben pricks up his ears and stands stone still, I realize I don't have a gun with me. We quickly head back to the barn. After I take off his bridle, I go into the house and find my daddy's gun. I won't leave the house without it again. That night I listen, but never hear yipping and howling off in the distance. I don't think it was coyotes that got my Judy.

I'm cursing under my breath because my stirrup leather has finally broken. I was mid-mount when it gave way, and now I'm on the ground. Sitting in her sleigh, Mom is trying not to laugh. I knew that leather was going to give sooner or later, but I was hoping for later.

"Why don't you go on, and I'll catch up as soon as I fix this," I tell her.

"Take the leathers off my saddle. I'm not using them these days," she says, and clucks to Ruby. Little John is asleep in his basket on the seat beside her.

"I'll be close behind," I say and go to get the leathers.

After I get Ruben's saddle adjusted and get up on him, we set off at a nice trot. We don't want to be late for supper. The Adamses have been digging a new well, so they won't have to depend on the river or the iron well anymore. We're going to christen it with a party. We plan to spend the night and come back early in the morning to do the chores. I've checked to make sure the animals are locked away safe from any critters that might come visiting. We've never found a trace of Judy, so I'm not taking any chances. I have Daddy's rifle in a sheath tied to my saddle.

The sun will set soon, and there are clouds directly overhead, but there's still plenty of light coming in from the west. Ruben and I hear something ahead of us that sounds like Ruby whinnying. Then it sounds more like a scream. Ruben snorts, and I kick him in the ribs. We take off at a fast gallop, me clinging to his mane and letting him have his head.

The cougar is on Ruby's back. The horse is wild and screaming in her traces. Mom is using the reins to beat at the cougar—where is her gun? No, she can't shoot the cat when it's on the horse. Ruben skids to a stop near Ruby. The cougar panics and jumps off the horse's back and onto my mom. It has to claw itself free of the reins it's tangled itself in. The second it hits the ground, Ruben rears, roaring his stallion challenge and striking the big cat with both hooves. I manage to hang on to him as he stomps again and again until the cougar is dead under his feet.

I jump down from Ruben and run to my mother. Ruben goes to his mother and blows into her nostrils. Ruby is quivering, sweating, bleeding.

The baby is screaming, but looks safe, still in his basket.

"Mom?" I lift her head.

When the cougar landed on her, it broke her neck against the back of the cart seat. Her eyes are open, but there's no life in them. I move her gently to the side and settle her in place, then pick up John and soothe him until he quiets. I don't realize I'm crying until a tear drops on his tiny hand.

I sing to him, a song my mother used to sing, until he's calm, then I put him back in his basket.

"Come on, Ruby, we have to get to supper," I say to the mare, trying to calm her, trying to keep myself calm.

She's still quivering, but her ears turn back to me.

"Let's go see Lazarus. You like Lazarus. Let's go, girl, please." It's hard to keep my voice steady, but Ruby and Ruben begin to walk. A thunderclap startles us all, making Ruby rear in her traces again, but she settles and keeps walking. The rain falls.

It's been two years since my mother died, so I know I was crying in my sleep, wasting water. I can feel the dried tears on my face. I hear a soft tap at the bedroom door.

"You awake?" It's Nathan.

"I'm awake," I say.

He comes into the bedroom and hands me a damp cloth to wipe away the tear tracks. I scrub my face and smile at him as he sits on the daddy side of the bed.

"I got the chores done already, so you're off the hook."

I yawn and stretch. "It's Sunday. Lunch with the family today," I say. He lies down and curls himself around me and my bulging belly that is our baby, a planned baby like little John and Teresa, not a surprise like Ruben and me.

"Unless you want to stay home and wear pajamas all day."

"I'm not wearing pajamas," I say, looking down at my naked self.

He grins. "I've noticed."

I laugh. "We should go. They'll be expecting us. Will Luke be coming this week?" I ask.

"I think he's going to try," Nathan says.

"We'll have to make sure he has plenty of eggs and cheese to take back with him."

Luke really misses little John. He can't wait until the boy is old enough to go to school, so they can be together downriver, but in the meantime, Nathan's folks are really good parents to Tess and John. I like Luke better now than I ever used to. He has stuck by his family the best he can, even when he is so sad and lonely.

Nathan and I hold each other close and listen to the wind outside.

"Do you think it will rain?" he asks.

Since my mother died, it has rained exactly four times if you count the one snowfall. The river has dried up near the Adamses' place where the fish farm is once more up and running. The fields have withered, and the firebreak is dusty again. We've repaired the catchments for the fruit trees, and we water the ground poles of the electric fence when we have to, use the well water carefully.

"Probably not," I answer. "It does this sometimes, but it doesn't usually mean rain."

He gently strokes my belly.

"Do you think we'll be good parents," I ask. It's something that's been worrying me lately. "I'm not so good with people."

"You're good with animals, though, and babies are a little like animals. They can't tell you what they need, so you have to guess," he says. "Besides, we've had good teachers."

"I guess so." I might not be as good a mom as my mom, but I have Nathan to help me, so I'll be okay.

"Will we need to come home early, so you can get your homework done?" he says, getting out of bed and reaching for my hand.

"No, I finished and uploaded it last night so we can stay awhile," I say.

He pulls me to my feet. He wraps his arms around me again.

"I think I might declare a major in horticulture."

He looks surprised. Everyone has been expecting me to study veterinary medicine.

"There are so many mistakes in those books in the university's online library," I say. "I need to straighten some of that out."

His mouth has gone crooked like it does when he's trying not to laugh at me.

"What?"

"You're not even done being a freshman, and you're already rewriting the textbooks?" He's grinning now. He's a happy man and can't help himself sometimes.

"Mistakes can hurt people," I say.

His smile fades, and he kisses me softly on the forehead, then rests his head against mine. "You teach the world what you know, how to live, how to survive. That's a good plan."

I like the feel of his arms around me. It makes me feel strong, able to do anything, even be in a town surrounded by people, maybe even swim in the ocean someday.

Nathan pulls away and says, "You get dressed and have some breakfast, and I'll get Lazarus hitched up."

Now that I'm so pregnant, we take the cart to go visiting. Ruby has gone to live at the fish farm because, once Ruben discovered he was a stallion, even though she's his mother, he wouldn't leave her alone. Horses have no sense of decency. I smile, thinking, it took Ruben a long time to grow up, but I probably have no room to criticize.

My overalls are too tight to be comfortable, so I look into the closet to see if I can find something of Nathan's I can wear. Clear at the back of the closet is a dress of some light flimsy stuff, a Christmas present from a long time ago. I slip the dress on over my head and look in my mom's mirror. Looking back at me is one of those women, those pregnant women who is beautiful and serene. It's probably an illusion caused by the morning light, the soft dress, being in love, but it's a nice illusion, and I'll settle for that.

AVALANCHE

Jason Morphew

Somewhere above
cold plans
to bury you
dead boy
ice arcing
like a rainbow
to your eyes
God's promise
never to flood the world
with love to keep
life a terrible surprise.

BRIDGE OF THE GODS

Chris Ketchum

Its trusses frame the Pentecostal
Stage: Portland, our summer loge,
Is loath to name what hostile
Habits set the blaze. Is age
To blame? One bomb-tosser
Sparked the flame's baptismal
Course through oak and Douglas fir—
A pyre laid of Eagle Creek's deadfall.
The city supplicates like abbots
With hoods drawn: our cottonmouths.
Azalea-lustered dawn and its
Gray bank predates the drought.
We convene upon steel beams to grieve
The fire-flood, our holy-curtained scene.

RUINATION DAY: WHAT THE GREAT DEPRESSION TOLD US ABOUT CLIMATE CHANGE, AND WHY WE SHOULD'VE LISTENED

Eric Shonkwiler

There was a lie, told and retold about the center of America: that the land east of the Rockies, heretofore known as the "Great American Desert," a treeless, arid plain that had long been unsuitable for farming, had changed. Its climate was permanently bettered, in part by the hand of man, as it was known that "rain follows the plow," that the land held in a wealth of water, and once turned over, would release that moisture to fall again as rain. This was the latter half of the 19th century, and the Homestead Act (and its ensuing expansions) brought settlers to the region, desert or otherwise. They built homes of sod, dugouts into the earth, and farmed. They found life manageable, if difficult. In truth, the Great American Desert was seeing an unusual and extended period of rainfall—one that would extend, in fits and starts punctuated by temporary drought, into the 1920s.

Wheat, corn, and cotton were planted, grew. With that little life, men saw fit to sell the region for something it wasn't: verdant, thriving, paradisaical. Plots were sold in the East, and suitcase farmers arrived expecting towns, cities, trees, but found none of these. This lie folds into the first, a campaign of misinformation that would eventually create the breadbasket of America in a land that was once considered uninhabitable. And behind this lie is an admission of truth—however wrongheaded—that we seem incapable of understanding today: we have a hand in climate change. Settlers in Oklahoma, in Kansas and Colorado, thought that they were multiplying their chances by breaking open the soil, that they were bending the land to their will, that it could be bent at all. The downfall of the region has the same origins, and it prefigures the coming onslaught of climate change upon not just the Great American Desert, but the world.

In the wake of the Great War, the region that had been known as the Great American Desert was habitable farmland. Endless fields of buffalo grass—a robust, hardy plant that prevented the equally endless winds of the Plains from blowing the soil into the Atlantic—were plowed up for cropland. Market forces encouraged farmers to go all-in, and the land rewarded their work. The 1928–1929 wheat crops in the region were phenomenal; records were broken, and boom harvests were reaped, until, almost at once, farmers were dealt two blows. The Great Depression finally reached west, sinking the wheat market, and the rain stopped. In the span of a year, the bushel price for wheat plummeted from $1.00 per, to around .60. Despite a boom crop, farmers struggled. Faced with half their income, farmers decided to work twice as hard: they doubled their output, doubled the work of their plows—doubled the land turned over. The farmers had forgotten, and some never knew, that the rains were an aberration.

The parallels here are simple, and the face of the Anthropocene on this era clear. Economic pressures forced the adoption of reckless farming for the sake of livelihood—those same pressures force a fiercely efficient and still-consumptive practice today. The climate reversion of their time is our climate change, plowed land our CO_2.

The dust storms began at the start of 1932, a normal part of the climate of the Great American Desert, but for the exception that now thousands upon thousands of acres of land had been turned over and exposed. Rainfall slacked, equally normal. But with all the families, all the new farmers, and all the towns now situated in the once-Great American Desert, the drought brought misery. Over the course of just a few years, the entire face of the landscape changed. Dust storms scoured and buried great swaths of Oklahoma, Kansas, Texas, and Colorado. The story of the Okies is known, the migration, the suffering of those who left—what is more difficult to grasp is the essentialness of humanity to this story. Without the relentless turning of the earth, there would be no Dust Bowl. High winds would have no dust to gather from the unbroken sea of buffalo grass, and the soil, thus guarded, would keep its moisture. Fed the lies of a permanently changed climate, though, of the adage that rain follows the plow, farmers can hardly be blamed for wishing to keep their homes, to keep their families fed. And when the storms began, they were quick to understand that this was their own doing—they recognized their own soil as it was swept away.

Today's agricultural practices all but ensure that the Dust Bowl is unrepeatable, at least in its economic effects. Farmers use water far more efficiently, and the soil is much less susceptible to erosion from poor plowing. But the practices themselves are more widespread, and their effects are far-reaching. Agriculture is a sizable portion of America's carbon footprint, with soil and livestock emissions alone accounting for nearly 10% of the U.S.'s overall output. And while the Dust Bowl itself may not occur again, a similar effect is wrought by climate change. Atmospheric instability increases with temperature, resulting in more numerous and damaging periods of heavy rainfall and extensive drought. When these conditions combine, the soil is easily eroded, carried away just as simply as upon a wind. And the effects of climate change are not limited to water and lack thereof: all manner of stresses are on the rise, from diseases, pests, to shifting life cycles as plants struggle to acclimate to temperatures outside of the natural rhythm.

By 1935, the great storms of the Dust Bowl are ubiquitous, nearly endless, and the days without wind strong enough to scour bare legs and paint, or to blind you with sand, are numbered fewer than the days with. The young and old succumb by degrees to dust pneumonia, the creeping plague of dust storms—particles so fine as to be unstoppable—and to a one you cough, spit, sneeze black. April 14th is a Sunday—known soon enough as Black Sunday, and it begins as we recognize most days like it: with a calm. Residents of the region plan picnics, put out the wash, go to church.

It's not rain, but breathing without a mask is good enough. Seeing the barn out back is good enough. When the storm arrives, it is with the same warning a duster always brings: sight alone—a wave of black from the north, 200 miles wide, and churning ahead at 60 miles per hour. It covers the land for over an hour, kills at least one: a young boy, running home. Cars stall from the static charge, drivers blinded anyway. Fencewires glow with St. Elmo's fire. When it is over, 300 million tons of topsoil have been scraped off the Dust Bowl and thrown to the south and east. Woody Guthrie sings about this day. Gillian Welch, watching over history, notes also that Lincoln was shot, and the *Titanic* sunk, on April the 14th, thus she dubs it "Ruination Day."

There are nightmarish projections from various sources that suggest mega-droughts are coming to the United States, recreating the Dust Bowl and giving cause for digging out the old nomenclature of the Great American Desert. California, until recently, made these models credible when an intense drought sucked reservoirs dry, tapped the snowcaps, and pressured residents. Then, months later, Los Angeles saw over 200% of its normal accumulations for the months of October through mid-January. Long Beach broke a daily rainfall record. Washouts and erosion followed accordingly. Whether we can count on the nightmare scenarios or not, we can be assured that climate change has turned our weather boom-and-bust. Not only are long-term shifts coming—floods and droughts—but extreme weather patterns increase, as well: tornado outbreaks in February, hurricanes knocking early, cold snaps and heatwaves. Oklahoma tied a record high in February, reaching 99 degrees. It's not necessary to have a ten-year dust bowl when a decade of storms comes in a single year.

The Dust Bowl would not fully abate until 1941, when the drought finally gave way to real rainfall across the Midwest and Great American Desert. An estimated 75% of topsoil had been blown away in some parts, and the economic repercussions were felt for decades to come. And though practices changed, they did not change on the grounds of responsible use—of understanding the land. Practices changed due to economic engines: deeper wells, better irrigation, more efficient equipment, a bigger dollar. Farming in the Dust Bowl was about survival for most, but by the end, it quickly became a land-grab for bankers and distant companies, and that ethos persists today. It will take years, but water usage in Mid-America is draining the Ogallala Aquifer, a fantastically precious resource that allows the region to persevere through droughts much like those that would initiate a dust bowl. Feedlot methane (and runoff), corn subsidies, pesticides, the simple trucking of goods putting CO_2 in the air; these problems are legion, and they will make life very difficult for farmers in the region—in particular those smaller farmers who haven't yet been pushed out by the corporate entities. The hits will come, rapidly and repeatedly, and while we may never see another dust bowl, or a decades-long mega-drought, the damage will be done by a thousand cuts.

The lie, ultimately, is thus: that humanity has some kind of supremacy over the land—It began as the simple folly that the beneficence of God would prevail upon the climate and make land habitable and fruitful for mankind, that we can turn over the earth and expect it to stand still for us. Today that ethos has evolved into the complex web of modernity—lies about the cause of climate change, lies about the effects, lies about preventative measures, all in the service of the supremacy of man—or, more likely, a few men. For farmers in the Dust Bowl, their punishment was immediate: rip up the earth, and it will blow away. For this generation, and for generations to come, Ruination Day may pale against the bevy of storms, the floods and droughts, the extreme events that punctuate the creep of dust of the Anthropocene.

SOUTHERN CRYPTOZOOLOGY: ALTAMAHA-HA

Allie Marini

Location: Georgia

Status: Unconfirmed

Description: Sturgeon-like river hominid

Once they left the rice fields,   I was alone
                    —each strand of the network of streams
Becoming   cleaner & fresher   year by year,
the dull gray of my skin   livening up,   deepening green
to match the riparian buffer & the corridors
                    taking me deeper & deeper
                              into the forested waterways.

Though   I sometimes miss the ready meal of rice,
          I do not miss   the noise,
                    the fragmentation of the green,
               or   the way my skin grew tougher under their runoff.

They knew   to look for & take caution with
                              the vainglorious gators,
                              always sunning themselves
                              on the banks.
They never knew   to look for me,
                    until I slithered up from the river bottom,
                    their own nightmare
                              of ecology gone awry.

DATE IDEAS FOR
THE POST-APOCALYPSE

Madeline Grigg

1. We go to the sea one weekend, just to see it in person. Its blue could carve the bones out of my body.

2. We comb the beach for melted seashells, sea glass flashing under our gloves. You find most of the skeleton of a fish, the bones braided together. I find a waxy oyster shell, nacre and purple running together like freshly spilled lava.

3. I invite you to the bee exhibit at the museum on half-off Friday. There, we marvel at jars of honey. We hold hands over the husk of a fossilized bumblebee. In the dark room, the honey glows like candlelight.

4. You cook dinner: delicious mealworm fried rice, served with twice-purified water.

5. We stay up until dawn to watch the sun rise, its light softened by the city soup. We stare directly at the sun.

COLOR BLIND

Caralyn Davis

The Panamanian golden frogs died first. Extinct but for a few stray specimens stored with hermetic seal in zoo laboratories. Scientists fretted, as
did some intrepid reporters from *National Geographic, Smithsonian*, and
The New Yorker. The Panamanians were devastated. They considered the
golden frog their national emblem and put its likeness on their keychains
and coffee mugs. No one else cared. After all, the golden frogs were frogs,
not puppies, and other things were golden: daffodils, tomato blossoms,
the sun, Big Bird.

I used to watch *Sesame Street* with my youngest daughter, Harper, when
the two older children left for school. I worked from home after she was
born; I finally had the professional standing. We'd cuddle on the couch
for an hour before the babysitter arrived, and count and spell right along
with those puppets.

"What's the point?" my husband said one morning when he was running late. He liked to needle me back then. "Bert, Ernie, and the Cookie
Monster are shadows of their former selves, and Baby Bear, Abby Cadab-
by? What the hell are those?"

"Don't judge the puppets, Harris," I said.

"There's no continuity. They don't follow the number nine or the letter
G through an entire episode anymore. Generations of children have stunt-
ed attention spans, and Elmo's a whiny little freak."

"I can't argue the Elmo thing, but ratchet down the hatred," I said. "It's
basic education, not a portent of doom."

Silence. Harris tended to find mommy-me a tad prosaic.

All the other frogs and toads died. Again, a global yawn. Amphibians
didn't inspire save-the-animal campaigns in quite the same way that polar
bears and wolves did.

Honeybees disappeared. People shifted in their easy chairs and grum-
bled. Even the meanest intelligence knew that bees did something important for plants. Still, plenty of other flying insects were on the job. Honey's
status as a universally enjoyed golden element faltered under the weight
of modern lifestyles. Most people deemed zero-calorie sweeteners devel-
oped in test tubes to be an equal if not superior substitute.

Harper's favorite snack was honey on buttered toast. I was a good mother, limiting that treat to twice a week. The rest of the time, she had to eat fruits and vegetables. She was desolate when honey production ended. I searched the stores, standing in line to buy cane, sorghum, molasses, maple, agave.

"Yucky," she'd say. "Bad."

She stopped eating toast.

"Be glad she's not popping a tantrum." Harris kissed me. "It's out of our control."

The bats went next, expiring en masse as they hibernated. Scientists hiking through their home caves watched the last ones drop from the ceilings and flutter sluggishly before they joined the thigh-deep decay on the cave floors. They named the disease white-nose syndrome because the dead bats had a villain-twirling mustache of white crystals.

The scientists identified a fungus as the culprit but didn't connect it to the frogs and bees because the corpses of those animals decomposed too quickly for the autopsies to find the white. They also thought hibernation played a key role in the proliferation of the disease-mongering fungus—not 30-degree temperature swings in a day, flooding, drought, or anything that could impact people. "Bat flu" wasn't destined to be a true newsmaker like humanity-imperiling bird flu or swine flu.

Even when Harper started walking, she kept me at the center of her world. Several times a day, she would toddle into my office, her babysitter trailing behind her.

"Mama!" she'd cry, goofy with pleasure at finding me. "Dance, Mama, dance!"

If I had time, I'd flip on some music, Noot d' Noot or Purkinje Shift usually (my brother's bands), and the three of us would twirl around the room.

Vultures. Hundreds of thousands fell out of the trees where they roosted in the heat. Autopsies showed they died from visceral gout a.k.a. bird kidney failure. White crystals coated their internal organs. The fungus had evolved.

Harper pretended to be a bird sometimes, inspired by the congregants eating at the feeder outside our kitchen window. She'd zoom around, flapping her arms, singing, "Tweet, tweet, tweet!"

"What a pretty little bird!" I'd say. "Hope a kitty-cat doesn't get you, sweetie bird!" Throwaway words purloined from the mouths of cartoon characters, ill-equipped to last a lifetime.

Then I'd grab her and tickle her stomach. How she laughed.

Hyenas, monkeys, bears, wolves, deer, larks, pelicans, whales, animals ad infinitum. White Death spread. Sometimes visible, sometimes hidden, the white fungus turned up everywhere. Average humans began to express concern but wouldn't concede to all-out alarm. Maybe natural selection was involved. Maybe wild animals were just past their cosmic due date.

Her eyes were blue. Not bluebells or sapphires, those Cinderella fantasy colors. An aqua overlaid with a hint of gray, like a lake on an overcast day. Inventive yet practical—part me, part Harris. The eyes of a future scientist or physician, of someone who could have found a way to save us even if *Sesame Street* hadn't given her appropriate mental discipline.

"What do you want to be when you grow up?" I'd ask her.

"You, Mama, you!"

Chickens, pigs, dogs, cows, humans. White Death went up and down the food chain—except for cats. The Family Felidae escaped unscathed. Every other species teetered toward extinction. Some, though, climbed out of the biological ruins with a spark of life intact. That survival instinct is how I ended up in this hollow in the north Georgia mountains, fenced in with Harris and our two surviving children on his family farm.

Harris socked me in the jaw. He's not an abuser. He knocked me out to get me in the car to leave Atlanta. Harper had gone to a birthday party, by herself like a big girl. I was about to go pick her up when one of the other mothers called and said everyone had gotten sick. I phoned the hospital, on hold, on hold, on hold. Finally, a harassed woman.

"Don't come," she said. "Too many sick. Infection."

"Tell me where Harper is," I said. "Is she okay? What's going on?"

"She's already dead. Turn on the news."

I was screaming, so Harris switched on the television, and we saw what was happening. I planned to go to the hospital anyway. I couldn't leave Harper there, alone, without her mother. That's when Harris hit me.

The human world—what remained of it—divided into three camps: people who ate cats, people who worshipped cats (the lion-headed Egyptian goddess Sekhmet experienced a resurgence in popularity), and people who befriended cats. Thanks to a modicum of intelligence, Harris and I could see the folly of the first two options. We took the third route, and that friendship saved us.

We have six cats. I don't know if they see it, smell it, or hear it, but our cats can spot the infection anywhere. They yowl an alert if White Death comes near, ensuring we know who or what to let on our land, when to put on our gas masks and hazard suits, and when to institute disinfection procedures.

With few insects, we pollinate our fields using paintbrushes dipped in pollen. Gold means food, survival, so people pay attention to it now. However, gold also can bring death since insects no longer eat their share of the pollen. The excess combines with severe thunderstorms to create pollen events that verge on tornadoes. You can choke to death in minutes if you're caught out in one. The cats help us there, too, sounding a warning.

My favorite cat is Brownie, an orange-striped beast that likes to rub his furry brain box on my forehead. He's named after Harper's teddy bear, a handmade toy that wasn't backed by a brand or a marketing campaign. I thought its anonymity would foster her creative spirit—Harris' concerns about *Sesame Street* had wormed into my mind. Brownie the bear was the color of a Hershey's bar, with a low-pile pelt that was perfect for snuggling without causing sleep-time sniffles. Harper was prone to allergies.

"Kisses for Brownie, too," she'd say when Harris and I tucked her in at night.

"Three apiece, that's the going rate for baby girls and brown bears" was Harris' standard reply.

One, two, three from us both on each soft cheek. Sometimes proper kisses, the ones that live the name smack or smooch. It's the pecks I regret. Rote kisses, but at the time they seemed a product of multitasking efficiency. Now I wonder if she heard our silent screams: "I have to unload the dishwasher" or "I've got to finish my presentation" or "I haven't shaved my legs all week—just go to sleep."

"Why did so much die?" my son, Danny, asked last night during dinner. "I miss Harper and Grandpa and Grandma. I miss my friends. Why did this happen? When can we go home?" He laid his head down next to his plate and cried into the tablecloth.

My other daughter, Emma, appeared stricken. Harris held out his hand; she got up from her chair and went into his arms.

"Gold and white, Danny," I said. "The colors of angels. We didn't think they'd let us down like that."

I reached over and smoothed his hair. I felt a little silly offering parental comfort. Danny and Emma had seen its fallibility firsthand. Mommy had let their sister die. Mommy couldn't always make things better.

"We should have new colors, for new angels," Danny said. Tears and fabric muffled his words.

"We'll work on it," I said. "Hush, now. Don't disturb the cats."

Late at night when the odd feline footfall is the only sound that breaks the stillness of the house, sometimes I see Harper. She's in a cotton-candy heaven. Generations of family members surround her and try to keep her safe. The White Death has crossed dimensions. It looks like a Santa Claus convention, white beards blooming from every mouth. But Harper dances. She spins, she swoops, and tiny golden frogs keep time 'round her feet.

METAPHOR

Kunjana Parashar

Sometimes I think of the old legend of the musk deer—
how he searches madly in the forest for the musk he creates,
and on not finding it, leaps to his own death. It is a metaphor
for chasing happiness outside of yourself. But when I have
a daughter, and there will be no musk deer left roaming in
the Himalayas, what will I teach her about happiness? When
people confuse a metaphor for literality and go hunting
for musk pods within the soft, white bellies of these deer, how
am I to make her understand what a metaphor is? Darling,
know this: Musk deer don't jump to their deaths. They don't go
looking for the light outside of their own bodies and homes.
The biology of their scent glands is not their own doing.
They leap, hiss, mate as musk deer do. We are the ones
trespassing with wire snares and traps, looking for something,
anything, that we can mar and maim to extract a lonely sac
of happiness.

DRY LANDS, NEW MEXICO

Deborah Kelly

ekphrasis on "Felt Umbrella and Moccasins,"
Maria Hupfield, IAIA, Santa Fe

The snow basin is dusty at the end of winter,
where color-changing hares hide white winter fur,
best they can, from predators.
Already, piñons shrink from the sun.

My forehead aches in half, with absence
of the high-running Rio Grande,
to see Pueblo Peak worry over Blue Lake.

I hike near a reservoir, a low pond now
with old frogs, who know
why stones in the arroyo cramp.

I make ceremony with wool
from Spanish sheep that overgrazed here.
In the absence of rain, I carry a thirsty felt umbrella.
In the absence of snow, I walk in thirsty boots.

A TRAY OF ICE CUBES
I MADE MYSELF

Anna Kaye-Rogers

"Ice is the perfect murder weapon," and you probably think it's one single icicle, perfectly sharpened to a point, one final exclamation of impassioned planning. When the weapon melts, so do the fingerprints. Is the Arctic Shelf Mother Nature's perfectly sharpened pinprick, waiting to melt and kill us all—a perfect murder weapon we sharpened ourselves? No fingerprints, only underwater bones fossilizing where humans once stood. An iceberg once took on the culmination of human folly: triumph and hubris clinking gold-rimmed glasses together in celebration. The ice cubes made the alcohol sparkle in the chandelier light, human icicles dripping from the ceiling, and then the band played on. They made ice for their drinks, their pleasure, their comfort, and it killed them.

"When Hell freezes over," we say, like it hasn't happened before. The planet has been encased in ice ages, glaciers carving off chunks of the planet the way we cut ourselves in high school. Maybe the ice hurt before, when it ripped earth and solidity out of the way with a slow intensity, the dreaded peel of duct-tape and Band-Aids, but when it was over, it left soft soil to reboot and reset. Now the ice will save her from us, ripping resources indiscriminately as we do. We've replaced ice cubes with plastic silicone that freezes, aching for human control as we break bones and bust foreheads open. We harnessed nature to heal ourselves until the Giving Tree had nothing left to give, and then we collected colored cubes filled with watery substances and built freezers meant to stay cold but not frosting. Icicles form on our gutters, and we knock them off, salting our driveways to prevent lawsuits. Children jump on ice puddles and crack off pieces, yet we ask why the polar bears need saving. Ice is not allowed to exist naturally; it must be carved into castles and displayed at weddings where we watch it melt throughout the night.

A water droplet could have become the raging force of the river that carves through plains, spending centuries etching the natural bone structure of the earth into pointed cheekbones and a perfect jawline; it could have rushed through the Grand Canyon or poured over the Niagara, my cup overfloweth. Instead it is perfectly frozen, preserved until death, in an ice stalactite hanging over somebody's house; a nuisance to knock down. It could have been powerful, could have been part of a mighty force. Instead it's forced to assimilate at a temperature it cannot withstand without changing itself completely. The lifespan of a water cycle is the search for meaning at a 9-5 abruptly ending from a patch of black ice you couldn't see, couldn't predict, and then it's over.

But ice isn't always freezing. It's a burning sensation at the touch, a sudden violence akin to fire, an extreme that remains at opposite ends of the spectrum but elicits the same response. Ice water in the shower is a stab in the back, and when the coldness kills us, we die feeling warm. Humans were meant to keep moving, designed to stay at an internal body temperature. It is the extremes that kill us; snow and sand, and ice is not the opposite of flame we once believed. Ice is the opposite of contentment, of safety, of a warm, happy feeling inside. Ice is frozen dreams and seasonal depression, the cold parts of winter humanity hates, for while we value the crystallization on an unbroken snowfall, we despise the broken dirty slush we made ourselves with our own killing machines. There is a function in vehicles, but a danger, our homemade ice cubes times a thousand.

We struggle with being vulnerable, building walls to keep others out. Passion is hot, impulsive; those taking visible ecstatic joy at being themselves used to be "flaming." Ice is the frigid bitch, the frosty response, the icy tone. Someone is cold and unfeeling "as ice." When I am afraid, ice runs through my veins, the same coldness I feel in the shower when the laundry gets turned on. But the chill heats me, enables my fight or flight—only I always end up freezing. My own blood struggles to reach my fingertips; my circulation is poor. I succumb to frostbite easily, my fingers moments from turning blue the rest of the year, unable to fight back against the encroaching cold. I am never warm enough. The delicate plumbing of modern life requires heating apartments to a certain degree or ice will burst your pipes, thousands in catastrophic damage and flooded memories. It is the poor families who can't afford ski trips and diamond jewels who struggle with bills in the winter, who wait longer to replace hot water heaters and furnaces. Ice creeps at windowpanes, kept at bay with plastic wrap clinging to window frames, while the kids in the better school district have birthday parties at ice skating rinks. The ice in fantasy novels is as strong and solid as bulletproof glass until it's required to break and crack, and then it collapses in on itself, and the bodies are put on ice. Death again.

Water, in its benign form, is meant to save us, to source life and replenish in our hour of need. It draws blood through blue-tinted veins, nourishes cells, keeps the skin elastic to the touch. We are made of water, and when they bury us, they avoid the local well supplies. But water is monsoons and hurricanes, flash floods and thunderstorms, tsunamis and riptides and strong currents. Our bodies are made of water, and yet if the wrong caverns and passages flood, we drown ourselves—too many punctured containment cabins and the whole vessel goes down. Yet ice was meant to last forever, and someday the satellites that orbit out in space will be frozen forever, nothing more than parasites and viruses safely encased in fragile glass, and the danger in the permafrost will be set free as the water retakes all we took from the seas. When we are gone, perhaps the ice will come back, for to ice we are the murder weapons, our bonfires sending fireflies into the skies.

There is no common perception that every ice cube is different, the way it is with snowflakes. Ice cubes are common, ordinary, nondescript, and plain. They are made with sturdy plastic, bent akimbo on itself to pop imprisoned water into lemonades and sodas we can only drink cold. One mold is filled until it overflows with the others, and the water does not care where it is sent to go. The droplets go down together, freezing as a unit, thin lines between sections and thin cracks in every piece. Each a different piece on its own—sometimes bought, sometimes crushed, sometimes cubed, all coming from the same source. Each is an idea clinking around in a glass we hold up to examine in the sunlight, delighted at the sparkle that catches our eye, and then drown them in their own kind, hoping they melt into one incoherent puddle of an idea, when once they formed glaciers and watched us drown ourselves. They flow together and reform among themselves, redefining form each morning sunrise and evening frost.

WATCHING SANDY ON THE WEATHER CHANNEL, OCTOBER 2012

Robbi Nester

The cowlick in my son's close-shorn scalp
swirls like the storm
I have watched for hours
on the computer's small screen
the low-pressure center
spreading its nebula arms
at this moment across the map.
Real people live in these places.
Real water rises in dark cellars
like a scream, while outside
the shattered windows
a gray sky congeals
thick as liquid silver
poured into a jeweler's mold.
In the charmed light
of the autumn moon
the beautiful abides with the terrible.
The buck, driven from drowned woods
onto the beach, standing
hock deep and still
though sky and sand
shift around him
flees from a person
who wants only to help him
escape from the swelling sea.

RONALD REAGAN WAS AN IDIOT (AND OTHER OBSERVATIONS ABOUT MY BIRTH YEAR)

Rota

I was born late. I could give any number of reasons I wanted to stay put.
Every birth is a bad hair day for the baby. The star of *Bedtime for Bonzo*
had been elected to lead us through the Cold War. Maybe I wanted
to stick it out until Christmas. Jews born on Christmas wind up a pretty
big deal sometimes. Plus, the world can be a scary place. My mom saw
The Shining while I was in utero. In my cocoon it must've sounded like a
 whisper wielding an ax.

There's nothing more sinister than a secret. How it makes the ears twitch
like a dog barking at an earthquake that's not yet shook. I wonder if
 I mouthed *Here's Johnny* as I burst into the world.

I was born in the winter of 1981 to a twenty-below windchill.
In other words, I was born into a world where we still had winter.
They don't tell children their plans to keep us warm, to poison the air
until the snow melts so the mosquitos can fly their violent love
 anywhere they wish.

When I was born, the president was an idiot. Chalking this up to dementia
is an insult to dementia. But when you're born into the right skin
to parents who can tell the churches what to teach,
you can go from shitty actor to shitty governor to shitty president
and still die to become the deity so many pray to when they're lying
 awake at night fearing demographic shifts.

There's nothing more sinister than a secret we all know
but pretend to forget. How every newborn is the property
of their ancestors' access to wheat. How the cradle can be the grave.
How the grave can be a magic phonebooth that makes men perfect,
 redacts our flaws like a designer toupée.

Every funeral is a good hair day for the dead. Even the most
desperate combover appears at peace. But the seas are rising.
The ground is thawing. And the warm flooding earth
 doesn't preserve anything.

THE DARKENING EARTH

Travis Madden

*Note: The following is a transcript of
Dr. Madeline Williamson's lecture on climate change
at Morgan State University, February 24th, 2056.*

[The lights dim, and a young, black woman walks onto the auditorium stage. She is wearing a bright, sleeveless flower-print dress and thick-framed glasses. Rings adorn most of her fingers, and her hair is made-up in long dreadlocks that reach midway down her back, kept out of her face with a headband. The audience applauds her, and she smiles and waves, but her face takes on a more sober countenance as she gets to the podium in the stage's center.]

Good evening, everyone. My name is Dr. Madeline Williams, and most of you probably think I'm here to talk to you tonight about climate change. Well, you're right. Sort of. What I have to talk about tonight has to do with climate change, but it's really about so much more than that. It's not about the science, but the social aspect of what's happening to us. It's not about cloud patterns or increased rainfall, it's about what's happening inside our bodies. It's not about rising sea levels and ice shelves breaking off, but about what's happening to our children. It's about what our planet—what *we*—are all going to become, in just a couple generations.

It's about how we're all going to become black.

Of course, I can't take credit for this discovery. The woman to first publicly discuss this link was, of course, Dr. Regina Perry, from Howard University.

[An applause goes up at the sound of her name. Dr. Williamson lets it grow and diminish, adding her own applause, before speaking again.]

Yes, thank you very much, Dr. Perry. Wherever you are. If you can hear this.

Eighteen months ago, Dr. Regina Perry published a research paper. And I say "published" in only the loosest sense of the word, because within days of its publishing, it was suppressed. And just in case anyone asks, yes, suppressed is the exact word I meant to use to describe what happened. That paper was called "The Darkening Earth: Climate Change's Undeniable Impact on Race," and her thesis was this: that because of the planet's warming climate, it would only be a few generations before everyone on Earth starts to look more like me, and less like someone like, say, the president. Not exactly like me, mind you, but *more* like me. A general darkening of the skin, a changing of the features. The climate would change everyone on the planet into an entirely new, dark-skinned race.

Only a few people read that research paper before it mysteriously vanished from Howard University's website. Before all copies of it in the university's own library were checked out by a patron who was later discovered not to actually exist, the copies never found. Before both Dr. Perry's personal and school computers were infected with a virus that made recovering any files impossible. Before purchased copies were stolen from the houses of individuals who bought them, including my own.

Many people, including myself, attempted to find and interview Dr. Perry on her suppressed paper. But no one, not even her family, has heard from Dr. Perry in over a year, since just after her paper was published. She seems to have simply vanished off the face of the Earth. Unfortunately, as some of us are all too aware, no one except family and friends is going to invest much time in trying to find a young, black woman who went missing in Baltimore.

[Dr. Williamson looks as if she's going to say more, but instead stares out at the crowd, letting her words settle over everyone. She stretches the moment out almost unbearably before she speaks again.]

Of course, conspiracy theories abound about what actually happened to Dr. Perry. The most common is that she was arrested by some sort of secret police force, that I often hear called the Bureau of Special Services. What really happened to her, we may never know.

Of course, there's also the official story, which says that Dr. Perry was last seen in Baltimore City and. ...

[Dr. Williamson shrugs.]

That's it. Like so many young women and girls across the country, she appears to have simply vanished. Which seems ... odd to me, in the Information Age. Or, in what some people would call the Surveillance Age.

[There are murmurs from the crowd. Many heads nod.]

Where was her last phone signal? Did a CCTV camera spot her? An ATM? A traffic cam? Someone else's cell phone camera? A satellite? No one should be able to disappear like that anymore, not in this age. And yet it happens.

Some of my more ... shall we say *suspicious* ... colleagues even went so far as to tell me not to give this lecture, for fear of what could happen to me.

[There is an awkward silence in the crowd. Heads swivel around, as if looking for hidden threats.]

But that's crazy ... right?

In a great majority of disaster movies, there's always a certain character that reoccurs, a character I call the Chicken Little. You know the one: The crazy scientist living alone in his office, surrounded by papers. Or the hermit doing esoteric calculations out in the woods. But one thing is always the same, no matter the movie; no one ever listens to them. Not until it's too late, at least. They die on their respective hills.

America, we had hundreds—thousands—of Chicken Littles. Every single scientist, regardless of political orientation, agreed that climate change was happening.

You know, maybe if Al Gore hadn't grown that crazy caveman beard, things would've been different. I really think they would have. If an actual scientist had come forward with it instead of a politician. Not that I'm trying to diminish Gore's accomplishments by any means, please. If you're somewhere listening to this lecture, Mr. Gore, I applaud you. But if a scientist, not a politician, had come forward with this, we wouldn't be having this discussion now. I wouldn't be here.

We wouldn't be here.

But we can't think about what was; we can only think about what is. What is, is the fact that after years of denial, people finally listened. And they listened to Dr. Perry.

And in listening to her, they told us what really mattered to them. What mattered wasn't the fact that New Orleans, that the entire state of Florida are currently underwater. What mattered wasn't that thousands of people died because of this sudden shift in weather, because of floods and hurricanes and tornadoes. What mattered wasn't the giant ice shelf that broke off and slammed into Greenland. Nobody really cared that historical sites vanished or that the economy was tanking; nobody could afford gas at seven dollars a gallon and new green technology was too expensive, because new technology always is.

What mattered was that they were going to change. Their children were going to change. Into something that, to them, I guess was undeniable. Was unacceptable.

[Dr. Williamson stops speaking for a moment, seems determined to let the nervous silence in the audience linger.]

The United States experienced an emigration crisis like nothing it's ever seen before; people were fleeing the country in record numbers. Canada took them. Sweden took them. Denmark. Mexico. Everyone went to places that were actually doing something about this crisis.

Still, that didn't matter to the people in charge. Let the other countries take their undesirables, as far as they're concerned. The people they didn't want left the country and left them to build their walls and keep everyone else out. And then Dr. Perry published and, well ...

[Dr. Williamson chuckles briefly, wipes under her eye. She smiles, but it does not touch her eyes.]

Everyone sure listened to that.

So, what is it that actually makes people black? What makes skin darker? Well, I'm sure you all know; you're sitting here in the audience, which I can only assume means you've read Dr. Perry's paper, maybe even some of my work. But for those who haven't, or for those listening at home, first we actually have to understand what makes people black. Why am I darker than this gentleman here in the front row?

I'll give you the short version, since we're not here to talk about science. Not really. A pigment called melanin is largely responsible for what makes me, and people like me, dark. Ultraviolet radiation also plays a part in darkening skin tone. So, what do you think will happen if more and more ultraviolet radiation keeps coming into our atmosphere? If it keeps getting hotter and hotter?

You've all seen the "color map" of the world, I take it?

Please.

[Dr. Williamson nods toward the man in the control booth. Another light clicks on and a projector hums to life, illuminating the wall behind her. A map of the world appears. The landmasses closest to the equator are a dark brown hue, lightening the closer they get to the northern and southern poles.]

I see these maps pop up on the Internet a lot, and while some of them are pretty inaccurate, they at least get us in the direction of a larger point we need to be discussing; skin color is a result of ultraviolet light exposure, of the amount of melanin in our bodies. Basically, of little more than circumstance.

But we didn't come here to talk about science. At least, not really. We came here to talk about society. Because *this* was the information that finally pushed people to action. The fear that their children or their children's children would one day become dark-skinned.

Now ... why is that such a bad thing?

SHE DOESN'T SMELL LIKE DEATH

Hannah Blaser

She is living, though I do not know how.
There are those, she says, *who take and take and
take.* There are those who do not know how
death sometimes looks like sunshine and birds
chirping against blue skies. My grandmother
says the worst days come right after the best,
and I would sit with breathless worry the whole
day after Christmas, just to be safe.

Something's dead, or dying.
Crows circle overhead welcoming
the stench, the spilled guts that spring out of
a ripped-open chest like bubblegum coils
and spill around like thick red paint.
This is a recognizable end. We point.
We stare. *Did you see it?* We ask,
grimace, and then carry on. Miles to go.

She is living, though I do not know
for how much longer. While stirring
sugar cubes into his coffee, the man says,
*If she was really dying, I would be able
to tell. She would tell me.* She is the Silent
Sufferer. I want to scream her impending
death from the mountains she has built,
but I am too often too quiet. Meanwhile
she blooms and blooms and blooms.

WATERSHED

*after the 1,000-year Flood of
Elk River, West Virginia, June 2016*

Never give your heart to a body
of water. Like a wayward lover,
it will only hurt you in the end.

I was courted in adolescence, bare
skin in a cool, calm cove. I poured
tears of grief in supplication and

found solace in a glacial white lull,
pain floated away in paper lanterns.
Sounds of weariness, of wonder.

One morning, I awoke to find
the river curling around my bed.
The bank broken in wild abandon.

Terror too terrible a kiss. A bond
asunder in fear, in uncertainty.
The mirthless waltz of water.

THE NEW WORLD

Ryan Napier

I.

In the early sixteenth century, Ponce de León led several expeditions to Florida. He was searching, according to legend, for the Fountain of Youth. He never found it, of course. One of his men did.

Lazaro Valdés was a sixteen-year-old sailor from Asturias. Against his mother's wishes, he joined Ponce de León's final expedition. She wept for days, but Lazaro knew she would cry with joy when he returned with his arms full of gold.

Two ships sailed from San Juan. On the first night at sea, the experienced soldiers told stories about the swamps of Florida and the poisoned arrows of the Calusa warriors. One of the soldiers had lost an eye on the last expedition, and he forced Lazaro to put a finger into his empty socket. Lazaro vomited, and the soldier laughed and laughed.

Lazaro did not want to have an empty socket for an eye—or, worse, to die, with a poisoned arrow in his chest, knee-deep in a swamp. He did not want his mother to be right.

And so one night, in the middle of the second watch, he stole a jug of water and a handkerchief full of biscuits, crept abovedeck, lowered one of the boats into the water, and watched as the two ships sailed toward the setting moon. When they had passed over the horizon, he took up the oars and rowed in the opposite direction.

He hoped to return to San Juan, and from there, find a passage back to Spain. But the next morning, his boat was caught in a current, which pulled him toward a small, rocky island. He heard a long scrape, and soon the water was pooling at his feet. He took off his boots, swam to the shore of the island, and watched his boat break on the rocks.

Lazaro sat on the beach for hours, squinting at the horizon until it was too dark to see. He knew that the ships would not pass by—but then again, what if they did? Perhaps another sailor had deserted: Lazaro would swim out to him, kiss his hands and face and feet, and row them all the way back to San Juan himself. Or maybe Ponce de León had noticed his absence and sent a rescue party. Lazaro would wave them down, too, and accept his punishment. No amount of flogging would be worse than dying here on this rock, alone.

He waited on the beach until sunset, and then he continued to wait.

He woke up wet—the tide had come in. He retreated up the beach and ate a few bites of wet biscuit. His mouth hurt with thirst. He walked inland. The island was flat and hard—gray limestone and brownish grass. It had a few trees, which bore small unripe figs. Lazaro picked one, but neither his fingers nor his teeth could break its thick, green rind.

At the center of the island was a long, narrow opening in the rock. Lazaro bent over it and heard water splashing on stone. He lowered himself into the opening, kicking until he felt the rock below. It was a cave. Water trickled out from one of its walls and collected in a little pool. Lazaro scooped some of the water into his hands and sniffed it. It smelled like nothing, so he drank it, and became immortal.

Lazaro didn't know this, of course. But that hardly mattered: the fountain worked anyway.

He drank again, and washed his face. It was now the hottest part of the day, so he lay down against the wall of the cave, out of the sun, and listened to the water dribbling into the pool. When he woke, the sun had just set, and the sky was purple and orange.

He had eaten nothing all day except a few bites of wet biscuit, but he was not hungry. Still, he knew that he should eat, so he left the cave and searched for food. As he was walking across a plain of rocks at the northeast corner of the island, he felt the ground shuffle beneath him. He had stumbled into a colony of iguanas. When he realized what they were, he grabbed the nearest iguana by the tail and whipped it against the rocks until he heard its back snap.

He brought the iguana back to the cave—*his* cave, as he had already come to think of it. With dry grass and sticks, he built a fire, and in an hour, the iguana was roasted. He decided to start with the tail, which seemed meatier than the rest. But when he raised it to his mouth, the smell repulsed him. There was something dead in it.

He told himself that he would try to eat again when he woke, but he wasn't hungry in the morning, nor the morning after that. And yet he felt perfectly fine. Another few days passed without any hunger, and he understood that he no longer needed to eat.

The island was a few miles long and a few miles wide. Lazaro could walk from one end to the other in less than an hour. Sand, iguanas, grass, figs, cave—that was it.

Lazaro spent his days at the southern tip of the island, which was, he guessed, the closest point to San Juan. He kept a smoky fire burning on the beach as a signal to any passing ship. The island's grass burned poorly, so Lazaro had to feed the fire every few minutes. This annoyed him for a few weeks, but later, he was thankful: it was something to do.

And so he lay on the beach and tossed grass into the fire and thought. What had happened to him? He had not eaten in weeks, and did not want to eat. He looked at his reflection in the pool, and found it was still the same. His hair and nails did not seem to grow. To test this, he bit his right thumbnail—three days later, it was still ragged.

Was God punishing him for deserting? Was he in hell? Or maybe he really had found the Fountain of Youth. But wasn't it supposed to be a grand fountain of gold and silver? Where were the naked, deathless girls that were supposed to play in its waters? These and other explanations flitted through his mind. But what did it matter? He was here.

Sometimes, he swam out from the island, but he never let it out of his sight. The only thing worse than being stuck on the island was being lost on the sea.

After a few months, he decided that he was on the wrong side of the island, and he moved his signal fire to the western shore. Another few months passed. He convinced himself that he had been right the first time, and returned to the south.

Then the rainy season came, and the hurricanes. He was driven into the cave for days at a time. He lay on a thin bed of grasses, listening to the rain and the trickling of the fountain, somewhere between sleep and waking. He had long, pleasant dreams that he never remembered.

The rains ended, and he returned to his fire. But what was the point? No one would come. Why sit in the hot sun and wait and worry? Why not dream in the cool of the cave?

When the rains returned, he found he was almost content.

By the fifth year, he no longer kept the fire. He spent most of his days in the cave, neither asleep nor awake. His drowsy thoughts blended with the faint drip of the water from the wall, and for hours at a time, he drifted somewhere between his body and the water, dispersed and suspended in the cool, still air.

For the first decade or so, he talked to himself and sang and hummed. But as the years passed, his words ran together, and his humming became slow and tuneless. Ideas and questions receded. More and more, his life was like that of the iguanas—still and silent.

By the end of the century, language had died out in him. He had spent sixteen years hearing and using it, and seventy without.

He had not aged. The face that was reflected in the pool when he drank looked the same as it had when he came to the island. This should have shocked him. But to be shocked at his appearance required him to recognize that the thing reflected in the water was *him*. And he did, sometimes, if he stared long enough. But more often the face in the water appeared to him as a strange watcher—some *other* who darts and looms and stares.

117

He was not entirely alone. Besides the iguanas and the migratory birds, the island had a few human visitors. In the middle of the seventeenth century, a Taíno woman escaped the hacienda in a canoe—she had dug it herself, in secret, and had hidden it in the roots of a mangrove. She rowed as far from the hacienda as she could, hoping to find somewhere that the Spanish had not yet discovered. She stopped for a few hours on Lazaro's island, but decided it was uninhabitable and continued west. Lazaro was asleep in his cave.

Sixty years later, the most feared pirate ship in the Caribbean was *Prince Charlie's Fancy*. Its crew mutinied and voted that the old captain should be marooned on the nearest deserted island, which happened to be Lazaro's. The captain was left on the shore with a jug of water and a pistol with a single bullet, and *Prince Charlie's Fancy* sailed into the sunset. Lazaro woke to the sound of the shot. He found the captain's body on the shore, stared at it for some time, returned to the cave, and slept.

By the nineteenth century, the island appeared on maps. Haiti called it Dessalines; the United States and Britain called it Georges Island. All three countries claimed it, though none very vigorously. The U.S. asserted its claim under the Guano Islands Act of 1856, which gave it sovereignty over all Caribbean islands with significant guano deposits. A Coast Guard ship briefly visited the island in the early twentieth century, but they found little guano, so the U.S. did not pursue its claim.

Lazaro's island didn't matter. For all the world cared, it might sink into the sea.

Which, of course, it would.

II.

In the early twenty-first century, a U.N. report identified Dessalines/Georges Island as "imminently threatened" by rising sea levels. Even if warming was limited to two degrees Celsius, the island—and thousands of others—would be underwater by 2050.

The U.N. report was the top story on major news sites for almost two hours; in the afternoon, however, it was preempted by even bigger news: the president had called Portugal a "dump." Nonetheless, the report was not forgotten. Important organizations noted its findings and began to work with speed and alacrity.

A month later, Duchess Cruise Line announced an "intriguing and groundbreaking opportunity." Soon, it would offer a new experience, which it called the Sunset Tour. The Sunset Tour would visit only locations that the U.N. report deemed "threatened" or "imminently threatened." These included many of the most beautiful spots in the Caribbean, and they were only available for a limited time.

Duchess' promotional materials stressed the Sunset Tour's social value. The cruise would be an act of witness, and Duchess would donate three percent of each booking to resettlement efforts for those affected by climate change. In addition, the Sunset Tour would provide its guests with a holistic approach to wellness, including a spa, fitness center, and at least four onboard yoga instructors. At sea, there would be countless opportunities for personal growth, including painting and poetry classes, wine tastings, and mindfulness workshops. In short, the Sunset Tour would be a powerful, once-in-history experience, done in style and comfort.

The Sunset Tour was contentious. *The New York Times* and *The Atlantic* debated the ethics of climate change tourism, while Fox accused Duchess of succumbing to political correctness. #BoycottDuchess rose and fell. But as Duchess anticipated, demand was strong, and within a week, the Sunset Tour had sold ninety percent of its bookings.

The cruise's route was determined in large part by the existing cruise infrastructure; many threatened locations, such as Key West and Grand Turk, were already well equipped to accommodate large ships and their passengers. But for the more adventurous guest, Duchess offered daytrips to smaller islands, some of which were entirely untouched by human hands. These off-the-beaten path excursions could be added to any Sunset Tour package for only $90.99 for adults and $85.99 for children.

One of the excursions was to Dessalines/Georges Island. A team of Duchess associates had scouted it one November morning. They rated it poorly in terms of natural beauty, though the iguanas were seen as a "plus." However, the island had the advantage of being entirely untouched, and its location made it ideal for a daytrip from Grand Turk. It was evaluated against several other possible excursions, but its convenience ultimately outweighed their more scenic qualities. The Sunset Tour brochure called the island "a paradise of unspoiled nature."

And so, on the fifth day of the inaugural Sunset Tour, a boat carrying the excursioners left from Grand Turk and landed in the late morning on the shore of Dessalines/Georges Island. Many of the guests wore hiking boots, and some carried collapsible trekking poles. Before they left the boat, a Duchess associate gave a brief natural history of the island—when it was formed, what kind of stones and trees and wildlife it had, when it was expected to be underwater—and warned the guests to walk with care, reminding them that they had signed waivers indemnifying Duchess for any injuries received during the excursion.

At first, the guests hung around the shore. They took pictures of the iguanas and the horizon and their feet in the sand, and plucked figs from the trees and asked each other if they were safe to eat. A group decided to hike inland. Soon enough, they found the mouth of a cave and took pictures of it. The flashes of their phones and cameras lit the cave, and several guests swore that they saw an animal—something long and hairy. One of the guests—the owner of two New England Subaru dealerships—turned on his phone's flashlight, lay on his stomach, stretched out his arm, and shined the light into the cave. Some of the guests told him to move to the left, others to the right, and there it was—a young man, naked, sleeping. Someone shouted, and the owner of the two New England Subaru dealerships dropped his phone into the cave.

A portion of the group returned immediately to the shore, their hiking poles left scattered around the mouth of the cave. But the owner of the two New England Subaru dealerships had lost his phone—the new iPhone 10X. His wife turned on her phone's flashlight and pointed it into the cave, and she and her husband shouted—first in English, then in half-remembered high school Spanish—at the naked man, asking him to give them the phone. The naked man blinked and squinted.

Eventually, a Duchess associate arrived at the cave, and he, too, shouted in English and half-remembered high-school Spanish at the naked man. The naked man continued to blink and squint.

The owner of the two New England Subaru dealerships wanted to climb into the cave and retrieve his phone, but the Duchess associate discouraged it, fearing the media nightmare that would ensue if a guest were attacked by a confused or hostile presence. No, the island had now become an unstable situation, and Duchess Cruise Line guidelines were clear: the excursion had to be cut short. The owner of the two New England Subaru dealerships protested—it was the new iPhone 10X—but nonetheless, they returned to the boat, which left thirty minutes before its scheduled departure time.

The Subaru dealer's wife had taken a video of the naked man, and when she returned to the cruise ship's reliable Wi-Fi, she posted it to Twitter (along with several other posts alleging that Duchess had "allowed" the naked man to steal her husband's iPhone 10X). Within an hour, the video had been retweeted 3,500 times.

Duchess' rapid response team went to work. It promised to buy the Subaru dealer a new iPhone 10X, and apologized, noting that the naked man's behavior did not reflect the values of Duchess Cruise Line. But the team also noticed that many of the replies to the video were positive, describing the naked man as "cute" or "hilarious." A still image from the video soon became a meme: the naked man's confused face was paired with captions such as "Me when I wake up before 9:00."

Duchess' team was nothing if not professional, and recognized the potential for positive brand associations. The naked man provided an opportunity to demonstrate the social values that motivated the Sunset Tour and Duchess Cruise Line more generally. And so, the next day, Duchess announced that it would personally arrange for the naked man's resettlement.

A team of Duchess associates and a translator were sent to the island. They found the man sleeping in the cave. The translator spoke to him in

English and Spanish and Creole, but the man did not respond. One associate climbed into the cave, and the man remained calm and gentle. The associate placed a rope around the man's waist, and the rest of the team pulled him up. The man allowed himself to be led to the boat, and before the island was out of sight, he was asleep again.

The team brought the man to Grand Turk, and from there to Ft. Lauderdale, where Duchess' headquarters were located. He was taken to the hospital for evaluation. Doctors pronounced him perfectly healthy.

There were, however, two problems. Duchess had hoped to find a translator for the man so he could be interviewed by the media and express his gratitude for the life that awaited him in the U.S. But the man would not speak. His vocal cords were, the doctors said, undamaged; he simply didn't use them. Several of the doctors compared the man to a cat —he looked at you when you spoke, but with no real interest.

The other—and more concerning—problem was food. The man refused to eat. His body did not exhibit ketosis or any of the other signs of malnutrition, but the doctors and Duchess worried, and counsel for the hospital warned of enormous potential liability. And so it was decided: if the man continued to refuse food, a feeding tube would have to be inserted.

The doctors explained this to the man. He continued to stare at them and pushed away all the food they offered. They were left with no choice: the man was sedated, and the tube installed. When he woke, he could not or would not understand the doctors' explanations, and at great pain to himself, he tried to remove the tube. Accordingly, he was connected to an IV, which kept him in a state of moderate-to-deep sedation.

In the meantime, Duchess released a media kit about its efforts to resettle the man and its commitment to sustainability and global citizenship. The kit included pictures of the man's rescue from the island and statements from the Duchess associates who had helped him. A press release noted that despite a language barrier, the man had communicated how happy he was to be a member of the Duchess Cruise Line family, and he looked forward to sharing his inspiring story with the world.

Journalists converged on Ft. Lauderdale. Dozens waited in the lobby for daily press conferences with the man's doctors. A *New York Post* photographer rented a hotel room that overlooked the hospital, and from there, snapped pictures of the man sleeping in his bed, which the *Post* ran under the headline "JUAN DOE." CNN gave hourly updates, and the *Huffington Post* offered full Juan Doe coverage—"Kylie's Reaction to Juan Doe is On. Point." *Buzzfeed* published an article that used Harry Potter gifs to speculate on the mysterious man's origins, and a Colbert clip in which Paul Rudd played Juan Doe amassed several million views.

On YouTube, a user called theodosius1488 uploaded an eighteen-minute video that analyzed the hidden messages in Duchess' media kit and proved that Juan Doe was not from an island at all: he was from El Salvador and a member of a gang, probably MS-13. Thus, according to theodosius1488, Juan Doe represented the newest strategy for illegal immigration: infiltrate the country in the guise of helpless climate refugees. This was the endgame of the globalist conspiracy of "climate change": cultural Marxists like Duchess Cruise Line could use the supposed crisis to help illegals enter the country and undermine American values.

theodosius1488's video received more than 300,000 views in twenty-four hours and topped YouTube's trending tab. The site removed it, but other accounts reposted it, and soon #BoycottDuchess was rising again. *Politifact* rated the claim that Juan Doe was an illegal immigrant "mostly false," and major media outlets published factcheckers and explainers on the theory. It continued to spread. The hospital began to receive angry phone calls and death threats against its employees. The president tweeted that Duchess was "very stupid" and "very bad" for helping illegal immigrants enter the country. Members of his own party expressed their surprise and disappointment, while liberals noted that immigrants like Juan Doe were hardworking and patriotic—many of them became entrepreneurs or served their country in uniform.

And so on.

The man remained in a state of moderate-to-constant sedation. Each time the doctors tried to reduce his level of sedation, the man attempted to remove the feeding tube, even breaking the restraints in which he had been placed. The situation was untenable: Duchess had already amassed nearly $900,000 in medical bills, far more than it had allocated for the man's resettlement.

Duchess had planned to offer the man a loan to finance career training and the down payment on a home, but in light of the medical debt, it reconsidered its strategy. Ultimately, it decided to offer the man a position with Duchess. Such a position would give the man both a supportive community—the Duchess Cruise Line family—and the opportunity to repay the costs of his treatment a little at a time from each paycheck. Despite his lack of training and language, Duchess was confident he could serve as a custodial associate on one of the ships—the company was proud to say that it did not discriminate on the basis of culture or disability.

The president tweeted about Juan Doe on a Tuesday. On Wednesday, everyone expressed his or her shock or disappointment. On Thursday, the president referred to the Japanese prime minister as a "chinaman." Members of his own party expressed their surprise and disappointment, while liberals noted that Asian Americans were hardworking and patriotic. #JuanDoe and #BoycottDuchess no longer appeared in Twitter's trending topics; only a few local journalists came to the doctors' press conferences. So it was hardly reported that on Saturday morning, the doctors removed the man's feeding tube and brought him out of sedation.

The man woke, and the doctors noted a change: the catlike indifference was gone. His eyes now darted and glared. The doctors explained that he would soon be discharged into Duchess' care, but before they understood what was happening, the man was out of the room. His IV stand trailed behind him—he tore the wires from his arm, and ran.

Nurses and doctors followed, shouting, but it didn't matter. He could smell the sea now. The automatic doors of the hospital slid open, and the man sprinted down Las Oslas Boulevard, onto the beach, and into the water. With long, chopping strokes, he swam past the bobbing children and the paddleboarders, beyond the sandbar, toward the horizon. The blue hospital gown slipped from his body, and the waves carried it back to the shore.

III.

For five hundred years, he had avoided swimming out of sight of his island because he feared being lost at sea. But now he knew that there was something worse than death, so he swam and swam.

The lights of the city disappeared behind him, and still he swam. He grew tired, but not hungry. The sun rose, and set, and rose again, and then he saw land. He came out of the water and onto the beach, and slept for fifteen hours in the roots of a mangrove. When he woke and looked around, he understood that this island was not his island, so he returned to the sea.

That was the northern tip of Bimini. From there, he swam east, and in a few days, landed at Gold Cay. He continued southeast along the coast of Andros Island, and then to Cayo Cruz.

But none of these were his island. Under the anesthesia, he had dreamed of it. The island had been drowned in cool, searing light, and in the air, he had heard an almost silent humming—a thousand soft voices twanging from the bottom of the cave to the tops of the fig trees. The island had appeared to him then as it never had before—bright and sweet, a home.

So he continued on, swimming along the coast of Cuba, avoiding the lights of cities and towns, past Baracoa, toward the Atlantic.

The odds were against him: he had never known where his island was, and now he was alone on a great sea. He knew this. But he continued.

He was, in a way, happy—much happier than he had ever been on the island. For the first time since the sixteenth century, he was not entirely hopeless. He did not know what he was doing, but he had forever to do it. It might take him another five centuries, but he knew that it would happen eventually: one gray day, after thousands and thousands of failures, he would see the island in the distance and recognize it as his own.

After a few years, Duchess stopped offering Dessalines/Georges Island as an excursion—the sea level had risen and risen, and there was hardly anything to see. The saltwater had choked the fig trees, and the colony of iguanas had dwindled to four or five solitary males. The excursion from Grand Turk was moved to another island, which had recently been deemed "imminently threatened." Fortunately for the Sunset Tour, there would be no shortage of these.

And so the tide came in, a few inches further every day. The remaining iguanas retreated to the cave and were safe for a little while. But the tide kept coming, always further than before, until one day, it spilled into the cave, and the water of the fountain mixed with the salt of the sea.

THE F'D WORLD

Lavina Blossom

The festering flowers did not worry them
much. Spring was fast becoming summer. The flies,
though, the fact they flourished while the bees
died out, fueled concern. And the fertile fields
become fallow, the forecasts
of fair weather proving fallacious: storm
fronts swept through with ferocious winds.

The few remaining frogs flopped from fetid
sinkholes to front doors, then back
to the frothing muck, back and forth
each day, bringing, in their frowning mouths,
bits of flotsam: parts of plastic forks and cups, fragments
of Styrofoam, filaments of floss, scraps
of synthetic fabric and fake fur.

Freak phenomena became frequent, became
the norm. Fog rolled in with the sound
of flutes and flugelhorns. Fissures gaped in freeways,
exuding foul fumes. Fish leaped above fjords in groups
of five or more then flipped belly-up to float and putrefy. Finches
quacked like ducks, flew in formation, then went off like firecrackers.
Snails fried themselves on flagstones. Floors fell in. Fences
flattened. Flamingos turned green, fingers fluorescent. Flags
snapped off at their stars.

There were quakes and conflagrations.
There was frenzy, flood,
famine, and plagues of fleas. Then,
fuchsia flakes of fallout,
followed by freeze.

BEYOND REPAIR

Deborah Marr

An iceberg
the size of Delaware
finally broke free
of the Antarctic shelf
this morning,
and it's all we can talk about.

I hear a neighbor say
you could see the crack
from space, widening
with the warming temperatures,
mile by irrevocable mile.

It's July in Los Angeles,
so hot that birds are falling
like stones to the ground,
and I skirt their bodies
stiff and frozen
all the way to my car,
its ample air conditioning.

Before we left for vacation,
I counted seven ducklings
paddling through the pond
only to return in a week
to one lone sibling,
swimming in his mother's wake.

How to accept these losses,
a world beyond repair.
How to believe anyone still cares
about such a place, in light of all we lose
and don't notice it's missing

until it's the size
of Delaware

until the damage we've done
is so deep
it can be seen from space.

NO FIRM FORTRESS:
READING AND MOURNING *MOBY-DICK*
ON THE CUSP OF CLIMATE CHANGE

Kathleen Rooney

If Herman Melville were still alive, he would have turned 200 years old on Thursday, August 1, 2019. This anniversary presents an occasion to reconsider *Moby-Dick; or, The Whale*, which Richard Bentley first published in the United Kingdom in 1851. Accordingly, this past January, snowfall making the ground as white as Melville's sea beast, the Newberry Library here in Chicago hosted a 25-hour *Moby-Dick* read-a-thon. By the end, a series of performers had collectively read the masterpiece aloud from cover to cover.

My spouse and fellow writer, Martin Seay, and I served as two of the readers, choosing passages from Chapter 32: Cetology. These infinitesimal observations on the characteristics of the various species of the order *Cetacea* are reportedly the most likely to be omitted in abridged versions. What a loss that would be; one would miss hearing, for instance, Melville's glorious description of the porpoise:

> [H]e always swims in hilarious shoals, which upon the broad sea keep tossing themselves to heaven like caps in a Fourth-of-July crowd.

As Ishmael concludes,

> If you can withstand three cheers at beholding these vivacious fish, then heaven help ye; the spirit of godly gamesomeness is not in ye.

Moreover, Chapter 32 is Martin's favorite; he's had hung next to his desk for as long as I've known him its concluding exclamation:

> This whole book is but a draught—nay, but the draught of a draught. Oh, Time, Strength, Cash, and Patience!

A confession, however: despite my enthusiastic agreement to participate in the read-a-thon and my strenuous assertion leading up to our performance that the cetology chapter was one of the finest, I had never read *Moby-Dick* in its entirety. I had attempted it one summer in high school, and once again during grad school, but never connected with it fully, though I could tell each time that I was in the presence of greatness. The looming read-a-thon and an attendant desire not to be a hypocrite caused me to endeavor the novel once more, and to be—at last—totally harpooned by it.

Reading *Moby-Dick* cover-to-cover turned out to be the best 10-day reading experience of my life. This novel is flawless and not to be abridged. I had failed before to apprehend how laugh-out-loud funny Melville is, and to admire the density and brilliance of every paragraph. It's the kind of book that feels like a friend. The kind of book that you miss when you're away from it. The kind of book where you know there are activities in life that may be *as good as* it is but none *better*. The kind of book where you don't understand why anybody does anything other than just read it all the time. It's the novel that William Shakespeare would have written if the novel had existed in English during the era in which he lived. Melville's masterpiece makes me deliriously, consumingly, uncontainably happy.

But it also makes me almost unbearably sad. Because the book is a lot of things to a lot of people, but in its deepest core, it's a book about a whale, and reading about whales in 2019 is an ineluctable downer.

In the years since Melville wrote the book in the mid-19th century (admittedly to an underwhelming reception), the whale has been construed as possessing almost endless symbolic meanings. The chapter on The Whiteness of the Whale, alone, must have launched an infinite fleet of PhD theses: so many vessels on the seas of interpretation. But the most profound answer to the question, *What does the whale represent?*, is: a whale. An actual flesh-and-blubber, swimming, breathing, miraculous mystery of the watery deep.

In her 2000 biography of Melville, Elizabeth Hardwick notes,

> The White Whale, ambiguously innocent as a virgin bride, ambiguously rapacious as a white shark of the tropics, is here a fictional creation of unparalleled inspiration.

Advocating in favor of the oft-cut cetology chapter and against reducing the whale to a symbol, she says,

> In this imaginative, developing story the whale is a central character, a human antagonist, as it were.

I'd go so far as to say that Melville characterizes Moby Dick as an inhuman protagonist, too. He continually gives us glimpses of the ecosystem in which the animal may be the hero of his own story, trying to live free of human predation.

Attempting to dissuade his captain from the lunacy of his actions, the first mate, Starbuck, cries to Ahab,

> Vengeance on a dumb brute that simply smote thee from the blindest instinct! Madness! To be enraged with a dumb thing, Captain Ahab, seems blasphemous.

Starbuck is right that Ahab's behavior is mad, but he's wrong about Moby Dick. This highly perceptive and rationally motivated whale pursues his aim of staving the *Pequod* out of intelligence and ethical drive.

In his 2018 book, *We're Doomed. Now What?: Essays on War and Climate Change,* Roy Scranton writes,

> [W]e need to give up defending and protecting *our* truth, *our* perspective ... and understand that truth is found not in one perspective but in its multiplication, not in one point of view, but in the aggregate, not in opposition but in the whole. We need to learn to see ... not just with human eyes but with golden-cheeked warbler eyes, coho salmon eyes, and polar bear eyes, and not even just with eyes but the wild, barely articulate being of clouds and seas and rocks and trees and stars.

Moby-Dick invites the reader to imagine the world as it appears to whale eyes.

An incredibly charismatic novel about an incredibly charismatic megafauna, *Moby-Dick* smites me with love for the whale himself. I feel more magnetically drawn to him than to any literary character since I read *A Tale of Two Cities* and discovered righteous antihero Sydney Carton. The way Melville has Ishmael speak about the whale is almost intoxicated, and certainly intoxicating. At the end of Chapter 1, when Ishmael accounts for his motives for signing onto a whaling ship, he cites above all "the overwhelming idea of the great whale himself" and "the wild and distant seas where he rolled his island bulk," declaring,

> the great flood-gates of the wonder-world swung open, and in the wild conceits that swayed me to my purpose, two and two there floated into my inmost soul, endless processions of the whale, and, mid most of them all, one grand hooded phantom, like a snow hill in the air.

Ecstasy aside, with global warming as dire as it's ever been and getting direr, my inmost soul was hit by how eerie and sad it feels to encounter Moby Dick, the exquisitely characterized white whale, in the Anthropocene, a term that the Nobel Prize-winning Dutch chemist Paul Crutzen began popularizing at the turn of this century. Crutzen, who won his award in 1995 for his work on the hole in the ozone layer, uses the label to describe this new epoch in which humans comprise a geologic force negatively affecting Earth and all its forms of life.

Melville's 200th birthday coincides with the human-made sixth extinction, as well as with the emptying, warming, and clogging up of the world's oceans via overfishing and the dumping of plastics. Such facts imbue his novel with renewed and melancholy relevance. Reading his book about a sentient, majestic, and desperate-to-live marine mammal in a period when the planet's whales—and all other creatures—are under such threat grants the work a grim ecological cast.

Melville seems neither to want to limit his leviathan to the antagonist role nor to want to consign him to the enemy side in a high-school-level categorization of conflicts, e.g. Man Versus Nature. Rather, Moby Dick possesses agency in his own right, troubling Ahab only because Ahab and the fleets of other whalemen have invaded Moby Dick's home in an effort to kill him and every other whale he knows and loves.

In giving his exemplar whale a name, Melville pays him an honor. The appellation derives from J. N. Reynolds' *Mocha Dick: Or the White Whale of the Pacific*, published in *The Knickerbocker* in 1839. Melville also borrowed from the story the idea that a whale could calculate revenge against hunters and their ships. From this inspiration rises Ahab's "white-headed whale, with a wrinkled brow and a crooked jaw," suffering protractedly from the onslaughts of man "with three holes punctured in his starboard fluke."

But Melville is not interested in Moby Dick as singular; all of his whales are capable of both cognition and affect in patterns easily recognizable to humans. In Chapter 87: The Grand Armada, he describes a pod of whales with such tenderness and admiration that it's worth citing at length. In the midst of a spate of their routine insatiable violence, the men of the *Pequod* spy a group of male whales exhibiting "a wondrous fearlessness and confidence, or else a still becharmed panic which it was impossible not to marvel at" as they circle together around female whales tending to their young and preparing to give birth:

> But far beneath this wondrous world upon the surface, another and still stranger world met our eyes as we gazed over the side. For, suspended in those watery vaults, floated the forms of the nursing mothers of the whales, and those that by their enormous girth seemed shortly to become mothers. The lake, as I have hinted, was to a considerable depth exceedingly transparent and as human infants while suckling will calmly and fixedly gaze away from the breast, as if leading two different lives at the same time; and while yet drawing mortal nourishment, be still spiritually feasting upon some unearthly reminiscence;—even so did the young of these whales seem looking up towards us, but not at us, as if we were but a bit of Gulf-weed in their new-born sight.

The paragraph concludes its identification of infant whales with infant humans thus:

> The delicate side-fins, and the palms of his flukes, still freshly retained the plaited crumpled appearance of a baby's ears newly arrived from foreign parts.

Yet even as he gives a meticulous account of the natural world and its seldom-seen features, Melville grapples with the mysteries and unknow-ability that it ultimately retains—how humans can scarcely comprehend what it is they're destroying. Ishmael sums this up in Chapter 79: The Prairie, when he puts the sublime brow of the sperm whale before his audience and dares, "Read it if you can."

Melville assuredly did not intend his novel as a cri de coeur against cli-mate catastrophe given that no one alive then knew the phenomenon existed, but that doesn't mean that it hasn't become one. In the introduc-tion to his 1960 book, *Permanent Red*, John Berger writes,

> [I]t is essential to remember that the specific meaning of a work of art changes—if it didn't, no work could outlive its period, and no agnostic could appreciate a Bellini. ... The meaning of the im-provement, of the increase promised by a work of art, depends upon who is looking at it when. Or to put it dialectically, it de-pends upon what obstacles are impeding human progress at any given time.

Climate catastrophe and the irreversible mass death of countless spe-cies with which we share the planet are a monumental set of obstacles. A new use to which latter-day readers can put *Moby-Dick* is as a meditation for thinking about and grieving the Anthropocene. We probably can't atone for causing the horror, but we can consider Melville's novel as a con-duit for processing our complicity, as well as for seeing the wonder in the ecology we were part of and violated.

In Chapter 105: Does the Whale's Magnitude Diminish?—Will He Per-ish?, Melville has Ishmael muse with misplaced optimism,

> whether Leviathan can long endure so wide a chase, and so re-morseless a havoc; whether he must not at last be exterminated from the waters, and the last whale, like the last man, smoke his last pipe, and then himself evaporate in the final puff.

He concludes that a variety of factors forbid "so inglorious an end." Ishmael argues that although humans have noticed whales' numbers de-clining, there's no cause for worry:

> [I]f one coast is no longer enlivened with their jets, then, be sure, some other and remoter strand has been very recently startled by the unfamiliar spectacle.

Then, in the most brutally sad passage for this 2019 reader, Ishmael asserts,

> [The whales] have two firm fortresses, which, in all human prob-
> ability will for ever remain impregnable. And as upon the inva-
> sion of their valleys, the frosty Swiss have retreated to their
> mountains; so, hunted from the savannas and glades of the mid-
> dle seas, the whale-bone whales can at last resort to their Polar
> citadels, and diving under the ultimate glassy barriers and walls
> there, come up among icy fields and floes; and in a charmed circle
> of everlasting December, bid defiance to all pursuit from man.

Writing in the middle of the 19th century, Melville had no way of knowing how badly he'd misplaced his faith, that humans are precisely who have caused the icy fortresses of the poles to become not merely pregnable but virtually nonexistent. The ice caps and sea ice continue melting at appalling rates. Not only is there no longer any "everlasting December" anywhere on the globe, but December itself becomes ever less December-ish as we log year after year of "hottest on record."

Contrary to what Melville—or at least Ishmael—believed about the species' invincibility, the Endangered Species Act lists the sperm whale as endangered and the Marine Mammal Protection Act lists it as depleted. Admittedly, Ishmael is sort of correct in predicting that it's not exclusively hunting, per se, that will drive whales to extinction. Rather, it's the fact that they, like every other living creature, will not be able to survive in the overwarm toxic death slurry that human activity has made of the oceans.

The granular texture and frolicsome tone of the lavish attention the book pays to its whales serve to underscore the reality of all that we're extirpating. In Chapter 81: The Pequod Meets the Virgin, second mate Stubb remarks quite cutely upon the marvel of whale farts. Watching "a huge, humped old bull" of a sperm whale, Ishmael notes,

> His spout was short, slow, and laborious; coming forth with a
> choking sort of gush, and spending itself in torn shreds, followed
> by strange subterranean commotions in him, which seemed to
> have egress at his other buried extremity, causing the waters
> behind him to upbubble.

Stubb calls out,

> Who's got some paregoric? ... he has the stomach-ache, I'm
> afraid. Lord, think of having half an acre of stomach-ache! Ad-
> verse winds are holding mad Christmas in him, boys. It's the first
> foul wind I ever knew to blow from astern.

Melville's obvious affection for these beasts in all their dignity and earthiness alongside his accounts of the whalers' gluttonous bloodletting resonates sickeningly with news[1] that 87 percent of the world's oceans are dying because of climate change and reports[2] that our oceans are "on a precipice of a major extinction event."

Like Ahab, we humans pursue our own demise with a fevered

monomania; like Ahab, we could choose to stop, but we won't. As Hardwick writes,

> In this way, Ahab can be seen to have fallen into idolatry, an unwholesome worship of the claims of his private destiny, a blasphemous disregard of nature, the seas, and the creatures within it.

It's true that some individuals and smaller groups serve as estimable exceptions, but because climate catastrophe is a collective-action problem, it is only solvable on a mass-population level. It's not defeatist to say that it's already too late, as the bromides go, to *Save the Whales* or *Save the Earth*; it's a realistic way to deal honestly with the circumstances we've created. Our relationship to the natural world is almost exclusively destructive, and our incapacity, as Americans anyway, to be compassionate to migrants at our Southern border affords little reason to hope that we'll be anything but cruel in our response to climate refugees.

Climate trauma is a real affliction, and by now you can probably see that I've got it. Our present catastrophe is a bummer to bring up. People worry about you if you do, which is nice of them, I guess. But climate trauma, to me, seems a reasonable response to our ongoing, colossal loss. Back in 2009, the National Wildlife Federation convened a forum to assess the effects that global warming would have on the public's mental health in America as a result of the psychological impacts of direct experience and the anticipation of future harm. In February 2012, the NWF issued a report that synthesized the forum's findings, concluding,

> Global warming in the coming years will foster public trauma, depression, violence, alienation, substance abuse, suicide, psychotic episodes, post-traumatic stress disorders and many other mental health-related conditions.

Climate trauma manifests in thousands of small and large ways over the course of a day, but one of its reddest flags is that lately, every time I hear that someone is having a baby, I think, *How sad*, and every time I hear that someone has died, I think, *Lucky*. When I express that aloud, friends and acquaintances rush to tell me that such a viewpoint is wrong. That it can't be as bad as I think. But it is. Admitting the devastation can be a way to maintain the ability to go on.

I thrill to Melville's awe-filled descriptions of his valiant whale, as when Moby Dick is about to defeat his would-be killers in the book's final passages:

> Suddenly the waters around them slowly swelled in broad circles

then quickly upheaved, as if sideways sliding from a submerged berg of ice, swiftly rising to the surface. A low rumbling sound was heard; a subterrous hum; and then all held their breaths; as bedraggled with trailing ropes, and harpoons, and lances, a vast form shot length-wise, but obliquely from the sea. Shrouded in a thin drooping veil of mist, it hovered for a moment in the rainbowed air; and then fell swamping back into the deep. Crushed thirty feet upwards, the waters flashed for an instant like heaps of fountains, then brokenly sank in a shower of flakes, leaving the circling surface creamed like new milk round the marble trunk of the whale.

But I cannot encounter such passages without other descriptions springing into my mind unwelcome. One from *National Geographic* in 2018 tells of a 31-foot sperm whale carcass₃ on the coast of Eastern Indonesia with 13 pounds of plastic in its stomach. The level of detail in the whale's abjection feels novelistic: 115 drinking cups, 25 plastic bags, and two flip-flops.

I resent and envy Melville for being dead and therefore not having to contend with this crisis of our making. I am jealous of his having gotten to live in a time when it was possible, however wrongheadedly, to believe that no matter how bad anything else got or how divided we became as people, the planet upon which we all dwelt would remain inexhaustible, eternal, perpetually fine.

Nathaniel Philbrick, author of the 2010 book *Why Read Moby-Dick?*, delivered the keynote at the Newberry read-a-thon. In his bright and insightful speech, he said that it was something of a mistake to make anyone under 30 read Melville's masterpiece, even though he read it in high school and was taken on the best possible Nantucket sleigh ride. I couldn't disagree, especially as my own experience tracked with that advice.

But hearing him say this made me even sadder, because when I think about young people, I think about doom. I refuse to have children for a number of reasons, but a big one is climate catastrophe. Philbrick quoted the passage from the novel in which Ishmael asks,

> Why is almost every robust healthy boy with a robust healthy soul in him, at some time or other crazy to go to sea?

My nephew, Luka, fits this description at four-and-a-half. He's crazy to be a marine archaeologist. If you were to visit him at his home in landlocked Oak Park, Illinois, he would climb into your lap with his books on the wreck of the *SS Edmund Fitzgerald* to explain his theories for why the mighty ship sank in Lake Superior just seven or so miles from safety in 1975. He spends a significant portion of each day drawing ocean life, especially sperm whales, their cartoonishly large heads well suited to his tiny hands.

Luka will be 30 in 2044. The United Nations' Intergovernmental Panel on Climate Change reported last year that failing immediate and intensive action, the worst effects of the climate crisis—mass coral reef die-offs, food shortages, wildfires, massive coastal flooding—will arrive by 2040. Aesthetically sound as Philbrick's advice may be, I'm not sure that Luka (or anyone) should wait to read *Moby-Dick*.

Moby Dick leads the *Pequod* on a merry, fatal chase through almost every ocean that washes the globe, but in the end, of course, it's just one massive sea. There is no firm fortress, no retreat for us. However old you are in this year of Herman Melville's 200th birthday, you should read—or reread—his jocular, perturbing book while you still have a chance. For the "draught of a draught" that we humans have been writing is coming to an end, and it turns out the story is a tragedy, the white whale's horizontal tail a vanishing horizon.

The only whale left to see may soon be the constellation Cetus—the distant, starry outline of a beast we loved and hated enough to place in the sky while removing it from everywhere else. At least we can never kill that one. At least that celestial memory can remind us, along with *Moby-Dick*, of what we had and what we did to it.

1. *"87% of the World's Oceans Are Dying: Report,"* Joe McCarthy and Erica Sanchez, Global Citizen, July 26, 2018, globalcitizen.org/en/content/87-of-worlds-oceans-are-dying-climate-change; 2. *"Ocean Life Faces Mass Extinction, Broad Study Says,"* Carl Zimmer, The New York Times, January 15, 2015, nytimes.com/2015/01/16/science/earth/study-raises-alarm-for-health-of-ocean-life.html; 3. *"Sperm whale found dead with 13 pounds of plastic in its stomach,"* Laura Parker, National Geographic, November 21, 2018, nationalgeographic.com/environment/2018/11/dead-sperm-whale-filled-with-plastic-trash-indonesia.

HORIZON

C. W. Buckley

after Richard Russell, August 11, 2018

The trail marks the path, as the salmon swims
Through wood and wetland, and finally
To fence, where it rises
Away from water and over tracks
Guarded by a suicide warning

> *I just kinda wanna do*
> *A couple of maneuvers*
> *See what it can do*
> *Before I put her down*
> *Y'know?*

Silence descends with water
To the Sound
Where it opens to Olympic vista
Just over the footbridge

> *Just did a little circle around Rainier*
> *It's beautiful*
> *Um, I think I've got some gas*
> *To check out the Olympics*

It takes both parents and an uncle
To talk one child down
Grated metal steps to the beach

> *Yeah, I'm not quite ready to bring it down just yet*
> *But HO LEE smokes I gotta stop looking at the fuel*
> *Because it is goin' down kaWICK*

Children flock, a colorful murder
Of crows, to the bridge, squealing
As the engineer toots once beneath them
From his deadly rolling pipeline, snaking North

> *This is probably, uh*
> *Like jail time for life, huh?*
> *I mean I would hope it is*
> *For a guy like me*

Hopeless cars, like men, loaded
Rolling, under pressure and ready to burn
When derailed, despoiling the beach
All the way to Burnaby

> *I would like to get some, uh*
> *Make it, make it pressurized*
> *Or something*
> *So I'm not so lightheaded*

There's one combing the beach already
Sweeping morning sand for what we lost last night
Another is close behind, detector in hand
Shouting "Fortune and glory!"
All the way down to empty sand

Uh, minimum wage
We'll chalk it up to that
Maybe that'll grease the gears a little bit
With the higher-ups
Maybe. Uh, yeah

Now at this lowest of tides, a trick of the moon
Pulls Salish waters back like a blanket
Rocky, blinking green beckons gulls and ravens down
For easy pickings

Hey, you think if I land this successfully
Alaska will give me a job as a pilot?
Yeeah, riight
Nah, I'm a white guy

Joining those grounded birds reveals
Life and wonder all around
Its primordial grind and squish flexing up
Through boots, onto bare calves

Hey, I want the coordinates of that orca
With the, you know?
The mama orca with the baby?
I wanna go see that guy!

Something gapes beneath the sand
Naked seafloor, suddenly a geyser-bed
Spurting, arcing all around
Eternal mollusks spew in seeming celebration
Of the very predators they call down from the sky

I think I'm, uh
I think I'm gonna try to do a barrel roll
And if that goes good
I'll just go nose down
And call it a night

But that's how they've lasted, see
Since before the People were

                                           Y'know the sights?

                                      They went by so fast

They dig deep

                                      I was thinking

Down

                    Like I was gonna have this moment of serenity

Cycle after cycle

                       And I'd be able to take in all the sights

Feeding, breathing

                       Uh, there's a lot of pretty stuff, but uh

And when the water's gone they shoot to the sky

                  I think that they're prettier in a different context

Like smoke, rising from Ketron Island

On August 10, 2018, baggage-handler Richard Russell took a Horizon Air plane from Sea-Tac airport, eventually crashing it into Ketron Island. The italicized words of Russell's are transcribed from publicly available recordings of Sea-Tac Air Traffic Control.

LOST TO THE SEA

Wendi White

"All I ask is that you remember me,"
a headstone pleads, wet with rising seas.
They live with their dead on these islands.
Graves like garden plots in backyards cling
to what's left—land that will soon succumb:
docks, fields, ridges and dunes, to the waves
of our own making, that soon will send
three hundred years of English history packing
on the final ferry. And we who've found ourselves
tangled in pound nets and crab pots cast
by Tangier's past will be cut loose, unmoored
from the lines we thought would hold us steady.

HONEYMOON IN TEMPORARY LOCATIONS

Ashley Shelby

Well, V, I'm sitting in the front parlor of the Glensheen Mansion, finally in the Promised Land. Let this missive serve as confirmation that I've safely arrived in a Climate Impact Resettlement Zone. Spread the word to those who were wondering if I ever made it—with patience and persistence, and a valid Environmental Migrant Residency Permit, they, too, can be successfully resettled in the bluffs of Duluth. There are familiar faces here. One of the first I saw was our good friend Cedar. He was standing at the top of West 5th Street with his longboard, trying to decide if careening down a 45-degree angle into two lanes of traffic was the best inauguration for a successfully resettled refugee. Luckily, a cop stopped him before he went for it. It was Cedar, bless his artisanal gin-loving heart, who gave me your email address (my phone was destroyed during the trip under circumstances which I'll now share with you). He wanted me to mention that you still owe him for that borrowed carbon credit from last year.

I have a story for you. I should warn you that this story differs from the ones we swapped at that dirty bar on Vandam Street pre-Breach, gobbling stale, fecal-dusted Goldfish mix from bowls and double-fisting vodka tonics on Ladies Night. Whenever I think of the Great Manhattan Seawall Breach, by the way, I can coax out a laugh by imagining how the Hudson must have washed through that hole in the wall, turning our beloved fish-shaped crackers into swollen monsters, and setting them free to explore upstream. Swim, little fishies, swim! Anyway, all this to tell you that this story isn't like the ones you're used to hearing from me, and I you. This isn't about the origin of your mysterious bruises or my late-night adventures in the bathrooms at the Cubby Hole. No, this is a tale of existential confusion, and I want you to caper down the road to oblivion with me.

I don't think you know that I married that girl about a month after you left New York, and a couple weeks before Superstorm XY came roaring through the city. And although I do have our certificate of marriage in my possession, along with our resettlement papers, I now avow that I was never married, and that my wife never existed. I will lay out for you the evidence of this nonexistence. And by the way, I'm not peddling that Simone de Beauvoir nonsense I wore like a dime-store prom dress in college. This is quantum physics. I am proposing that my wife was a wave-particle duality in human form.

First, the girl: You remember her. She was the Chapstick lesbian circulating at Grant's Net Zero party, the one who gave the toast about the carbon neutrality of biomass and how Grant's achievement of personal net zero was a "proof positive" of continuing human ingenuity. You ridiculed her reckless use of air quotes around proof positive, and that was how she came to my attention. (So I do, perhaps, have you to blame for all this.) Anyway, when we talked later that night, I wasn't immediately smitten.

Still, she was interesting enough to accompany to the IRT that night, and I don't know, but something she said when we were standing there, under the rusted trestles, ignited something (my own biomass, perhaps?). She made me laugh, and you know how that goes with me. Anyway, it was the funny thing she said, or the fact that the first rolling blackout of the night had just started or that we were close enough to the waterline that I could hear the river lapping against the dikes on 96th Street, or the low-grade humming of the generators so reminiscent of my battery-operated girl-friend—it was any or all of these things that pushed me into the abyss of infatuation. The feeling was returned by half—I suppose that she felt aerosol dispersal management was a stable job sector and that my wagon was as good as any on which to hitch her pulsating death star.

As you already know, I had been making plans to follow your example and apply for a residency permit in one of the Non-Impact Regions. My bride mentioned she had family in Duluth, but she had lost their contact information—much as I did yours, in fact—when she dropped her phone into our composting toilet. This was slightly inconvenient—as you know, your residential permit application is fast-tracked if you have family in the Non-Impact Zone to which you're traveling. But since her parents had gone radio silent since joining that eco-village in Bellingham and could not be petitioned for the contact info, we simply followed the typical bu-reaucratic channels until one day, when she told me she'd located her aunt's address and phone number in a rigorous online search. We called the number in the listing, but no one picked up. Our messages, left at the behest of a robotic voice spewing out their telephone number, grew in-creasingly dramatic, I confess. These also went unreturned. Meanwhile, we waited for our papers.

Our hand was forced by the storm surge, of course, and we were rounded up, along with the others on our block, and transported to the Migrant Transport Center up at the Cloisters. We were told to wait there for "unscheduled buses" that would take us to "temporary locations." I was too exhausted to ask how a location could be temporary, though now I've come to consider this question hopelessly naïve.

We slept on cots in the Unicorn Tapestries Room—where, it seemed, they'd installed all the gay couples "out of abundant concern for our own comfort and safety." Three days we spent here, waiting for buses, for pa-pers, for any indication of where we were headed, and in the meantime becoming very knowledgeable about the use of wool warp and gilt weft in medieval South Netherlandish tapestries. All we knew was that Manhat-tan was being evacuated and that each migrant would receive a resettle-ment notice eventually, but probably not until we had arrived at one of those mystical "temporary locations." Those who had left earlier, and of their own volition, like you, had a say in the matter of where they resettled. Us stragglers were at the mercy of the green *politburo*. This experience, incidentally, was the extent of our honeymoon. As we were sleeping in separate cots, I was only able to cop a couple feels by reaching across the cold marble floor before a security guard approached with a scowl.

Eventually, though, we made it to Chicago, the environmental migrant's Grand Central. She bore the whole adventure with a kind of dreamy optimism, saying little, but holding my hand all the way from the Pennsylvania turnpike to the Indiana toll roads. Not even the roadside signs announcing MIGRANT SCUM, KEEP DRIVING punctured our connubial contentment. We were a couple miles past Gary, the ZEBS bus (Zero Emission Bus System) idling in a miles-long jam headed into Chicago, when she disappeared to visit the onboard bathroom. When she returned to her seat, her entire demeanor had changed. Her words were frosty, her face impassive, even cold. She asked to exchange seats with me so she could be next to the window. Once seated, she turned her back to me. She began to sob. "How could we have left him behind?" she cried. "The poor kitty. He'll never know why we didn't come back." I was taken aback. Her sorrow was immense; her face was wet with tears. We had no cat. When I gently pointed this out to her, she nodded. "I know. I know. But what if we'd adopted that tabby from the Humane Society. Can you imagine? He'd be pacing the apartment, crying for us, wondering why we'd abandoned him. I can't bear to think about it." She turned back to the window to look at the endless line of hydrogen-fuel-cell vehicles glinting in the relentless midday sun. It wasn't worthwhile, I felt, to point out that we had never visited the Humane Society.

We arrived at Union Station, where we spent several hours in several different lines, making our case for a temporary residency permit for Duluth. As a Non-Impact Zone, Minnesota is in high demand among migrants from the East Coast cities for obvious reasons (you know what happened to Wren and Lennon when they ended up in Green Bay). Thanks to her mysterious and unresponsive Duluth aunt, we were given approval papers and directed toward a St. Paul-bound train. We had to make our way through a boisterous mob in possession of lots of handmade signs and a single tooth (ha), and one of our cohort got into a shoving match with a guy who called him a "taco jockey" (the man was a Syrian-born professor of antiquities at NYU).

The ride was unremarkable for the first two hours. The towns along the route were all official environmental migrant resettlement sites, taking advantage of that generous federal subsidy about which you argued with me so vehemently at the Mets game we attended last summer. Eventually, the train pulled into a Wisconsin town called Tomah. We'd run out of food by this point, so I disembarked alone in search of provisions (she was still too distraught about the nonexistent cat to leave her seat).

I was gone a total of four minutes, but when I returned with a fistful of energy bars, the train was gone. When I went to inquire at the ticket office, the agent was instantly agitated. He sprang up from his swivel chair and jabbed a finger at me. "You had no right to get off!" he bellowed. I wandered over to the train tracks, and as I looked down the line toward St. Paul, my phone chose this moment to make its escape from the unzipped breast pocket of my Carhartt utility vest (one of *Glamour*'s "Must-Have Pieces for Evacuation Journeys"). It landed with a sickening thud on the gravel between the wall and the third rail.

Thus began my bureaucratic nightmare. I won't bore you with the minutia, but suffice it to say that since neither she nor I had a phone now, I took the next train and got off at the next resettlement stop (the aptly named La Crosse, Wisconsin), but she wasn't waiting for me at the station as I'd hoped. I returned to Tomah—perhaps she'd gotten off at La Crosse and crossed the track to head back to Tomah in hopes of finding me—only to discover she wasn't there, either. As I munched on one of the energy bars I'd procured for her, I thought about the cat. Might as well have been Schrödinger's. Was it real, and I'd forgotten? Or, more ominously, was it imaginary, and she thought it real? This would've been a fun brain-teaser for us in better times, but as I sat there on a bench in the empty Tomah train station, I entertained for the first time that my wife did not, in fact, exist, and that I was in pursuit of an entity that was no more likely to exist than the tabby for which she mourned. I dismissed the thought as the ravings of an exhausted mind.

I arrived in St. Paul the next day, and took a bus across the Mississippi to Minneapolis, where the New York migrants had gathered in a neighborhood called Longfellow—a place crisscrossed by old rail lines and rehabbed grain elevators. A uniformed resettlement officer gave me directions to the hostel where the rest of the New York diaspora had been relegated, and I checked in—asking, of course, after my wife. She had not been heard from, so I made my way to the Minneapolis resettlement office, hoping for better luck. There, I produced papers, our wedding certificate, and her own notice of resettlement, which I'd kept nestled next to mine in the left thigh pocket of my Dickies. Bureaucracy having received its portion, I was told again that no one had seen her. I contacted the police, who were of no help whatsoever. One officer, upon inspecting our marriage certificate, claimed it was invalid because the notary's seal hadn't completely perforated the paper. Still, he took down my information and claimed that he'd look for my "lady-wife."

That night, I ate dinner at the neighborhood café where my fellow displaced New Yorkers gathered to watch CNN's coverage of Superstorm XY, and to trade information about the friendliest enclaves for refugees. I learned that the Syrian professor had been taken into custody earlier that evening and was being questioned at the Hennepin County Courthouse for alleged ties to a carbon-trading scheme. I did not, however, learn anything about my wife.

I spent the next two days wandering around Longfellow, waiting for word. I was still awaiting my—our—temporary residency permits, and so I found I had a great deal of time on my hands. Minnesota was temperate in November, and I spent several hours walking through Minnehaha Park, marveling at the orange-gold and garnet leaves lifting lightly in what could pass as a harvest wind. Though the Minnehaha Falls had gone dry two years earlier, the rocky precipice over which the waters used to cascade was still something to behold. Even as things vanish around us, I remember thinking, their absence reveals a different kind of beauty.

When I returned to my room at the hostel that night, there was a message from one of the police officers, asking me to meet him at the YMCA downtown. The place was as seedy as you'd expect—an old SRO of the sort that used to haunt every city block above 96th Street, but which, in Minneapolis, is termed "transitional housing." I met the officer in the lobby, and he told me, "Your lady-wife has been found." I followed him up the back stairs to a room, where he burst in on a couple in bed. Needless to say, the woman in question was unknown to me. She and her bedmate, a doughy man covered in nautical tattoos, gazed back at us serenely, as if such intrusions happened frequently. The officer kept trying to get the poor woman to confess that she was my wife, until she finally said—and you'll appreciate the echo of Wren and Lennon's one-woman show in this—"I don't go in for that girl-and-girl stuff, officer."

I walked back to Longfellow alone, and it was at the tail end of this solitary amble that I spotted her at the end of a long line of people queued up at the back of a Red Cross truck dispensing blankets and ready-to-eat meals. When I called her name, she turned her head but stood rooted to the ground. I sprinted over to where she was standing and took her into my arms. Her first words to me were, "I hope these meals are vegan."

V, she told me a tale that night, one so banal that I hesitate to share it with you. But because it speaks to this question of nonexistence, I might as well tell you that after the train took off without me that day, she disembarked at La Crosse as I was speeding toward her on the second train to La Crosse, and took the next train to Tomah. Instead of braving the frothing rage of the stationmaster, she went straight to the Commissariat, which, in this case, masquerades as the Tomah Department of Environmental Migrant Management. They were no help, and as she had no papers with which to board the next St. Paul-bound train (I had all of our papers, remember), she fell in with a group of North Carolina refugees in a similar bind. They spent the night in an abandoned microbrewery on the outskirts of town, and the next morning she was able to borrow a carbon credit from one of the migrants and get on a ZEBS bus to Minneapolis. She'd been directed to the Longfellow neighborhood, and had heard from the patrons of the café that I had been looking for her.

I accepted this story, and we quickly took advantage of the near-empty hostel to engage in coital activities. It was in the middle of this, as her strong thighs flanked my head, that she became unresponsive. I ceased my efforts to see what the matter was, and was startled to see her gazing down at me impassively. "I lied to you," she said. "Before. When I told you about returning to Tomah to look for you. I met a man on the train. I didn't want to do it. He was a salesman."

Was this man the tabby at the Humane Society? Was he real? She wouldn't tell me more, but over the next few hours, as we lay together in a top bunk, and the other migrants straggled in, I got the story out of her crumb by crumb. You may wonder here how I was able to bear this. How I did not fall to pieces or storm out, taking her papers with me. It may sound strange, but I felt like I couldn't respond until I knew each detail, the way you can't judge if a rhinestone Christmas sweater is successful if a single stone has been lost. Until I had a full accounting, then I couldn't know how to handle it. In other words, because there was no way to judge, there was no way to feel.

She revised continually. What to believe? The first time they had sex, she said, was in the luggage compartment near the front of the train, and she'd been "too tired to care." The second time, the following morning, in the same place because she thought I'd deliberately left her and had no intention of returning. I probed, V. I was the Jacques Cousteau of sexual details—nothing was too insignificant to escape my notice. Had he bent her over the crates of ready-to-eat meals bound for the Twin Cities resettlement office, or had she sat upon the crates herself, opened wide her legs, and let him thrust against the cases of field rations? Was he a breast-cupper or a nipple-pincher? Was he a grunter? I half-hoped he was, because rhythmic ape-like grunting has always struck me as one important point of divergence between the straight man and the self-respecting gay woman. But even this she wouldn't confirm, telling me, "I wasn't listening."

Because of our paperwork problem, this back and forth between us went on for what seemed an eternity. The non-residency permits were being held up for reasons that changed every time I inquired. We were buried by paperwork, benumbed by documentation. I was up all night filling out online forms I'd already submitted several times, beset by a caravan of rainbow wheels of death. The images of her failed flood insurance salesman (this was a detail she let slip) and his grunting lust blended seamlessly into the chiaroscuro of government documents and bored regional officials unwilling to even look up our permit status.

It all came to a head one day when we'd left the hostel to make our daily check of our permit status. We decided to walk a few miles down the Hennepin County Regional Bike Trail. We were only about a mile in, when I dropped onto a bench and began weeping. She sat next to me, silent as a flooded generator. After I'd regained some semblance of control, she took my hand between hers and denied the whole thing had ever happened.

This marked the beginning of our estrangement, which, mingled with the emotional morass of displacement, created a feeling of complete isolation. I had no idea how much time lay before us, whether our permits would be ready within days, weeks, or even months. (The couple in the bunk next to ours had been waiting for a permit for an Iron Range relocation since last spring.) Because our fates were intertwined by paperwork, we remained together. I made the daily forays to the relocation office to check on our permits; she monitored the situation online. It was like living fulltime with a failed Tinder date. But it was worse than that. The first days of silence that passed during this contest between us were brutal and wintry. They formed a neat stitch of time that didn't close the wound, and I spent hours of every day trying to collect myself, as if I were scattered sand on a boardwalk. The best I could do was sweep myself into a little pile until the wind blew me apart again. V, your cynical, worm-eaten heart will scoff at this, but I loved her.

Now I come to the moment when I knew she never existed. Our permits were in. I left to retrieve them and to secure our seats on the Duluth-bound train. I didn't know how we were going to move past all this, but for the first time in two weeks, I was feeling sanguine.

When I returned to the hostel, she was gone. Her hemp-fiber purse, her two dresses, her duck boots—everything she'd brought to Minnesota had disappeared along with her. I looked for her everywhere, of course, and walked the paces—I asked everyone who shared our room if they'd seen her. Not only would none of them speak to me, they also seemed angry and disapproving. I was flummoxed. Finally, one of them deigned to talk to me, an elderly woman named Kate, who was wearing purple legwarmers despite the heat. "You are a terrible person for what you've done," she scolded with her trembling arthritic finger. "I've never heard of such behavior."

It turns out, V, I'm a boor. Turns out—again, echoes of Wren and Lennon, whom if they catch wind of this misadventure will co-opt it entirely—that she'd hooked up with a prepper from Mankato named Rosie (natch) who had promised her a luxury underground bunker, a migration-free life, and plenty of hot meals. (It is with no satisfaction that I remind you that the prepper plutocracy I'd loudly predicted those first months post-Impact has, in fact, been established.) Those hours when I was out at the relocation office, supplicating and petitioning, she was holding the talking stick at the café and telling tales of my refusal to grant her a divorce in order that she might fly away with Prepper Rosie. Apparently, I had not responded well to this news. I'd threatened murder-suicide. I'd denounced her love affair and said I'd rather see us both dead than to travel to Duluth alone.

The details my elderly scold shared were so pointillist in nature that I was unsurprised when, as our conversation came to a close, she gripped my wrist and made me swear not to rent a gun and take off after the lovebirds (whom, she told me, were already ensconced in a bunker beneath the terminal moraine of Blue Earth county). When I asked Kate if she'd ever seen Rosie the prepper-queen in person, she confessed she hadn't, but had been shown a blurry cell phone picture (where'd my wife get a cell phone?) and declared Rosie "rough but handsome." By this time, Kate had ceased pointing at me with her twisted index finger and had calmed down considerably, but just before I left, she rapped upon the side of the bunk three times with her bony knuckles and said, "One thing I won't forget, and will never forgive you for, is what you did to that cat."

I spent the days remaining before my scheduled departure trying to parse out whether the insurance salesman was the prepper-queen, whether it was the other way around, or, more horrifying, if none of them had ever existed, including my wife. I gave up looking for her at this point—searching the streets of Longfellow was pointless, and asking after her at the café would yield nothing, not now that the story of my apparent cruelty had spread throughout the New York diaspora.

A few hours into the train ride to Duluth, I met that Syrian professor who'd been taken in for questioning when we arrived in Minneapolis. He inquired after my wife, wondering if she had remained in the sleeping car because she gets motion sickness, as his wife does. When I told him I traveled alone, he simply stared at me. Thinking he hadn't heard me, I repeated myself. "Forgive me," he said, after a full minute's hesitation. "Perhaps I'm not thinking of the right woman, but I believe I saw your wife just yesterday, walking along East 26th Street. She told me you were on your way to meet her with your relocation permits, which had just come in."

I imagine this moment is the atomic nucleus around which this entire story revolves, the moment I knew for sure she was nothing more than a thought. And lest you think this wishful thinking, let me add that once I arrived in Duluth, and just before I saw Cedar teetering atop West 5th Street on his longboard, I went to the address she'd given me, where her relatives maintained a home, the basis on which we received our relocation permits. It was a bike shop with rooms on the second floor. The proprietor, who lived in said rooms, had never heard of anyone with her family name. He tried to sell me a fat-tire bike.

V, I remember thinking my life could be segmented neatly by subway lines, the ones now sunken beneath the brackish floodwaters—the old 1/9 that sliced through Manhattan lengthwise for the new arrival living in graduate student housing on 113th and Broadway; the polished steel six train and the steaming Astor Place Station during a summer spent in a windowless sublet on 2nd Avenue; the filthy B/C hurtling through Harlem and toward the foreclosed rental where you and I lived sans electricity and heat for six months, subsisting on Kerouac and Old Grand-Dad. You kept me buoyed, but sometimes I sank anyway. Back then I tried to slip past the bleak days the way I avoided the crush of bodies at Columbus Circle, without making contact. What kept me going was believing fervently, even urgently, that the days could not grow bleaker. You, my partner in misery, know as well as I do how bleak things would become, how many things this global inevitability took from us, even the hope we claimed we didn't need. And because you know this, I'm sure you understand the import of the question of whether this woman—my wife, this entity that I'm sure I loved—existed in the way I thought she did, or whether she's only that girl I met at a party once. Perhaps she's not even that; perhaps she's nothing more than a specter I conjured. Which would be worse, I can no longer claim to know. I know it's not on you to figure this out for me, or even to sympathize, though I hope I may depend, at least, on your sympathy. But perhaps you can weigh in on the question of my sanity.

RISING

Pinny Bulman

before the syringe dropbox was put up
as a mezuzah at the park's entrance
protecting the rusting car skeletons dotting the landscape
like picked-over carcasses,
this was a forest's edge

and in this spot
where you stubbornly refuse my help to stand
on legs still shaky
a bush once grew where a black bear
foraged for berries,
a doe and her two fawns weaved quietly
through the trees
on their way down to the river

yes, the same river that will one day cover all this
submerging our hubris in heavy silence
refracting our limits under a surface
masquerading as sky

but today the squirrels
are chasing each other among the wildflowers
when you put your tiny hand in mine
and lead me forward
step by shaky step

and as we quietly weave
our way down the slope,
you look up at me as if to say,
the river is rising
let us go to greet it.

STOP SAYING THE
WORLD HAS SHIFTED

Haley Lasché

replace shift
with moonlit mine stick
undercover explosive

not dynamite
nor dinosaur

but deeper than mantle
it is all revolutions at once
an eruption as only
Pangea could have dreamed
like a gene
bald in its hard drive
weighing down the code

GHOST DIVISIONS

Andrew M. Howard

Josh and his father couldn't stay on the island. So soon after the storm, the hotels were all closed, so they got a room at the Holiday Inn in Mannahawkin, a stripmall-and-highway town just before the bridge and the first stilt-standing beach houses. The hotel was like every other that Josh had previously been in. He sat quietly on one of the lobby couches, listening to faint Christmas music while his dad talked with the woman behind the counter. Josh was tired from navigating, and, even though he'd eaten Slim Jims and Fritos all day and had barely moved from the truck's passenger seat, he had an empty, hungry feeling. The sun was setting soon, and dinner would surely follow. Thanksgiving night, and it was cold in New Jersey.

As they gathered their things up to the elevator and then to their room, Josh could hear his dad mumble to himself. This was something he had been doing more and more. He looked a little worried, breathing out the words. The only thing Josh could make out was "One-seventeen." Caught, his father looked down at him. "Expensive," he said. "Maybe we'll only stay a couple days."

Josh's father had split the trip into two days, since the drive from Macon was so long. Having left late and rushing as usual, they had to spend the night in another chain hotel in some North Carolina town, the name of which neither of them caught. The plan had been to help, to do some cleanup, but Josh wasn't too sure why. "It's important to help," his father had told him, after spending hours in front of the television, watching news reports from New York and New Jersey, the reporters in rubber raincoats blown over and pelted by rain and wind, the boats that carried people through city streets.

They ate dinner in the hotel restaurant, a dark-walled diner occupied by a few sad travelers and short, squat waitresses in black polo shirts. Josh ordered a patty melt, and then his dad did, too. "We'll save the turkey special for next year," he said, winking. Their waitress told them good choice in her New Jersey accent. She seemed nice to Josh, like she was happy with no particular worries to weigh her down, even on a holiday. Like serving strangers in a weird, too-empty restaurant was really what made her feel complete. Josh was generally unable to believe something like that could be true, but the idea was a comforting one. When she brought out their Cokes, she called him Handsome and his father Honey. Josh admired something about her, her lack of pretense. She emanated sincerity, something that he had missed at home, even though the women in his life— now mostly teachers, or his friends' mothers—seemed to like him well enough. They didn't call him nicknames or ask how he was doing. Mostly Josh would feel like he was fading into the background. So far, he liked New Jersey. In Mannahawkin, he was Handsome.

While the two of them ate their food to the nostalgic sounds of Bing Crosby, some men in heavy work clothes collapsed in the corner a couple of tables down from them. They were familiars, it seemed, workers who had been staying at the hotel for weeks, carrying on loudly with the waitress before she brought the menus they didn't have to look at.

"Happy Turkey Day, fellas," she said, and the men laughed, grunting light disapproval. "Yuenglings for you guys?" she asked, smiling.

"Oh hell, Deb," one of them said, a man with cracked squint-lines brimming from his eyes and a white college ball cap that had been worked and sweated through to a dull beige. "We've been working around enough piss and swamp water all day—we don't need any more."

"Okay, Hon," she said, and laughed, and Josh noticed her walk to the back without taking a drink order.

He watched them. "No more of that fucking Jersey swamp water," the man in the hat said, reflexively smoothing out the bill and bobbing his head up and down. They were tired, but they were talking quickly. Josh had no idea what they were saying, but he could tell they were talking about work. Real work—digging and moving things, working outside in the bitter cold where you had to wear those thick, orange jackets and dark, knit caps.

When Deb came back she had beers for them—apparently not Yuenglings, which was something Josh had never heard of. They raised their glass. "To Sandy," one said, and in unison they cheered, "Bitch," before taking a long gulp. One of the guys suggested another toast as the rest of them took their drinks. "To Mannatwat," he said, and the others placated him with throat-clearing. The name made Josh laugh, then his face reddened. He looked at his father, who, like him, had been watching the men. He looked back at Josh, a bit skittish, and raised his eyebrows. Boys will be boys.

And maybe that's what this trip was about—boys being boys. But Josh knew that there was something more to it. His father had been palpably distracted since moving into the apartment complex with the never-open pool and the iron staircase leading up to their door. Since it became just the two of them. His father was trying to act fun, to make Josh comfortable and to appear easygoing, but he seemed to be pulled by some plaguing need.

On the long ride through the eastern states, Josh and his father talked about helping out, about what that had meant. "Well, first we'll see your Grandpa Jack, see if the beach house is okay. They said LBI got hit pretty bad." Josh knew this was the pretense for the trip, but still he felt that there was more. "Then we'll see if there's anyone else who could use our help. You remember what happened in New Orleans?" he had asked from behind the wheel, doing that thing he did where, out of nowhere, he would turn down the radio to almost nothing and start talking.

"You mean Katrina?" Josh answered, remembering not so much the actual storm—he couldn't have been more than five—but the way people would still talk about it.

"That's right. You were a kid. Remember one time I went to New Orleans?"

"Not really."

"Sure you do. It was a couple years after. You must have been in," here, he paused for a second, then forced out the words "second grade." He was trying not to look like he was guessing.

"Did you go to New Orleans to help out?"

"Nah, Scout," he said, checking his mirrors and changing lanes. Josh thought that his father was used to talking to someone without looking at them, but not always that good at it. The more he looked away, the more uncomfortable he seemed. "I had a presentation at this conference. You know, teacher stuff. But I got a chance to see some of the damage. You know there are still houses that are abandoned?"

Josh thought about that for a second. He'd seen plenty of abandoned houses in Georgia. Along route 49 especially there were houses that were half-burnt out, houses that looked like no person had lived in them for years. "Like that house on the highway that you said was a meth house?"

"Which one?" his dad asked, laughing a bit.

Josh wasn't sure why he laughed.

"No, this was like whole neighborhoods. Like if our old neighborhood was gone, but the houses were still there. Just no people. Then all the weeds and grass would grow, and all the houses would start falling down."

"Like ghost divisions?" Josh said.

His father looked at him for the first time in a while, for a moment too long. He started talking again when his eyes met back with the road. "Where'd you hear that?"

"School."

"From a teacher? Who?"

"Miss Barnes. She was talking about how in Florida, how no one buys houses anymore or something."

His father laughed again, a slight and quick sound. "You guys discuss the debt ceiling, too?"

"Yeah," Josh said, not sure what was funny. "Miss Barnes spends one day a week on current events. Sometimes she plays these radio shows, though, and everybody falls asleep or, like, text each other under the tables. We talked about ghost divisions one time, how there's, like, neighborhoods with no people in them."

"And that's why you will never go to my school." Josh's father taught at the public high school, and would often say that Rutland High School paid him the big bucks so that Josh would never have to go to Rutland High. "That's a bit different, though. Most of those are supposed to be nice neighborhoods from the get-go. The houses I saw, they were old."

Josh could see his father's eyes tighten and squint at the memory.

"It seemed like a lot of them were already falling apart, then the water came in and just killed them. Like dead houses still standing. They were all boarded up, and they had *FEMA* spray-painted on the boards. And numbers. I guess to designate them. This number gets that service, that number gets another. Frankly it looked like they should all get torn down."

"What about the people that lived there, though?"

"Yep."

"They could fill in all the empty neighborhoods in Florida," Josh suggested. It wasn't a terrible idea. There were all these houses just sitting there, from what Miss Barnes had said.

"Just send them all to Florida? But what about the ghosts?"

That was a stupid joke, Josh thought. "Dad," he said. "That's not why they're called ghost divisions."

Josh's father looked at him again, this time cocking one eyebrow all the way, the way he did when he was being slick, or when Josh was trying to be slick and his father caught him at it. "How do you know I'm talking about the ghosts in Florida? New Orleans is known for ghosts, you know. Or did Miss Barnes not get to that yet?"

Josh turned his head toward the passenger-side window, watching oncoming raindrops hit the glass and slide. They would hold out for a minute, skidding slowly across until the velocity of the truck would send them off again, back into the world outside their little Ford Ranger, like they were jumping off on their own motivation.

His father was still talking. "A lot of ghosts in New Orleans," he said, but Josh didn't think his father was exactly talking to him anymore.

In the morning they drove over the bridge. They were supposed to see Old Barney, a lighthouse that Josh had been to once but didn't remember.

What he did remember was from the old house in Macon, a photograph in a silver frame with *Family* etched into it in fancy script. His mother thought the frame was cheesy, but she liked having a picture of everyone at the shore. In the picture Josh was probably four or five, and all the people in it—his mother, Grandma Rose and Jack, the cousins with Uncle Jim and Aunt Linda—look like they're having the best time. They're all sitting around a picnic table, dressed in summer clothes and laughing around the remains of a birthday cake. Josh is making one of those wide smiles that kids make, his chin pointed up and the corners of his mouth pulled back as far as they can go.

Grandma Rose, who was always sending them family things like that, had sent the picture. Josh can remember staring at the photos on the end tables in the old house, putting together little narratives for each one he couldn't remember. He'd asked once why his father wasn't in it.

"Someone needed to be the Ansel Adams for a moment," he had said, but Josh didn't follow.

His mother had called in from the kitchen. "Ha," she said. "Your father's just a paparazzo with your Grandpa Jack's camera. Last time we were all at the shore, he spent more time on that thing than he did talking to anybody." Josh could tell she was trying not to use her annoyed voice, the voice that made his father wince and whine. Which would, of course, make her stop talking entirely, and everyone would spend the rest of the evening in separate rooms, waiting for the oppressively quiet night to end.

The annoyed voice was in Josh's head as they crossed over the bridge, not saying anything in particular, but intoning something, some vague dissatisfaction. The houses by the shore stood on stilts; they'd survived the storm. Pale houses, gray and blue and the color of vanilla ice cream with red roofs bunched up by the water. The November sun glinted across the morning water. This place looked like a good place to Josh, like a home he almost remembered.

When they got to the island, Josh's father tried to make a joke. "Looks like a hurricane blew through here, all right," he said, but with none of the commitment with which he usually told his jokes. What had been inside the beach houses now lined the streets—ruined carpeting pulled from the floor, soaked couches, cabinetry rippled and stained with seawater, ripped from the walls. Piles of sand filled parking lots and other places where sand should not be. Demo crews worked everywhere, hauling things out of buildings and moving great trucks around, but aside from a few folks cleaning the surf shop parking lots and readying the book and souvenir stores, Josh couldn't see any locals; though quietly busy, the whole island seemed abandoned.

They stopped near the beach, parking in a hotel lot. "Let's check out the beach, Scout."

Walking the beach, Josh trailed behind his father, trying to decode hidden messages in the scrawling tracks of fat seabirds. The wind blew loud and heavy, but the sun was out, and a few men in waders stood by fishing poles lodged upright in the sand. Driftwood jutted out from the sand throughout the beach; a lot of it, Josh noticed, had been painted and was splintered instead of worn smooth by the water. He picked up a piece of wood from between his bare feet, looked at the screw holes. A sad thing, he thought, people's kitchens torn from their houses and strewn throughout the sea and spit back at them. He wondered if he would see any forks and knives pushing through the sand, silver picture frames with families.

Grandpa Jack wore a turtleneck sweater that clung to his belly, parting a tweed sport coat. His hair, as always, was shiny and effervescent, a great slicked-back mass of silver curls. Josh was surprised to see him, but when he arrived at the restaurant, he did his usual punching at the air, pivoting at the waist and yelling, "There's the champ!" at Josh. He had done that since Josh could remember, and though he was too old for the routine, he still loved Grandpa Jack's Jersey accent and too-loud voice.

Grandpa Jack did not seem as happy to see Josh's father, however. The way they shook hands was perfunctory, and they greeted one another in low, muted tones. The mood matched that of the restaurant, which was dark and under-populated, as if it were running on half power.

They sat in a booth, Josh and his dad on one side, facing Grandpa Jack. "Can you believe this mess?" Grandpa Jack asked them. "Christ knows when Irene blew over we had it bad back home, but this." He sighed. "Jesus, this is the worst I've seen since I can't remember when." When the waitress came by, he called her Sweetie and asked her questions: how she was dealing with the storm, how her family was. Josh couldn't tell if they knew one another, since this was the way Grandpa Jack talked to anybody, as if he happened to be long acquainted with everyone he came into contact with.

Josh liked his grandfather, the way he filled a room. He watched his own father shrink in the booth as Grandpa Jack made idle talk about the storm, the repairs he'll have to make to the beach house, how even though they'll have to replace the living room carpet and a lot of the furniture, they had it easy by far compared to some of the other Long Beach Island families. That Rose and Eileen have been real troopers, not only cleaning up but holding everything together.

Eileen? Josh thought. *Mom's here?* A quick, wet heat built within him. He hadn't discussed any of this with his dad, but he could see where this was going. One night in a hotel, a walk on the beach with his father. His head went swimmy for a moment, and when he checked back into the conversation his father was speaking.

"I talked to Miss Barnes, all your teachers. You can work out the rest of the semester online, so you don't need to worry about school. And then you'll be back in Maconga at the beginning of the new year."

Maconga. That was their word for home: Macon, GA. To Josh it sounded like something far more exotic than it really was, like a conga line ready to burst out spontaneously. It was a place that his mother always called slow, sleepy. His father didn't seem to like it much, either, but as he had often said, one way or another it's home. Josh knew what he should do now, what most other kids would do. He could burst out himself, ask why, ask what his father was going to do, ask why he was being sprung with this information now, too late to do anything about it. But this was how his father handled things, and like his father, Josh kept quiet.

"You'll get to spend Christmas in the city," his father said. "Take a picture of the big tree at Rockefeller Center." He tried to smile reassuringly at his son, but Josh could see the anxiety building within him. They had only packed for three days. Josh would run out of clothes to wear immediately.

"Jesus, Preston," Grandpa Jack said. "No wonder the kid looks dumbstruck. Did you not tell him what we all decided?"

"Hey, I'm not dumb!" Josh said. He was kidding, the way his father kidded him, but neither man at the table got the joke. His face went red at the embarrassment, which didn't help the confusion. Grandpa Jack apologized, explaining what he meant, that Josh had the deer-in-the-headlights look all day, and Preston grabbed Josh by the shoulder, hugging him tight.

"It's just for the holidays, Scout."

"Unless you like it in Orange," Grandpa Jack said. "Your mom can get you into the school she teaches at if you like."

"Jack," Preston said, cutting him off.

"Look," Jack said, shooting a brief, uncomfortable glance at Josh, then honing back in on Preston. "I know you two haven't settled everything—I don't know why you haven't put everything in order yet—but this is only fair."

"She didn't have to leave, Jack."

"Didn't she?" He paused, said, "All right," then looking at Josh, said, "It'll be fun. We'll have you for the holidays. Your grandmother is delighted. She and your mom are waiting at the beach house. Hope you don't mind sleeping on the cot tonight. They'll take you home tomorrow morning. I've still got some work to do here on the island."

Josh nodded at the half-eaten plate of food. His father hugged him into his shoulder again. "Just for the holidays, Scout."

In the parking lot, Josh watched his dad and grandfather handle the negotiation handing him off. They shook hands again, brusquely, and for the first time, Josh took note of how tired his father looked. He was unshaven—sure, it was a holiday—but instead of giving him an air of casualness, he just looked old and exhausted, whereas Grandpa Jack was put together, clean-shaven, and smelling of a drugstore men's hygiene section.

Preston crouched down to meet Josh at eye-level but ended up only chest-high. "Shit," he said, embarrassed. "Call you when I get home. I'm sorry, man, but it's been rough this year, you know that. I wanted you to have a break from the apartment, you know, from us just hanging out together." He laughed a little. "It's been getting kind of sad in there, I know."

Josh thought of things he could say, how the two of them were taking care of each other and he liked it. That he felt like part of a team, just him and his dad, but because of the savage speed of this turn, the sloppy way his dad handled everything, big or small, he just nodded. "Okay," he said, noticing the lighthouse beyond the restaurant parking lot. Old Barney, his grandfather had called it. He didn't see what the big deal was; it wasn't even that tall.

"Look, you'll have a great time in New York. I wish I could have taken you, but this is as far as I can go right now." Before Josh could reply, his dad went to the truck, pulled out both of the bags they had packed. "This one's got your stuff in it, too. Let me know if you need anything else from home; I'll ship it out super-quick."

They left. In Grandpa Jack's maroon Lincoln, Josh watched his father drive behind them, his truck small in the passenger-side mirror, until it turned away on the central road, back to the shore, to Mannatwat, all the way back to Maconga. All these silly names. His father would call early the next morning, before the sun came up, after driving all the way home in one go. But before then, Josh would have to make it to the beach house, past all this wreckage, past all these things just waiting for someone to come by and try to put them back together.

ACCIDENTAL GENOCIDE

Josh Daniel

"When one tugs at a single thing in nature,
he finds it attached to the rest of the world."
—John Muir

In South Carolina,
a pesticide designed to pierce
a stormcloud of mosquitos
inadvertently killed
millions upon millions of bees.

The horror a beekeeper must feel
when the walk to the hive
is filled with oppressive silence,

the routine life-buzz snuffed
out overnight

and "so what?"
you say,
"So what?"

Bees are responsible
for one out of every three
bites of food we eat.

No bees
no fruit
no honey

No, honey. It's true,
I swear it.
Even the clothes you wear
at some point
probably
came into contact with a bee,

and I lied earlier
about my dad going to jail
and maybe about
the pianos
but listen
my god
we have got
to save the
bees.

READING *ALTURAS DE MACHU PICCHU* BY THE LAKE ONTARIO SHORE

Tracy K. Lewis

I.

It was my lot to be a man
of many tongues beside a lake
as wide as were the tongues
I spoke, and wider, for its
inland ocean was to me
a cipher of infinity, and I, a petty
wizened shard upon its shore,
curiositer of verbs and morphemes
in the gabble gabble of lands and peoples
I was not. What, who was I then
in all my knowing but an orphan
on that shore?—and more an orphan
even than the scat the seagull
drops to bleach upon the rocks,
for even scat reverts to wave,
to fish-flesh fueling seagull body
making scat again, but I, simply
whitened on the rocks. Despiser
of the race of moral midgets that
among its many widgets made
me, I made no widgets, sought
no place in boardroom or assembly
line to make or sell the next Big Thing
now flotsamed under stinking algae
by the mighty lake, CDs of has-been
rockstars, cell phones, tires, syringes
junkies left in gutters of Gary
or Chicago, beer cans, always beer cans;
I wanted none of it, eschewed
my birthright as a widget captain,
assumed instead the podium of words
and classes, disquisitions on the Word
made flesh of Baudelaire or Roa
Bastos, and still, I whitened on the rocks,
and had no circle in the turning
waves.

II.

And from my rock I read
another man of words who stood
upon a rock, his an Inca height where gods
and lightning sported in a thousand years
of air, and I mused in casual dessication
on my rock that once that selfsame air
sported on the flanks of glaciers in their
mile-deep march to make this lake,
to grind these drumlins from mountains
like so much dough before a kneading
fist, and something stirred me in my
torpor, the merest cracking of a seed-hull
somewhere under earth, and the lake
rose mightier in my mind's hyperbole
even than those Andes that he
sang: horizons of horizons of ice
scarring bedrock to a template
of waters from Superior to Gaspé,
seeding the deep-gouged trenches
with rivulets, rivers, north-draining
fingerlakes, gem-facet tarns
in the sun, moraine for marsh and meadow,
forests, forests. Came moose and mountain,
lion, mosquito, kingfisher, and salamander.
Came turtle basking and wolf mating. Came
tribes of salmon reversing gravity
up draws of crashing spume and boulders
large as asteroids. Came men. Came
tribes and hunts, wars, turfs, vendettas,
snake-haired tadodahos bidding minions
suck the scabs of rivals, and power
had no edge of mercy on the salmon-
teeming shore. Came then
a stranger in a stone canoe
who made a greater miracle than floating
stone, tamed the viper tresses, made the worst
of men coauthors of the best of Laws,
made power prosper on a principle
of Peace. So grew the Longhouse
of the peoples, a metaphor that might
have been for mine, as well,
but for ...

III.

    Again I felt in me
the farthest smallest moving of a thing
remote yet not, as if that seed-hull
scarcely cracking somewhere under earth
made pressure on my inner ear,
and pricked me in my solipsism
on my rock. I read again the man
upon the other rock, who trailed his finger
on the edges cleft by slaves
and trailed his pen along the stone's
hypoteneuse of blood. Came other strangers
to the Longhouse shore, men in trumped-up
enmity with muskets and the mortal
trace of microbes, faux emulators, bare-
faced slayers, all to one end walled
the Longhouse off in token statelets,
admired then consigned the lofty genius
of balanced-powered peace to asterisk
and museum basement, dreaming selves
exceptional built in the lie of their own
superiority a Yankee Longhouse droned
by mammon-seekers, queened by greed
co-opting freedom's face. Flowed
from their fingers every manner
of contrivance in the synthesis
of needs not real, forests fell, bedrock
fracked, wolves fled, fast-food fried,
the very air warmed in the frictions
of so much contrivance and seeded
with demise the far-off seed-ground
of the glaciers.

IV.

The man upon
the other rock spoke again to me
on mine, called to slaves long dead
in cleaving Inca stone to skein again
the braid of days unskeined in fingers
crushed, in nights unslept upon a bed
of welts, to rise, to be again in poetry's
eternal now, to live again in blood
of now, in fingers crushed of callused
hands of now. A breeze traversed
the bluffs across the bay, roiled
the pages on my lap, stirred again
the gull-wail and the stench of algae,
pressed again upon my inner ear the sharp
impinging of that seed-birth ever less
remote. The waves owned me
in their circle, the ghosts of forests and glaciers
owned me, Peacemaker owned me
in his stone canoe, and all my musing
of multitudes was not musing but my
body palpitant upon the palpitating rock,
a part at last of Place.

V.

                         I breathed,
and the air riffling the mighty waters
subsumed my breathing in an epidemic
of whitecaps and thousand thousand
lappings on the breakwall, and the Place
inhabited my flesh and I it. And the air
upon my summer rock moved my
throbbing mind to winter, and I
thought of snow as it boils from these
waters in the paroxysms of January,
lifts warm to cold in the updrafts
of meteorology and rides cold and colder
in Canadian foreplay and falls abhorring
every vacuum in white coitus across
spent fields of corn stubble and curbstones
and steeples of closed churches and rust-belt
sweatshops courting tax breaks, falls
on the pinstriped lawyers en route to power
lunch and the stubble of the spent
fields of the faces of the bums culling
bottles from dumpsters for tomorrow's
hit, falls on the meth-makers and the mothers,
on gangbangers and cops and legislators
and haberdashers, on malls and the buses
I ride to work. And I looked in my new mind's
seeing in the faces of the riders and saw
not the race of midgets I'd despised
but man, and in their plastic widget-
scrabbling not greed but fear and the despairs
of love. And the seed far-near I'd heard
within my cochleas burst and burned
those syllables upon my brain
and bones, and the glaciers' breathing
sifted in the milling snow like hope
through the vast lattice of our mistakes
and gathered in the cup of my eyes,
and I prayed man's virtue will
outspeed the snow's demise. And I
closed the other man's book, and my
rock became a stone canoe,
                         and floated.

UNPLUG

Shanna Yetman

Evanston, Illinois

Numbers swirl around her, and they all surround her consumption-guilt. Before the spill, Pam used to have consumption-guilt about food. Too many carbs? Too many calories? Now, it's the electricity grid. Six watts for charging her iPhone. Unplug. Twenty-four watts for her morning coffee. She always unplugged the pot and dumped the liquid into a Thermos after brewing. Sixty watts per hour for her laptop. Unplug. Unplug. Unplug. No hybrid vehicle to drive, but the Transit Authority did introduce those biodiesel buses. She's adjusted accordingly.

On.

Her apartment lights up with a laughable, CO_2-emitting certainty. *Jesus, it's like eating cake.* She feels like an energy-slut; a power-consuming whore. Outside, she can taste the dirt and soot pouring through the last coal-fired power plant in Illinois. Three years ago, she might've said she liked the industrial grit, liked being a stone's throw from her company's biggest plant. But that would've been the money talking. She looks out her window. Why is that one still there? Coal plants were turning off all over America.

With the lights on, she feels like an overweight person obsessed with counting calories and always cheating. An unaccounted bite here, a cookie unrecorded. So, off they go. Her apartment dims. Dinner by sunlight? Nah. She'll eat in the dark, later. There's a beach close by, and the sunset is nice. Somehow the grime doesn't make it up that way. She slips into linen pants and sandals and walks breezily through her parking lot to Lake Michigan. Waterfront view—an amenity from her former job. She'd bought the place outright. *Good thing.* Now, she can enjoy it without worrying about the mortgage. But she knows this, too, is dirty.

She sets her towel on the sand. The lake will be warm, perfect for a foot soak. She rolls up her pants and walks in—water up to her calves. Shallow at its recesses. Her toes trudge through the sand. She lifts her foot to admire her pink toenails, and there it is. *Coal-ash.*

Where did this come from? She examines her foot by turning it over and over. Her cuffs have fallen down, and dark gray sludge covers the linen. Wet, thick, heavy. *It shouldn't be here. There are contingency plans for this sort of thing.* This particular plant's ash pond was a good ten miles away from any water source. *How did this happen? God. If there's another spill, people need to know.* Too much arsenic, aluminum, selenium, so many chemicals. She shouldn't be exposed to this, either. Nobody should be in the water. Her feet are stuck.

The last time this happened, three years ago in North Carolina, there'd been so many TV crews. Everybody wanted her to say something, and she couldn't. She was flummoxed; their pipe had broken. It was her company's fault. Her fault. But she'd held it together. After all, she'd taught the course on crisis management and the media. "You looked so sad on TV," her boss had said to her. "You were the perfect spokesperson." He'd even given her a raise.

Now, she's drowning in it. *Where did it all come from?* She watches as a boy plays tug of war with his dog. The boy yanks the Frisbee loose and throws it toward the lake.

"Not in the water," she yells. "Dog out of the water." She feels like the police in *Jaws*. People stare, shake their heads.

If she looks at the water a certain way, she can see a plume of coal-ash making its way toward her, rocking gently to her with the waves. She's managed to remove herself from the sludge and almost runs toward families, almost tells people the water is unsafe. They must go home. They must stay away.

It's the sunlight that does it.

North Carolina never looked this way. That red, pink, and purple horizon shines brightly on the sandbank, and she sees her plume for what it really is. Sand disturbed by her constant movement.

SHIFTING LANDSCAPE

Leah Angstman

I wake one morn to snow,
the next to sunny mids.
To the snowcaps, I wonder how they stay—
the people below fretting floods "like those
year back." They're still restoring drainage beds
in ye-old-mining country, where
corporate courts, not the Constitution,
decide who can protest fracking. She's a swell
in a field of wells—
a sleeping policeman, Mom would call it,
and the swells to the west are what remain
after we don't.

Today I wake to the snow gone that landed yesterday,
delicate balance shook by sky and shock,
opened in acorn cracks, burst shells of mugworts
loosed from dust too old and ornery to hold,
too escapist to bury her roots in it.

Sagebrush once held us all in place.
Now we blow to the coasts and out
and out and out to the Atlantic and don't
come back again.

FIRST LIGHT JUNE

Helena Lipstadt

I.

first light, June, and the apple tree
is empty.

where is white throat?
every other year

her voice
peabody, peabody.

where nuthatch?
every other year

upside down
on east-flung branches

hiding seeds of spruce
and spider legs,

for later.
where woodpecker?

with your blood-red patch,
where chickadee?

you rascal bandit
your whole face a curiosity.

where bold and spunky phoebe,
goldfinch, vireo? where are you,

guild of foragers?
where?

2.

forty spring equinoxes
forty junes

forty years of birdsong,
of densities

of fledge and flight
of indispensable beauty

on the coast of Maine,
three thousand six hundred

days of summer
and one morning,

I suddenly notice.

Was it a marrow-saving
numbness

a refusal, a disbelief,
a failure to grasp,

to admit, human hubris,
desperate ignorance?

It doesn't matter.
This morning, I notice

there is no full-throat chorus at dawn
no thousand birds singing

hallelujah to the sun
no more solitary loon

from McHeard's Cove
(already rare, but still)

I don't hear you
and I cannot undo
the Not-Hearing.

3.

On this night's
midnight ramble

I meet skunk.
Her black-white face

and pebble eyes
gleam up at me,

her paws together
for the warning drum.

Do you want me
to look up, skunk?

to the whole picture,
the overstory?

or down, where white webs
scabbard under grass

and miles of mushrooms
raise their clean white fingers

from the musky ground,
and slippery worms

stir air into the clay
to light their hiding places.

and I know this:

I cannot Live
without You.

4.

Hunkered down in rocks
you, vole, what do you want me to see?

Rocks growing like slow potatoes
like underground root children

spreading polish
on the hips of worms,

to iridesce their hiding places
to grow fatter and slower

since no robin comes to pull.
Or are you thin and weak, worm,

without robin exercising you
in tug-of-war.

I squint up, to sparrow-empty sky
that couldn't be empty

that is not empty
that will never be empty
of wings.

until it is finally,
empty.

and I know this:

I cannot Live
without You.

ALIVE WITH THE OTHERS: STELLER SEA LIONS

Ellery Akers

I'd never seen a stillborn sea lion pup before. In 1994, I'd been working as a volunteer for a month on the Farallon Islands, 30 miles off the coast of San Francisco, when Peter Pyle, one of the island biologists, brought the body into the lab on a sheaf of newspaper. That morning we'd both noticed the dead Steller pup slumped next to its mother near Sea Lion Cove. The mother cow who had miscarried looked tired and grumpy; she snapped at a gull that swooped down and landed beside her, its pink feet spread out, hoping to get a meal.

I thought the fetus would be a mess, a loose scarf of blood, but when Peter laid her gently down on the table, both of us fell silent in front of her. She was translucent and perfectly formed. The only thing she was missing was fur. It seemed as if she could come back to life any moment, and was waiting patiently for instructions. She was rose-colored, about two feet long, with brown flippers at her side, and her nails and wax-colored whiskers looked chiseled. I'd never seen anything so still in my life; she looked peaceful and obedient, as if she were listening to something I was unable to hear.

"Thought you'd like to see her," he said.

Peter, a wiry, intense biologist with curly, black hair, had worked on islands all over the world and was able to spot a shearwater in the distance just by the way it flew. He was one of the mainstays on the Farallones, a national wildlife refuge that was home to thousands of seabirds and marine mammals. Consumed by his work, he didn't make much small talk, but was happy to show volunteers anything important. I'd been volunteering off and on for years for Point Reyes Bird Observatory, now called Point Blue Conservation Science, which hires a team of biologists to live on the island to study birds and marine mammals for the United States Fish and Wildlife Service. I wanted to help out because I felt Point Blue scientists were making a difference; they'd collected information about marine wildlife since 1968, and if anything could persuade lawmakers to protect the ocean, I thought, it was those piles of data.

In my years as a volunteer, I'd seen corpses—elephant seals that looked charred, their pelts covered with flies, their eyes gouged by gulls, the nails on their flippers still gripping the sand—but this was different. An adult sea lion has felt the wind on her fur and sniffed the sea air, has heard the slosh of waves against rocks, has felt the shock of cold as she dropped into the water. But this pup had never experienced anything; she looked pure, like a holy statue. Even Peter felt it. He was reluctant to take out his surgical saw and start the necropsy, so we both stood there, staring at her moist, closed eyes and delicate eyelashes, surrounded by calipers and strings of bird bands and instruments.

Outside the lab, sea lions were climbing up the rocks, coarsened by life, but in here she would remain as she were, interrupted.

I suddenly became conscious of the holes in my jeans, the stains on my hat. She made everything on the island seem worn—the old lighthouse keeper's house with its flimsy, guano-covered windows; the cogs of machinery at North Landing, which had lain there, rusting for 40 years; even the Boston Whaler, dented from lunging through surf and scraping against rock.

Finally, Peter started to dissect the pup to send tissue samples to a lab on the mainland, along with identifying information: *aborted Eumetopias jubatus, March 17, 1994*. I turned away before the blade sliced into the body, though I could hear the whine of the saw. I knew it was necessary; scientists needed to study those samples to figure out why so many Stellers were miscarrying.

And eventually, they did find some clues: heavy metals and pesticides full of organochlorine pollutants were seeping into the ocean, and it looked as if a virus were also involved. But biologists were becoming more and more concerned about other challenges the sea lions seemed to be facing: overfishing, warming ocean temperatures, climate change, and dwindling fish populations.

That night at dinner, when we started talking about the dead pup, Peter seemed dispirited. I remembered something he'd once said: "By the end of the night, the conversation on the island always turns to one of three things—shit, barf, or death. Maybe because we're surrounded by it."

In 1974, when I first went out to the island, long before so many females started miscarrying, the Stellers were everywhere. Every morning I sat by the sea and watched as rafts of Stellers floated past, snorting, sticking their flippers out of the water to cool off, diving and sighing loud whiskery breaths as they rose to the surface again. Steller pups splashed in the tide pools, learning to swim, venturing out into the waves for a few minutes, and then climbing back to the safety of the rocks.

Most people are familiar with California sea lions, *Zalophus californianus*. They are brown, and about half the size of the Stellers, but to my mind, the larger animals are more beautiful; on land, their pelts are golden, and their dark facial marks look shocking in their pale faces, which are the color of straw. In the water, their pelts shine and turn platinum. The first time I saw them swimming, I thought the sea was striped with silver.

The Californias are the goofballs of the sea lion world; they bark and play a lot, and for that reason, they are popular in zoos and circuses. Underwater, they chase their own exhaled bubbles of air.

But the Stellers are heavier—the bulls weigh 1,500 pounds—and can't walk as quickly. They're more solemn and stolid; they have *gravitas*. The Stellers seemed so much calmer than the Californias that when I first saw a Steller bull swaying slowly from rock to rock, moving past a pod of noisy, darting *Zalophus*, I couldn't help thinking that he looked like a king, tolerating the antics of his courtiers.

One of the happiest afternoons of my life was a summer day in 1974, when the Stellers were still abundant. I watched two Stellers swim after each other in the ocean—a mother and her pup. I was standing on Lighthouse Hill, the highest promontory on the island. My job that day was to clock the soundings of a gray whale as he dove and surfaced, but as I circled the lighthouse building, I spent most of my time watching those two silvery-blond sea lions.

Every few minutes, the cow's head broke the surface of the water, her whiskers dripping, and she turned and growled, encouraging her pup, who growled back as he swung after her in the water. Every so often, they touched noses. I stood staring at them, trying to hold my spotting scope steady as it shuddered in the wind, and I felt completely alive. I loved the way she encouraged her pup to swim and to follow. I loved the way they glinted in the water as they dove and sank and rose again. I loved the way she seemed to be showing him the rocks and shoals and fishing spots.

It was windy enough that day to blow through the holes in the rusted metal railings along the path until they shook and moaned, windy enough to stop me when I turned a corner. I huddled in a crevice beside the lighthouse, pulled on my hat, and pounded my gloves to keep warm. Gull feathers blew around me. Gulls squatted so they wouldn't topple over. A gull shuffled off her nest as I walked past her and then nervously squatted down again, but not before I saw the fuzzy polka-dotted chicks she was trying to hide; they wobbled as they hunched in the wind. Down below, lines of cormorants flew low over the whitecaps. One of the biologists was walking down the path, bent over, his sleeves blowing, waggling his hand over his head to keep gulls from shitting on his baseball cap.

Pigeon guillemots flew into their nests below me in chinks in the rock, whistling as they streamed past, their beaks full of fish. Elephant seals trumpeted in the distance. Then the murres began to call, *Agh, agh,* a low moan, a wild gargling sound rising from a thousand bird throats, a sound that told me a marauding gull had just passed over the murre colony, looking for a stray egg or a chick. It was all noise, abundance, sparkle—elephant seals yawning and blowing bubbles in the sea, and on the rocks, California sea lions lying in their hundreds, and the Stellers in their hundreds.

I watched a Steller bull climb slowly out of the water and shake his massive mane, which glistened in the sun. He moved up the rock, stately and imperious, one slow flipper after another. His mane was scarred from fights with other bulls, and he looked regal as he stretched his head toward the sky and surveyed the cows in the colony. Then he stuck his pink tongue out and held it in the air for a few minutes, ruining the whole royalty effect, and I laughed, bent over in the wind. I was so alive, with so much life around me.

But that had been in the days of abundance, and this was 20 years later. For a few days after I'd seen the dead Steller pup, I couldn't stop thinking about extinction. I tossed the water sample bucket into the ocean every morning, and hauled it back up and poured a little bit of ocean into a glass bottle, and I thought about it. I took notes on the gulls, and I thought about it. In one El Niño year, many seabirds had stopped nesting in large numbers on the island, leaving the rocks silenced and denuded. In that unsuccessful breeding season, hardly any female cormorants showed up, and the males, who had built nests out of Farallon weed, got tired of waiting, and abandoned them. The murres arrived late, and only a few birds laid eggs. Though the Bird Observatory biologists cheered on these pairs, calling them by their scientific labels—"You go, X 12! You can make it, G 3!"—the numbers of murre chicks plummeted. And now, along the coast of California, the Stellers were becoming scarce.

I realized that part of my happiness came from knowing there was variety and abundance in the world—birdsong pouring from a thousand throats instead of just one; Steller sea lions and California sea lions and elephant seals diving into the ocean and jumping out of the water and splashing back down again, each in their individual ways. If the Stellers were to leave the world, I had a hunch it would affect me, even unconsciously. Perhaps one morning I'd wake up and feel oddly blurred in my life, all because one species of sea lion that swayed slowly over the rocks had vanished. I knew there was something about the depletion of a species —any species—that would make me feel diminished.

The last time I went out to the island in 1994, I spent an afternoon in a blind at the edge of the ocean, and the small shack smelled damp—the planks were coated with algae and guano. Clipboards full of data hung on rusted nails, and gull feathers drifted across the floor. I lifted out the wooden board that served as a windowpane and set it on the floor of the blind with a *clonk*. Wind poured into the open hole, gulls shrieked, and I leaned out and expected to see what I'd always seen: rafts of Stellers.

But there weren't any Stellers. Instead, dozens of California sea lions —their darker cousins—slid over each other in the water. A few were playing a game of catch—tossing a dead gull back and forth in the water, as its wings floated open in the tide. There were no Stellers on the sand, either. As I was scanning the island with my binoculars, a gull landed on top of the blind, and I could hear his feet smack the wood overhead. Finally, I turned and saw a lone Steller on the rocks, one gold animal in a crowd of dark alien bodies. His snout was blunt and squared off—he looked nothing like the Californias, with their gently sloping faces—and he was growling over and over, stopping and listening for an answer, and growling again. The Steller's call is low and gravelly, unlike the sharp bark of the Californias, and sounds as if someone is trying to start a tractor in a cellar, the roar of its engine muffled by stone.

That Steller called all afternoon. He swung his heavy head around—he had the beginnings of a mane—and looked restlessly out to sea, but there were none of his kind left at Fisherman's Cove. The Californias clambered around him and paid him no attention. They barked and scratched themselves with their flippers, and yawned, and nipped each other, and shuffled down to the water; their wet glistening bellies slapped on the sand. The Steller padded back and forth as he called, raised his head, and sniffed. Then he lumbered down the cliff, settled himself on the rocks, closed his eyes, and went to sleep.

By 2013, the eastern population of Stellers, off the California coast, had recovered to some degree, though the western population, off the Gulf of Alaska, remains endangered. But the Californias (Zalophus) have had trouble in recent years. Though the overall numbers of Zalophus are still abundant, over 3,000 starving pups washed ashore on the California coast in 2015. Experts believe this was caused by higher ocean temperatures and lack of food.

SPELL FOR TOLERANCE

Ann V. DeVilbiss

Smash the clock
and cling to the bed
long past waking. Let time
keep its own company.

Fasten the sill and
draw down every blind.
Send no mail and
open no letters.

The mailboxes
have washed away—
today, the flood.
Because the sky

forgot how to calm,
the river rises past
every floodgate, muddy
and insistent,

swollen with trash,
undulant belly
casting up scales of light
wherever it meets the sun.

The river knocks
on your door and
insists on staying:
its water becomes

a mirror, turns
your heart into a well.
Suss through ruin,
the mold and dirt.

Throw away what can't
be saved. Bear the weight
in pieces, as you'd walk across
a bed of nails, or how poison

should be taken gradual:
dosed over time, small
measure of the things
we get used to bearing.

MOUND BUILDERS

Donnie Welch

Jeremy snapped his spine
at an X-Games qualifier last year.
He had an offer from Monster.
It was a simple trick.
Superman. The first one kids learn
when they want to fly.
Now he's paralyzed from the waist down.
Spends his weekends playing wheelchair ball
at the VFW and joking about his jump shot.

The practice course he built
is being flattened.
Since it's nice and deep in the woods
his dad wants to plant weed
to help pay the bills
now that the mine is dry.

Everything here is being flattened:
the mountains, the towns, the people.
In the Bible, God had to command
Isaac from Abraham,
but America's just giving up West Virginia.

When the mine left,
a mound of waste stayed behind,
slowly eroding into the soil,
a monument to what this town
used to be. Last election,
the mayor put up signs all over
that people still keep in their yards,
simple white letters on a blue background
reading: "Friends of Coal."
I imagine Jeremy hanging in the air
arms stretched like wings
saying to himself:
I've got this.
I've got this.
I've got this.
Then, in an instant, darkness.

RAPTURED IN KUDZU

Allie Marini

It wasn't that it took three mowers to tame the grass. After all, they were push mowers; it wasn't like you could speed things up unless you had three bodies straining against the sun & by some miraculous intervention, all three mowers worked at the same time. It was never about needing three mowers; it was always about not having enough money to replace them with one mower that worked. The backhoe been rusting out since one of the cousins—Tre, who floated in & out of the family, & no one could ever remember if he was *actual kin* or just a relation by marriage of someone who'd long divorced out—well, one night the backhoe just showed up behind the tool shed, & Tre said, *Lookit, if the cops show up to ask 'bout it, act surprised.* It wasn't the kinda thing you could drag on down to Pawn Stars without an explanation, so there it sat. No cops ever *did* come round to ask about it, though they did eventually come looking for Tre. Momma used to strap the Spectracide on her back like a weird chemical baby & walk the length of the property to keep out the fleas & the silverfish that overrun the summer kitchen when it got up into the 90s. *Used to*—the whole weedy, overrun patch of property is a *Used-To*, the family is a *Used-To*, this whole place is *Used-To*.

Hard to say why I woke up in an empty house on an empty plot of land in an empty town crisscrossed by empty streets & empty cars. Even Tre disappeared when the whole town got Raptured—maybe—or maybe they just got swallowed up by the kudzu that'd been creeping up on us, scrub pine by sweet gum: closer, greener, more & more like hands wrapped around a throat. Cutting off the breath. If they'd been Raptured away, what was the design behind me being left here with a stolen backhoe, three broke-down mowers with no gas, & a partly used tank of pesticide for silverfish & fleas that all seem to have been Raptured away, too? Even the bugs found them some redemption. That's *gotta* mean something.

There are this many means of exerting your will on the world & only one very quiet, lush way the world wills it back in again. Under the scrub pines, I evolve: I hear every scale of rust flake from the backhoe & fall into the dirt like thunderclaps. A furious wave of cells, splitting & dividing—human, vine, rust, dirt. Kudzu encroaching, stealthy as a husband's hand under the bedsheets. A wave of fleas & silverfish riding weeds to the Rapture. Roots digging, tasting, ready to garrote any fleshy things left behind. Creeper vines encircle the structure of the toolshed, the backhoe, the mowers, these things meant to suppress them. This is the Rapture—I become something else, something that moves, greenly, without the human impulse to control the direction.

IT'S JUST NATURE
SAYS SOME YOUTUBE COMMENTERS

Dorie LaRue

"It's just nature," says some YouTube commenters,
when hyenas eat a still-standing, still-fighting
buffalo starting with the testicles.
And it is nature again,
when a male bull elephant in musth
whacks a baby into the air
to attract the attention of its mother.
All you bleeding-heart liberal vegans
can go to hell, they say, which must be nature.

Some days it seems nature is everywhere.
Maybe Pearl Harbor was nature, then,
and Afghanistan, the Gulf War,
Kennedy's November. Columbine.
Maybe lonely drunks are nature or maybe
buttering up your professor is nature,
and matched luggage that falls from a balcony
and kills your cat, and fever charts,
and pate's pale painful history,
and room-temperature Chablis,
decanted too soon,
a Romaine salad hiding botulism,
and people who drive slow in the fast lane,
and one-week brides and their grooms
dead on the turnpike,
their necks snapped like carrot sticks.
Maybe wife beaters are nature,
child beaters, and dogs who
lie down in fear in cages
in the laboratory, and the daughter
in the subway who jumped on top of her mother
(after she was pushed onto the tracks by
a crazy) before the train severed her spine,
her arms, one white running shoe,
her life as legal secretary
with, thankfully, disability.

Maybe nature was the crazy,
who couldn't afford bullets
but moved from the shadows,
his arms rising like smooth rifles.

All things considered,
there seems to be
no news in nature. Maybe
we should say, it's just history,
biding its time. Children starving
in Ethiopia could be nature,
and women executed in Afghanistan
with loose stones from labyrinths
we'll never solve, is nature.
The vestiges of landfills
in 9th ward low-income housing
sprouting children's ballfields
and the Gulf of Mexico, our newest dead sea,
is not only nature, but a new kind of primitive art
totally unavailable in the jeopardy-shared future.

If in medieval times,
female nature
once perverse but
become holy by chastity was nature,
and female nature
once chaste but
become perverse by holiness
was nature,
then maybe 1,500 years later
nature is still waiting,
gracefully calculating,
like some marmoreal-veined
musician, quietly tuning
his rent-to-own instrument.

Or ... maybe nature is the tenor,
and we are the vehicle.
The first order of business
seems to be to name first cause,
the chicken, the egg, the primogenesis
thinginess of things,
because if we aren't careful
"that's just nature" can be an excuse
for the worst of our worst.

Anyway, maybe nature isn't the driver—
ever thought of that? Maybe
nature is the passenger,
and the drivers—us—
are taking nature for a wild ride.
The *Enola Gay* guys
stuffed 15,000 tons of nature
into a simple gun assembly,
a militarily useful gadget,
twisted and evil as a mass murderer.
Wait—wait—it *was* a mass murderer.

Narrowly avoiding
the pathetic fallacy,
we can say, lives were saved
by nature. Trees blocked the blast wind.
Stunned grandparents and children in flip-flops
gathered under branches to escape
the summer heat.

Elsewhere,
the wind blast cleaved the branches
of 500-year-old camphor trees
from their charring trunks. Distance
from hypocenter, .8 km,
and the black trunks were also, handily,
their own tombstones.

But one spring new buds appeared
on their upper stories, and in brilliant
patient green. They were speechless
and not interested in what would happen
next, just patient, as I said,
as though something bigger mattered.
Only now we know just how fragile,
and inexperienced they were,
vulnerable to nature as slave,
as bully, as thing that can be made
to scorch, to vaporize,
disfigure for days, weeks, months, years. ...

And though the wind shifted
that day and controlled the fires,
as though the pathetic fallacy
were not so pathetic as rumored,
what comes up now and again
is the specter of some bigshot God
with his finger on the scale.
God must be nature then.
To try to beat nature back
with a stick, must be nature.
Yet, if we, admitted airbags of false motive
that we are, can trick ourselves out of our own
evolution, offering our limp handshakes,
to the Thing That Is The Subject
Of This Poem, can we not see
how it surrounds us in mixed media
right this minute, arrogating,
curling up at our feet,
begging us to stop the cautery,
the ashes, the making beauty,
and the throwing it away, the making it,
the throwing it.

A ONCE RIVER

Dionne Custer Edwards

When a glacier retreats, it leaves a stunning blanket
of thawed everything.
A loose hem unraveling its insides.

A new line of quiet used to be an entire system living.
Until water run changed direction. Fed its wet limb into a new

channel. Disappeared and left a drought, in the middle of
a once river. Became an unfamiliar crawl.

A steeper gradient tunneling down to a new body,
a stranger pour.

At home the faucet leak reminds me
when loss is quiet, it gathers itself in a bank of unseen.

Slow looks like hidden gestures.
The river disappeared in plain sight.

Tumbled down a wrong way. No fault of its own.
Left worn ground formed. Stones and creatures exposed.

How serious a leak, unnoticed.
Something so slow it gathered into gone.

EMERGENT NORM THEORY AND POST-CLIMATE CHANGE IMPACT: APPENDIX A

Ashley Shelby

The following appendix provides four examples of Post-Climate Change Impact community communications via various forms of media. The authors include them in this paper because they reflect a rich blend of evolving and adaptive community and national norms while offering interested researchers further material for microsociological analysis of how climate change impacts are affecting four distinct areas: a.) Social Disclosure ("Post-Climate Change Impact Craigslist Ads") b.) Status-Directed Consumption ("Impact Cruises' Endangered Cities 7-Day Free-Sail Cruise" website text) c.) Perceived Incentives ("Unicorn Investment Newsletter: Subscription Confirmation") and d.) Functional Sociology/Adaptive Culture ("Three Rivers Park District (MN) Activities Catalog Text: 'New Friends at the Feeder'").

Fig. 1: "Post-Climate Change Impact Craigslist Ads"

Hot Van Time—m4w (Far Rockaways, NY)
Body: Fit **Height:** 6'3" **Carbon Status:** in compliance
I lost my Civic in the most recent massive flooding event so I opted for a van this time. No back seats, tinted windows. If you have a fantasy I can help with let me know. Can travel.

Damsel in Distress?—m4w (Greenwich, CT)
Body: Lots to Love **Height:** 5'7" **Carbon Status:** in compliance
Did Superstorm Zuzia send you packing? Looking for some help? Do you have a talent you can share? I live in a Non-Impact Zone and have a spare Environmental Migrant Travel Permit to share with the right lady. Must be from an Impacted Community. Prefer BBWs just a few pounds shy of the Federal Overconsumption Tax threshold.

Babe Looking for Jesus at Tinderbox Lounge on Halloween—m4w (St. Augustine, FL)
Body: Athletic **Height:** 6'6" **Carbon Status:** Under Review
I was dressed as a studly "FEMA Director Jesus" at Tinderbox last night and I kept seeing tweets from some girl looking for "Jesus" to meet her in the third stall of the bathroom. I was on my way to the johns to find you when the evacuation order came in. Your Twit Pics showed a girl dressed up as a Displaced Person of Middle Eastern Descent. Despite the problematic nature of your costume, I would love to bestow some heavenly

graces onto thou. Hmu if you're the girl I'm talking about. Hopefully you're hot. Willing to throw in a few Federal Fuel Stamps if you are.

Flood Relief Hottie—m4m (Charleston, SC)
Body: Dad-Bod **Height:** 5'10" **Carbon Status:** Suspended
You: National Guardsman working flood relief during most recent storm surge event. Me: stranded homeowner who should've known better than to buy near the floodplain. You were in the rescue bucket when the helicopter arrived, told me to leave my "man-purse" behind (it's an attaché, actually). Although it was too loud for conversation, I thought I sensed a spark. If you see this, tell me the name of the street my house used to be on.

Ride Wanted: Headed North (Santa Monica, CA)
This is a long shot, but putting this out there just in case. Like everyone else, I'm looking for a ride out of California, basically ASAP, until the fires die down. I'm not particular about where I'm dropped off, just ask that it be within the Federal Designated Safe Zone, preferably the Upper Mississippi River Basin. I am very good at gas jugging. Only luggage is my surfboard. Can help load or unload on both ends. Currently located at the Evacuation Gathering Point on the Pier. I'm the one with the Spongebob Squarepants shortboard.

Room for Rent: Impact-Free Home (Appleton, WI)
If you're looking for a handout, you can just stop reading right now. This ad is for EMPLOYED people only with NO Excessive Carbon Usage violations that will end up with a midnight visit from the feds. If you pass that test, read on: we're seeking a roommate for a laid-back house. Not many rules here, but there are two and they are VERY IMPORTANT. Number 1. No black market fuel in the house of any kind. We've been busted before, and it wasn't pretty. Save us all some grief and get your gas legally. Sure, it's hard, but people do it every day. Number 2. No violence of any kind, not even a raised voice. There have been a couple minor issues but we have worked them out MATURELY. If you're still holding on to some existential anger about runaway climate change, move on. We're okay with Environmental Migrants AS LONG AS YOU ARE EMPLOYED. Another important thing is paying your rent on time. Late payments will NOT be tolerated, and I don't want to hear any sob stories about long lines at the Bartered Goods Cash Conversion office. This is a cash-only thing— no produce or bulk foodstuffs will be accepted. C-A-S-H. My house is the only one with Christmas lights up (I hoard my carbon credits all year for this in case you're wondering). Also, liking the movie *Heaven is for Real* is a good sign.

JOB AVAILABLE: Sick of Being Evacuated? (Anywhere)
Has your local Evacuation Gathering Point become like a second home? Are you tired of waiting floods out on your roof? Why not experience emergency evacuations from the other side: apply to become a member of

the National Disaster Resilience Corps (NDRC). We are currently seeking highly motivated people who want to make a difference in the community for opportunities in the following project areas:
Ironic Hedonist Dispersal Project
Prepper Engagement Initiative (exceptional people skills a must)
Perpetual Evacuation Management
Vertical Farm Inspections Team, Soil-Free Division
NDRC corpsmen and women receive generous increases in Federal Fuel Rations for each six months of uninterrupted employment, as well as housing in Safe Zones for themselves and their family members. Monthly allotments of High Demand Foodstuffs and Endangered Grains are based on performance reviews.
NOTE: This is a branch of the United States military and enlistment is required.

Support Group for Recently Displaced Millionaires (Newport Beach, CA)
Are you one of the hundreds of wealthy Newport Beach homeowners whose beachfront properties were recently deemed uninhabitable under the Federal Post-Climate Impact Human Resettlement Act? Are you having a hard time adjusting to living fulltime in your second home? These changes can be difficult to handle. We invite you to share your stories of displacement in a safe environment with people facing the same struggles as you. In this group we will talk about how we face our changes in circumstance, examine our anger and helplessness in the midst of unexpected domestic downsizing, speak openly about forced interaction in mixed-income society, and share strategies for coping with the loss of square footage and ocean views. This is not a drop-in group. Pre-registration is necessary, along with a copy of your most recent tax return. Craft cocktails will be served.

Rants and Raves: Immigrant tide (Des Moines)
What exactly is wrong with Midwesterners? You want to destroy yourselves all because you think this country is a "melting pot"? Stand up like men to the environmental migrant invasion. We don't need Texans in Iowa.

Fig. 2: "Impact Cruises' Endangered Cities 7-Day Free-Sail Cruise" website text

Impact Cruises' Endangered Cities 7-Day Free-Sail Cruise
Cities include:
Boston
Baltimore
Norfolk

Charleston, SC
Savannah
Jacksonville (expires next year due to Complete Municipal Submersion)
Miami
New Orleans

The unexpected rapidity with which our country has been affected by Climate Change Impact has left many seasoned travelers reeling, soaked with regret over missed opportunities to explore our domestic jewels now threatened by rising sea levels. Others find themselves uncertain about the global regulations on the cruise industry and the mandated shift to carbon neutral, small-ship, free-sail cruising.

Impact Cruises offers the thoughtful traveler an unparalleled experience through its "Endangered Cities 7-Day Free-Sail Cruise," fashioning a cruise experience for our treasured guests that taps into their passion for the history, culture, and wonders of the pre-Impact world. From vanished Boston and the floating artificial islands of Miami to the last standing building in Savannah, Impact Cruises aims to give its guests a taste of the past, the present, and the future.

Immersion is a core principle of the Impact Cruises philosophy, and where possible, we invite our guests to come "ashore" to experience the charms of cities like New Orleans, Miami, and Savannah[1]. Our experienced dinghy captains will lead small groups around cherished landmarks, such as the proud spire of St. Louis Cathedral in Jackson Square and Boston's last remaining island neighborhood, Beacon Hill. In Miami, unparalleled SCUBA experiences await the avid diver, including excursions into the submerged charms of South Beach[2].

These cities will officially become Restricted Impact Territorial Zones (RITZ) in 2060. Don't rob yourself, or your family, of the opportunity to take one last look at our vanished coastal cities, while enjoying the luxurious appointments you've come to expect from Impact Cruises.

Terms and Conditions
Fares are quoted in U.S. carbon credits and are based on double-occupancy. Fares do not include pre-paid charges, optional facilities and service fees, or global carbon tax apportionment. Also not included are shore "excursions," gratuities, federal geoengineering surcharges, state and federal Engineered Iceberg Deployment fees, and Sulfate Particle Dispersal duty.

All itineraries, including points of "embarkation" and "debarkation," are at the discretion of Impact Cruises and may be modified up to and during the voyage. Sea level fluctuations may impact the order in which cities are visited, or whether they are visited at all. Impact Cruises reserves the

---

1. *Not all ports of call are available for traditional disembarkation due to sea level rise and individual cities' State of Submersion (SOS)*
2. *Requires additional Release of Liability form*

right to amend, cancel, or make substitutions for any aspect of the voyage without prior notice to the guest. Sulfate Particulate Showers cannot be forecast in advance and will affect the timing of arrivals and departures. The timing of International Cloud Brightening Drone Missions are not disclosed to the public in advance and will affect levels of sunlight, in some cases for weeks. Impact Cruises regrets that it cannot offer refunds for any reason whatsoever.

Fig. 3: "Unicorn Investment Newsletter: Subscription Confirmation"

From: Jack Marcelo, Chief Imagination Officer, Unicorn Investment, Inc.
To: Jeffrey Meredith [jmeredith_812321@yahoo.com]
Date: November 2, 2036
Subject: Unicorn Investment Newsletter: PLEASE CONFIRM SUB-SCRIPTION

Dear Jeffrey,

Thank you for subscribing to Unicorn Investment's E-Newsletter: You have taken the first step toward making savvy investment decisions during this time of upheaval. As you know, times are "hot" for getting rich in a climate-challenged world. The question is: can you adapt, and if so, how quickly? RAs (Rapid Adapters) are in an enviable position when it comes to investments. Subscribing to this newsletter proves you are an RA.

Per federal law, you must confirm your subscription. Please click on **this link** to do so now.

If you're still reading, you likely have not clicked the link. Are you unconvinced? Fearful of adding more spam to an inbox already riddled with suspicious pleas from family members stranded in Impact Zones he or she should definitely not be visiting? Unicorn Investment's E-Newsletter is no carnival barker's cry trying to sell consignment carbon credits for pennies on the dollar.

Perhaps a few tidbits will tempt you.

What's next for the home insurance industry?
In short: collapse. Check your portfolio—are you tied up in these stocks? If so, have you asked yourself why you—or your investment adviser—are stubbornly protecting this aspect of your investment?

Renewables Sub-Sector Faltering
The only reliably strong industry post-climate change impact has, of course, been Renewables. But since last week's release of IPCC's latest report confirming a 3.5-degree rise in global temperature, Renewables stocks have plummeted, leaving the industry in disarray and mutual fund managers scratching their heads. With the feared doomsday scenario

confirmed, investors are stuck in a what's-the-point mentality. This massive sell-off provides RAs a rare opportunity to snatch up valuable stocks that are sure to roar back once investors have been able to absorb and accept the IPCC report. By subscribing to Unicorn Investment's newsletter, you will receive hot stock tips based on a subtle understanding of today's complex investment landscape, including abandoned Renewables stocks that will make you a fortune once investor confidence returns.

Shirk the Long-Term Asset Allocation Mix: Yes, we're serious.
Unicorn Investment is known for its contrarian sensibilities, but this one may shock even our long-time devotees: it's time to dump your long-term asset allocations. The writing is on the wall: investors no longer have the luxury of assuming a long-term horizon for their investments. In these unpredictable times, with time and manner of death basically a crapshoot at this point, short-term is the name of the game. Want to know more? Click the link.

If you've read this far, it's clear you still haven't clicked the link to confirm your subscription. Please be advised that this confirmation e-mail was sent at your direction. It's only because of our commitment to adhering to the jauntily named CAN-SPAM Act of 2003, signed into law by President George W. Bush, repealed by President Donald Trump in 2022, and reinstated by President Trump in 2023, that we're going through the motions of confirmation of your freely chosen subscription.

Still, you're a skeptic, and we respect healthy skepticism. So chew on this:

Special Situation: Wearables
Check your portfolio: do you see any investments in Wearables? If so, congratulations—and welcome to the RA world. Wearable Startups are huge. Take Portable Physician's insane $304M round in Q3. Some early investors were concerned about resistance among consumers—the "Blush Factor"—to the company's iPhone colostomy bag widget, but its ninth-generation Bluetooth technology has proven a hit with aging Millennials whose nostalgia for iPhones informs their buying decisions.

Are you a savvy investor who prefers investment advice in all caps, followed by a flock of exclamation marks?
PLEASE CONFIRM YOUR SUBSCRIPTION!!!!
We want you to Get the Wealth You Deserve© and Unlock the Doors to Staggering Profits™.

NOTE: Certain statements contained in this communication may be identified by terms such as "expect" and "believe" and "may" and "intend" and "possibly" and "will." Be advised that investments in companies mentioned here are considered to be extremely high-risk and that the material herein was designed for reading pleasure and water cooler conversation, not action.

Fig. 4: "Three Rivers Park District (MN) Activities Catalog Text: 'New Friends at the Feeder'"

Having a hard time identifying the new feathered friends at your bird-feeder? Can't tell a keen-billed toucan from a Nicaraguan seed finch—and wouldn't know what to feed it if you did? Intense biodiversity at Minnesota's birdfeeders is one of the few upsides to massive global climate change, but the arrival of mixed species flocks from the Southern Hemisphere poses unique challenges to the dedicated birdwatcher. For example, traditional tube birdfeeders may not be up to the task of feeding larger-bodied species, such as macaws, while bloody squabbles between squirrels and swallow-tailed kites over the Trader Joe's figs you tossed onto the ground feeder may strain your tolerance for intraspecies violence.

Join other dedicated birdwatchers in this day-long class at Richardson Nature Center, where we will learn all about these new critters, why sunflower seeds and suet just won't cut it anymore, how to accommodate large birds with destructive habits while keeping your sanity, adjusting to the chaos of mixed-species flocks, protecting your outdoor cat from visiting macaws, and why planting a fig tree might be a good investment for a robust backyard bird population.

We'll also deal delicately with psychological feelings of loss and despair common among Midwest birders who have lost the species they've grown up with, such as cardinals, blue jays, robins, and, yes, even sparrows. This will be a safe space to discuss feelings of grief and anger.

Plus, you'll walk out of class with your own homemade coconut "Tiki Bar" parrot toy.

From the broad-billed motmot to the fiery-throated hummingbird, this class will help you adapt to and enjoy our new native birds.

**Please note that the info session for the three-day "Birding at Superfund Sites, Abandoned Nuclear Plants, and Evacuated Coastal Cities" guided tour has changed to January 9th.

RIVERS THAT SEEK FOR SEAS

Chris Ketchum

He watches the sun crane its ruddy neck
along the empty timber-loading dock:
yew and cedar scent, Newport cigarettes
and coffee in hand like checks. They murmur
and turn the morning like a perfect globe
in palms gloved with bacon fat, congregate
for gulls' gospel of leisure and chatter.
Monday's breath hangs at the men's craggy lips,
two-ton hook and a gurney from the crane
where he will rest one day. Another plan
sawed fresh from the Northwest's open pocket.
He tightens the night's slack belt, crowns himself
the day's yellow-headed king, and suspends
his dreams from tomorrow's nether-gray hours—
a lightbulb loosely fixed in life today.

What does he hear in "Columbia"?
Someone's lexicon who knows another
river—Clearwater, Lochsa, the Salmon
and Snake. Driftwood and bones in the delta
unpacked like an old suitcase: photographs
like the dead fishes peeling, coat hangers,
the broken sturgeon rods, some creature's suit
mottled and adrift. These flotsam conches
carry desires beyond Hell's canyon:
a tugboat labors against the current
to Enterprise, the Wallowa snowpack
where a man drops a fly in a green creek,
reaches out, slips his boot across a rock
embalmed with the not-yet Columbia,
and listens for a message from the coast.

Enough of this moon! its silky folding
into the clouds between the Steller's jay
evening and Orion's saggy belt—
enough winds shake the leaves from their branches,
enough oak matter and lichen festoons
on a pond that remembers Narcissus,
the emerald surface, the faces returned
that cost nothing more than one summer's day.
To see god peek through the curtain of clouds—
an eye or window on the horizon—
so much as the skyline's only wrinkle
would signal his concern for all of us.
One man fishes off the promontory
into salt-stirred delta waters. He leaves
his bait for ravens to pick from the shore.

The blue plume of a Mallard's wing bobs once
in ripples where the river bottlenecks.
He sees the horizon's edge fade. It sinks
into cushions of grain, long direction
of light. All things flow to the Pacific
to swirl in the belly and the bowels.
How long can the quiet crow hover
before the ocean's thermals cool and wane?
Man in the young mountains, both of them proud.
Snowpack fire-dried by May, the low cliffs
keeping mist at bay. What season is this
that runs its craft long after the tide breaks,
what river offers shelter and passage—
the pearly twilight mankind takes and takes—
what endless act, what silhouette of day?

Season of December bloom, immortal
as the coal-fed barge. Pines in the flatbed
shimmer with a cadaver's waxiness,
Kesey-towns where the mountainsides shiver
fifteen miles off the interstate, the wind
dusting the village with a clearing's ash.
A veranda overlooks the red-wing
blackbird, a lunatic in the bulrushes,
bristling with riparian verdure.
White noise in Oregon's basin. The man
fishing brushes his hand along a dam,
its concrete thickened with algae and moss.
He extracts it like freshly shipped cargo,
cupping spoiled roe like an orange blossom
muddied in his Columbia River.

LAVOCATISAURUS AGRIOENSIS

Olivia Kingery

The day they discovered a new dinosaur
(I've nicknamed her Lav) tucked into a desert
where she did not belong, I realized no one
really belongs at all. And it got me thinking
about this dinosaur, found with her two young
sons or maybe daughters—what were they feeling?
Archeologists predict the group died together:
a family blasted, or forced, into the sand.
How we can keep digging and digging
into the earth and uncovering fossils and fuels
and dinosaurs completely intact, but we can't find peace.
We can't find what we are looking for, and hell,
who actually knows what that is.
                                    One day we will dig
through to the other side of Earth, unveil ourselves
in a Chinese kitchen, the flavor of rice noodles
welcoming us—we will wall up the hole, spew
hate and trash inside, and we will tell them not to come
through, that we are not going to allow them to violate
our country, violate our people, as if we had not dug
hundreds of miles in fossils and fuels and dinosaurs to get there.
As if we had not broken through the linoleum
of the family noodle shop and taken their noodles
and retreated, full of power and broth,
back to where we came from, home.
                                    Which is almost
as comical as the thought of a 12-meter-long dinosaur,
her young at 8 meters each, clawing in the same clay
for survival. Almost as comical as our ancestors tearing
at the very same earth, for any sense of home, any sense
of place. The day they discovered Lav resting in the dirt,
she asked them simply to cover her back up,
not to disturb her young, to leave her home alone,
to keep digging somewhere else.

AT THE COUNTY DUMP

Leah Kuenzi

One night when I was five or six years old, snuggled into my mother's bed for our nighttime routine, I learned the word "human being." She always read to my brother and me—usually storybooks, but sometimes other things. That night it was a periodical—*National Geographic* or *Sierra Magazine*. My mother subscribed to both. Curled against our mother's side, my older brother looked at the pictures. The article was about the rapid proliferation of landfills and environmental destruction in the United States. I closed my eyes and thought of sleep, comforted—at first—by the sound of my mother's voice. But as she kept reading, my mind seized on certain words that scared me. "Trash. Landfills. Destruction. Human beings. Responsible."

"Human beings" sent my mind running wild. I wondered: what was a human being? I formed a monster in my mind: Godzilla-like, hellish teeth, snarling, grabbing bird eggs from their nests and smashing them on the ground. Trees burning. Foxes scurrying away with their tails between their legs, wolves growling and showing their teeth, everything turned to ash and dust. Behind my closed eyelids, the forests burned and crackled.

I felt certain "it" would come for me next. My lips quivered, then I sobbed.

"Human beings is just another word for people," my mother said. "I'm a human being. *You* are a human being."

I am the monster my mother foretold. These days, my husband Daniel and I live in a brick ranch with a sloping, sickly lawn. When we couldn't get the grass to grow in accordance with the neighborhood standard, we hired a company with a green truck and a sloshing tank of liquid chemicals. The yard is serviced every other month. A technician sprays the grass. From the window I watch him empty a bag of fertilizer into the spreading machine. He throws the bag into the bin at the end of the driveway.

The weeds adapt, grow stronger than ever. The lawn is just weeds now, but so green it looks spray-painted.

The technician leaves the invoice—a wax-coated piece of paper, which cannot go into the recycling—stuck in the screen door. $34. Once I've paid the fee, the invoice joins the empty bag of fertilizer in the trash can.

I should call to cancel the lawn service, but the green is easy on the eyes. We win neighborhood contests for our green lawn.

At the county dump, large and heavy objects cost extra to dispose of, but not on "free dump day." My husband and I had been waiting months for it, the date marked on our calendar. When the day arrived, we spent the morning loading up our cargo trailer with the remains of our demolished screened-in porch. Rotted beams. Plexiglass roof. Mesh screen. In a photo I took with everything loaded, an old, cracked toilet left behind in our yard from the previous owners of the house sits atop the pile of construction materials. The wooden rails on the trailer bend visibly from the bulk. The trailer is connected to Daniel's car, a two-seat convertible with enough torque to pull the trailer, riding low on its tires from the weight. The wooden scraps are badly stained and molded from months of sitting uncovered in our backyard, awaiting proper disposal.

What is proper disposal? I hide damaged things (the cheap yoga mat from college—torn to shreds, sheds foam all over the floor; the mini food processor with the broken lid; a picture frame with a plastic edge that is snapped in half) in the corner of the guestroom closet to avoid throwing them away.

I'm well acquainted with the trash along my regular running route. Gerald, who lives a few houses down from me, does a weekly trash pickup on the main road just outside our neighborhood. There's always an exploded bag of garbage in the middle of the street outside of the Five Oaks apartment complex. Apartment residents routinely load their trash bags onto the roofs of their cars to drive them to the dumpster, forget to stop, and drive out onto the main road with the trash bag still atop the car. I run past Gerald in his reflective orange vest. I wave to him as he stoops and bends, a giant plastic bag ballooning out in the wind behind him. He waves back and lowers his long, silver pickup tool to the ground: Styrofoam containers. Coke bottles. Dirty diapers. An onion ring. *I should stop at his house on the way back and ring the bell, say, Hello, neighbor, I'm so thankful for what you do. Maybe I could join you out there sometime?*

"Don't use a Ziploc bag for that hunk of cheese! We're just going to pull it back out of the fridge in less than a day and finish it."

Each morning before the sun comes up a car arrives in my neighborhood. The driver proceeds slowly (never stopping completely) through the cul-de-sac. He leans out the window, throwing a neat little trash package into each yard. *AJC Reach*, officially known as an "advertising circular product" —it looks like a newspaper but isn't, comes in a plastic bag (to add insult to injury), and, though no one has asked for it, is produced and distributed by the *Atlanta Journal-Constitution*. Google yields dozens of angry responses.

One online complaint reads, "*AJC* is littering Lakes at Cedar Grove subdivision with the *AJC Reach* solicitations despite residents' repeated request that *AJC* stop throwing the solicitations in the streets, driveways, vacant homes, grass, and vacant lots. ... Because *AJC* has not responded to residents' requests, the community now has piles of wet, soggy papers and plastic wrappers in storm drains and retention ponds that lead to 5 waterways that feed the Chattahoochee River."

There are Facebook groups, webpages, and community-action initiatives. There are widespread calls for people to cancel their subscriptions to the *Atlanta Journal-Constitution* until the company responds to community complaints about their "advertrashing" practices.

One commenter writes, "They deliver it on trash day, so it's right next to my dumpster when I go to the end of my drive. Perfect timing!"

I read on one of the pages that concerned residents should email reachee@ajc.com to unsubscribe their address. On January 20, 2015, I write:

Subject: "UNSUBSCRIBE 123 Main Street from AJC Reach."
I would like my address, 123 Main Street, Tucker 30084 promptly unsubscribed from AJC Reach. We do not wish to receive any more litter in our driveway.

I receive no response. The papers keep coming.

There is no away.

Last year, my sister-in-law and I were walking back to our cars after meeting for dinner one evening. I was doing my usual rant against Styrofoam containers being the standard choice for restaurant leftovers.

"Yeah, I agree, Styrofoam sucks," she said. "Speaking of restaurant trash, did you know that there are entire social media profiles—like on Instagram and Tumblr and stuff—and all they do is post pictures of chicken bones that have been thrown in the street?"

"No way! That is wild! How is that possibly common enough to have dedicated social media accounts just to show chicken bone trash?" I asked.

No way is it common enough, I thought to myself. The next day, I was out for a jog. Just outside my neighborhood, I ran past a chicken bone stuck in a sidewalk grate.

Blueberries from California. Nectarines from Mexico. How many miles in a refrigerated tractor trailer?

As Daniel maneuvered the loaded-down trailer out of our driveway en route to the county dump, I wondered, Is this all trash?

Could we burn the wood? Cyanide and arsenic. Green with chemicals. Arsenic fire in Georgia in July?

Could the metal be recycled? Fee for pickup. Save some money? Wait? Ruffle the neighbors' feathers with our backyard trashpile?

No. Maybe next time. This time, the easy way out. I have a lot of excuses but no reasons.

"If the zipper on that bag is broken, you can always cut it open and use it like plastic wrap."

I'm well acquainted with the trash along my usual running route. I continue uphill toward a small clearing and see the abandoned treadmill in the woods. I'm sure it was easy enough to back a truck down the small incline and leave it there for someone else to deal with. *There's no way it still works, if it ever did, after sitting out in the rain*, I think, trying to come up with a possibility for rescue.

In fact, there are at least two Instagram accounts—@wingsofatl and @randomchickenbonesofatl—both dedicated to documenting images of fast food trash, mostly chicken bones, that are littered around Atlanta. On Tumblr: chewedupchickenatl.tumblr.com.

A March 2017 article in *Atlanta Magazine* titled "What's with the chicken bones all over Atlanta?" never answers the titular question. From an interview cited in the article, with one of the Instagram chicken bone documentarians, "People are hustling. That's the other thing, people have places to be. They don't have time to lounge around and work on their chicken. We're always on the go."

At the county dump, Daniel and I didn't see any actual trash, just a series of rolling green hills along a wooded path. At the end of the path, which led from the landfill entrance to the disposal area, we came upon a shaded pavilion with several rows of industrial-sized metal dumpsters. There was still no visible trash. The smell in the air was faintly sour, but not foul. An employee in an orange vest directed us to back in behind one of the dumpsters. We stepped into the hot sun and strapped on our work gloves.

The wooden beams made a hollow sound when they hit the bottom of the dumpster. *Thud. Boom.* The lady in the next car—the car covered in cartoonish drawings of children, hearts, flowers, and a name written in a swooping font—unloaded a trunkful of old TVs. Even daycare has upgraded to flat screens. *Crash.* The glass shattered but never settled, the sound a chain reaction as she hoisted one TV after another onto the ledge. My eardrums tried to retreat further into my head.

"You can just wrap the vegetables in the tin foil we cooked them on. Why even bother with Tupperware?"

The *San Francisco Chronicle* reported that, during the 2015 Olympics in Rio de Janeiro, a kayaker on a practice run hit a submerged sofa with his boat and capsized. The accompanying photograph shows a discarded sofa on the shore of Guanabara Bay. Is it the same sofa that thwarted the kayaker? If not, how many sofas are in Guanabara Bay? The sofa from the photo is surrounded on all sides by other kinds of trash: bottles, foam containers, the insole of a sneaker, a baby doll (its face streaked with dirt), a cardboard box colored with the pink and orange markings that I associate with Dunkin' Donuts. *Do they even have Dunkin' Donuts in Brazil?*

When I was a child, my mother threw things out of the car window. Apple cores, orange peels, peach pits, clumps of her own hair. The chicken bones, too, will degrade over time.

"I'm sending it back to the earth," she would say.

"You should be careful. That's illegal—you might get pulled over," I warned, just ten or eleven years old at the time.

"Pulled over *for what?*" she asked, indignant. "For enriching the soil?"

I'm well acquainted with the trash along my usual running route. Around the bend, the green and white striped awning of Northlake Gardens Assisted Living & Memory Care comes into view. Is there really a garden anywhere on the grounds, or is it just the hot asphalt parking lot and lineup of empty cat food cans? I sometimes see one of the old women who lives there shuffling around outside. She pops the top and sets the cans in a row around the water fountain. When my father died there—not there, exactly, but somewhere just the same—we kept the mementos and the valuables. We hauled his broken shower chair, warped computer desk, and half-used shampoo bottles (he always bought in bulk) to the dumpster out back.

"I'm going to research whether it's more environmentally friendly to wash Tupperware or to throw away plastic."

This is what you'll see posted on the accounts: chicken bones, picked cleaner than clean, against gray asphalt. A cockroach atop a bone with a little meat left. A chicken bone covered in so many ants they look like little specks of dirt, with a caption that reads, "We do lemon pepper wings a little differently here in Atlanta." Chicken bones next to cigarette butts and liquor bottles. A chicken bone at the bottom of a deep puddle. A chicken bone cast aside in a store, atop a shelf, amongst several bottles of men's shaving cream. Chicken drumsticks with one bite taken out. Chicken wings that look untouched: the crispy, brown skin still fully intact. A chicken bone tossed into the center of the fronds of a spiky, palm-tree-looking plant. A chicken bone on the cracked tile floor inside a convenience store. A photo of a large mural on the side of a building that depicts a hummingbird painted in a line-art style in shades of bright teal and purple. In the foreground, a drumstick, with a little bit of meat left at either end.

As we drove away from the county dump, nearly back to the main road, Daniel and I waved goodbye to the man in the guard booth, who gave us a sideways look as we pulled out of the parking lot: hauling a trailer with a sports car (the trailer is longer than the car itself) usually draws confused looks from strangers.

"Why would I bother getting a truck? This works just fine, and I own it outright," Daniel said to no one in particular.

"And the planet appreciates your thriftiness, too," I said.

The line to get in stretched around the corner, cars and trucks full to the brim. Toilets, mattresses, shelves, bicycles, lawnmower, wicker baskets, treadmill, TV stand, monster truck tires, chain-link fence, roofing shingles, plastic sheeting, packing peanuts that weren't held down well and escaped containment, fluttering and swirling around. What's the difference between the ditch outside the landfill and the landfill itself?

Where does everything end up?

Every weekend for the next month, the DeKalb County sanitation department offers curbside collection of bulk items, free of charge. I got a notice about this from our neighborhood association. The first line of the email reads, "Get ready to throw out your old mattress, DeKalb." I wonder how many people have gone out to buy new mattresses, just because getting rid of the old one would be easy.

This morning, the Kelleys to our left put two desktop-sized, ancient-looking oscillating fans out on the curb. This afternoon they added a third to the pile. A few houses down, a mattress leans against the long handle of a red vacuum cleaner. The Franklins to our right have set out several slabs of drywall, a charcoal grill, and a water heater with the metal bashed in on one side. The mass of cords and wires on top of the unit, all twisted together, resemble the arteries of a human heart.

I'm well acquainted with the trash along my usual running route. Waffle House is the last thing I pass before turning left across the I-285 overpass. On the ground in the parking lot, I see cigarette butts, plastic round lids made for to-go platters, a roll of foam insulation that blocks the sidewalk, a plastic water bottle filled with urine, a wad of greasy paper napkins, a shattered ballpoint pen, hairnet, some mangled ketchup packets.

Along the freeway overpass: a fully intact car bumper for a white Honda sedan, a pair of blue latex medical examination gloves, a large throw pillow with the image of a jack-o-lantern stitched on the front.

"I want to start composting the cat litter."

Good Afternoon,

After requesting to unsubscribe, I still regularly receive AJC Reach publications that litter my driveway and front yard at 123 Main Street. Again, I would like to be entirely unsubscribed from this publication.

No response. More papers.

"Did you know there are 93 million cows across the world as of the last cow census? 93 million damn cows just drinking all our fresh water and burping methane up into the ozone layer."

I'm well acquainted with the trash along my usual running route. Most of the houses I pass are tucked into neighborhoods, but three older homes stand just off the main road. The house with the coral-colored front door and shabby wooden boards that need repainting always catches my eye, the color bright and cheery despite its dilapidation.

I wonder how old paint is disposed of. If you took it to the landfill on "free dump day," would they just throw it into the ground?

The house's days are numbered: increasing property values, development company buyout. A few weeks ago, I sat in the audience at a rezoning hearing and ate a cookie and didn't say anything. New townhomes will go up in place of the house with the coral-colored front door. I wonder who lives in that house, where they'll go.

Hello,

There was a paper thrown into my driveway this afternoon, despite the fact that there were two papers still in the driveway and despite the fact that I have emailed twice to unsubscribe my address at 123 Main Street, Tucker, GA 30084.

The deliverer was driving a silver Kia Soul. Please notify all of your drivers immediately that they should not deliver to my home anymore.

I will continue to email you until this issue has been resolved.

I'm well acquainted with the trash along my usual running route. The smell first, then I round the corner and the sign for Southern Seafood comes into view. They must throw away more fish than they sell. Upwind of the odor, I stop along the low stone wall outside the building for a break, turn around, and head home.

Hard some days to drive, move, breathe, eat, drink, talk, consume. Heat death of the universe. Sit in the quiet dark for hours on end. Punishment for my crimes.

On the way home from free dump day, I pulled out my phone and opened Google as Daniel pulled into a gas station. I typed, "why is there no trash at the landfill" and read from the first article that came up, "When a section of the landfill is finished, it is covered permanently with a polyethylene cap (40 mil). The cap is then covered with a 2-foot layer of compacted soil. The soil is then planted with vegetation to prevent erosion of the soil by rainfall and wind."

"What constitutes a 'finished' section of a landfill?" I wondered aloud to Daniel.

"I guess it's when there's no more usable space in any direction," he replied, unscrewing the gas cap.

"Oh my God, you and the paper towels. You think you've got enough?"

It's deer season. More than the turning leaves or the cool mornings, the first thing I notice in October is usually a deer carcass on the side of the interstate. I hit a deer with my car years ago while driving to high school in broad daylight on a state highway. I would have sworn it dropped from the sky onto the left fender of my car.

The deer that I hit died. The police notified me of this when I went to the station to report the accident for insurance purposes. I was surprised, because I hadn't been driving fast, and it seemed to run away after the impact.

"It doesn't always happen right away," the officer told me, and I shrunk down in misery at the thought: everything slow, the suffering extended.

The easy explanation for this phenomenon comes from a popular saying, "Like a deer in headlights." Deer have incredible vision, especially at night. But in the face of oncoming traffic, they do nothing. They are blinded, frozen. There are some other explanations—for example, deer also have excellent hearing; when grazing near a busy road, they may hear a predator and be "spooked" into traffic—but paralysis in the face of certain doom is the only explanation I need.

In most places, the sanitation division, or some other offshoot of Public Works, is responsible for collecting roadkill. In my county, the website promises that roadkill collections are made within 48 hours of receiving notice. Sometimes they are incinerated. Sometimes they are taken to the county dump. When I read this, I pictured one of the black strappy sandals I threw away last week hooked over the horns of a buck, an odd composition of human recklessness.

I've not kept up with my email campaign to *AJC Reach* as I threatened. I can't help but laugh at my correspondence: how important I thought I was. I can't bring myself to trash the papers anymore, not entirely. Each week, a few go in the recycling and the rest I stuff into the cabinets above the washing machine. I use the pages to clean glass with Windex and protect Christmas ornaments in the box. I read online that if you wrap a green avocado in paper, it ripens faster. I'm not convinced it makes much of a difference, but still I transfer my avocados from my shopping bag to a few sheets of *AJC Reach* advertisements and fold the bundle up tight.

Reach for a square of paper towel even when a cloth rag would do the job just fine. Less laundry. It's just easier.

I read somewhere about a playground built over top of a "finished" landfill in Florida. The landfill is still there, of course—it always will be—the trash buried just below the monkey bars and jungle gym. One day, a little girl stretched her arms up to the metal bar above the slide, hung on for a moment, then shot down as fast as she could. Before she reached the bottom: the methane in the air, a bit of a spark from the friction of her clothes against the plastic, up in flames. I would swear to the fact of my reading this, but I can't find the source anywhere when I look for it now. Maybe I saw it in a nightmare.

CROSSING PORTAGES

Cynthia Gallaher

eagles soar over namesake marsh only once yearly,
in the state tagged "a great place to sleep!"
to those on cross-country road trips.

eagle eyes connect dots
that draw Asian carp fingerlings between raindrops,
across flooded portages that meander toward Erie.

before long, their massive fillets could backflip over Niagara,
like divers who catapult from Acapulco cliffs
with hidden, compact strength.

here in lolling headwaters, it's awfully quiet in Lime City,
where the old canal carved next to the new
waits smothered under buildings and concrete roadways.

when I put my ear to the ground
close to the banks of the Little River,
I'm not sure if I hear

the splash of thousands of fins on approach,
or these rivers, angry, twice invaded,
holding rally as New Madrid threatens

to split what George Washington sought
right down the middle.

EXTINCTION II

Robert René Galván

What will be missed?
Already the Tasmanian wolf
Stares at me with her glass eyes,
Dwarfed by the frames
Of behemoths long passed,
Almost unnoticed
In a transparent cell.

And what of the ghost bat
And his golden wings,
Asleep in a green tent,
Dreams of the rare fig
That sustains,

Or the toxic toad
Freed from its liquid chrysalis,
Drops fully formed
From the odd frond
Into the rushing stream,
Becomes a song of desire
That fills the cloud forest
With sadness,

And what of the orchid's
Vampiric beauty that drives
It to its demise,
A fragrant spirit wasted
On the ignorant air,

And the entire progression of life
Brought to a halt by avarice
Or catastrophe;

When all those eyes have vanished,
Who will be our witness?

THEY ARE STILL BUILDING IT

C. S. Malerich

The first time I saw the sludge was in our apartment bathroom. Standing in front of the sink, flossing my teeth, listening to NPR on the shower radio—

"According to climatologists, February was the hottest month on record. ..."

I lost the end of the headline, because a noxious smell filled my nostrils, and there it was, reflected in the bottom corner of the mirror. A smear across the floor behind me.

I turned around. It was seeping between the tiles and from the grout along the base of the tub. Thick, like coagulated blood, and rapidly spreading over the floor. I covered my nose from the smell, like burning rubber. I couldn't let it touch me. My feet were bare.

Kat found me standing on the sink, balancing with one foot along the edge of the basin and one wedged behind the faucet, my back pressed into the corner. I didn't remember climbing up there. All I knew was her shocked face and her voice shouting over the newscast.

"Nonie, what's wrong?"

"Don't touch it!" I shouted back.

"Touch what?"

She was right. I'd glanced from the floor to Kat's face for a split second, and when I looked back down, it was clean bathroom tile again. That was worse. I couldn't know whether to trust her eyes or mine, my memory or her voice. It felt like a feint, to get me back down. When Kat offered me her hand, I shook my head.

She needed to brush her teeth and do a final hair check, which she could have done with me standing there. Instead, she clicked the radio off, sat on the toilet, and talked to me calmly and rationally, until I came down on my own. After, she held me for a good long time, stroking my hair and telling me it was all right, that it was my imagination, until the terror faded long enough for me to put on my scrubs and leave for the clinic.

We were just 22 when Kat and I met, but already she was this shit-talking, put-together powerhouse who could back down men three times her age. I knew she'd be calm in a crisis, when one came along.

Sludge Day One, we were both late for work. I told Dr. Brenner it was an upset stomach. Something I ate. Another nurse had covered for me, so I bought her a little potted orchid from Trader Joe's. Purple. I don't know what excuse Kat gave, but probably she got chewed out anyway, because the whole office was geared up for midterm elections. She didn't say.

That night she told the downstairs neighbors we had a minor plumbing issue, and did they mind if we used their bathroom? They didn't. But the next morning I still couldn't go into our bathroom without shaking. So she said no problem—we'd just spend a few days at her parents' in Montclair.

By the time we'd packed the Xterra, I wanted to agree with her that it was my imagination. It had felt so real, though—the burning-rubber smell had stung my sinuses. When we got to the in-laws', I asked to borrow shower shoes. I couldn't stand letting my bare feet touch the tile.

After three days, my stomach unclenched, and I could think about returning to our apartment. It wasn't convenient to stay in Montclair. I could take the train to work, but Kat had to leave an extra hour earlier to make it to her office on time. She told me it didn't matter. But there was also our privacy to consider, and her parents' concerned looks. They were careful, ever so careful, not to say anything upsetting or controversial. Enough drama in that family already.

Inbox>Drafts>
To: NJ_Kat0222@gmail.com
From: BridgeWalker@riseup.net
(no subject)

By the time you read this, I'll be gone. Sorry to leave it this way but

I don't know why I saw the sludge, but Kat never did. Or never admitted she did. Inside all of us, I think there has to be a part, maybe an ancient crevasse in the cerebellum, that still notices the direction of the wind and the migration of animals. Evolution can't have bred that out of us yet, and *it* sees. It reads the signs.

On the train one morning, a woman sat down beside me and broke into hysterical sobs. No warning. In the newspapers, a police officer shot an unarmed man (black); and a West Virginia couple (white) went on an arson spree. Crossing the street in front of the clinic, I saw a single duckling (yellow and brown) in the middle of the intersection, all by itself. And all over, everywhere you look and everywhere you can't, they're building. Walls. Fences. Condos. Terminals. Pipelines.

People have always made structures, all the way back to the Stone Age. But around 1800, things really picked up. In 1830, the world had 300 miles of railroad. In 1875, there were 300,000. You think about that. 300,000 miles of steel, cutting across the flesh of Mother Earth, like twist ties across a wrist.

Kat did not agree that these events were related.

"Where was the mother duck?" I asked her. "Where were its brothers and sisters?"

"I don't know, honeybee. Things happen. It's not always a call for revolution." Then tenderly: "I'm glad the Humane Society could help. Cute little guy." Her arm went around my neck, and she held up her phone, so we could look at the Instagram pictures together. Duckling in a kiddie pool (plastic).

The second time, I was in the in-laws' kitchen. Kat and her parents and her sister, Brigit, were all in the next room around the dinner table, discussing Brigit's dreadlocks and whether she'd ever land a real job—topics intrinsically linked, from the parents' point of view. I'd only stepped out to get a corkscrew.

When I shut the drawer, the sludge below it surprised me. Same muck. It was seeping out from the cabinet under the sink, dripping onto the linoleum in thick dollops.

No! I commanded myself, before I could retreat. The sight had startled me, but I held it together and forced my feet to stay put, forced my eyes to look, waiting for the hallucination to disappear, like it had for Kat in the bathroom. The in-laws in the next room made me bold. I wouldn't make a scene in their house.

The sludge had a vivid beauty to it as it oozed into the kitchen. The color was dark, but not black like I'd thought at home in the bathroom. Here, it was more like melted rubies. I sidestepped and bent toward it, to get a better look, then the smell hit me. My throat thickened the same way as when I drank too much wine, until I was coughing. I dropped the corkscrew. It fell into the sludge, and backsplash hit my ankle.

Hot! Scalding hot!

Before even thinking about it, I'd put my weight on the countertop and boosted myself up to escape. I must have yelped or made some noise that got their attention, because when I looked up, they were all four crowded in the doorway staring at me.

Kat started forward, right toward the sludge's path.

"Don't!" I screamed. "It burns!"

Kat froze. "Nonie," she murmured. "What burns? What happened?"

"Don't you see it there on the floor?"

She didn't.

I shook my head. If you couldn't see it—if you couldn't *smell* it—it was impossible to describe and make it real. "You'll never get it off, never, never."

"There's nothing there, sweetheart." Kat's father.

Her mother just stared at me, sadly. A broken thing that couldn't be fixed.

Brigit didn't say anything, either, but she was looking at the floor, not at me.

I lay awake in bed, resting on top of Kat, one set of her fingers in my hair, while my cheek pressed in the crook where her neck and shoulder met her chest. We'd turned in early. Downstairs, dishes clinked together, as the in-laws cleaned up.

"They are still building it," I whispered. Repeated.

She hugged me, our clammy skin sticking together, and rocked me twice side-to-side. "They aren't. There's an injunction, honeybee. You won. Time to let it go."

"It was so real." I'd been repeating that, too, as if repetition could make her see what I saw. But why did I want that? So she could be terrified, too? I'd never seen Kat frightened of anything. Except maybe right before proposing.

In response, she only held me tighter and tucked her chin over the crown of my head.

There was a knock on the door, and I tensed. Together more than five years, and it still felt strange sharing a bed under her parents' roof. Illicit.

"Who is it?" Kat called.

"Brigit."

"We're in bed."

"I wanted to talk to Winona for a minute."

I stiffened even more, and gently shook my head, so Kat could feel it. In the past, I would have gotten up. I'd only met Brigit because I was dating her sister, it was true, but we got along so well that sometimes she teased Kat about which one of them was my real soulmate.

It was just teasing.

Kat gently rolled me onto the mattress and got up. At the door, I heard her speak. "Leave it alone, Bridge. She's exhausted."

"I just wanted to—"

"Maybe tomorrow."

The shadows changed position, and I could sense Brigit shifting her weight at the doorway, frustrated. Probably tapping her fingers against her thigh. Always in motion. Their mother told me she was diagnosed with ADHD as a kid.

The next day, Kat and I packed up and moved back into the Hackensack apartment. Whatever I saw, I was seeing it everywhere, so it didn't matter where we ran. On the ride home, I agreed to talk to a therapist. Kat pulled over while I made the appointment.

By evening, my ankle had reddened and blistered where the muck splashed me.

Before pulling up the duvet, Kat shrugged and said it looked like poison ivy to her. "If you stopped traipsing around the woods. ..." She rolled onto her side, away from me.

I held my pillow over my face and held in a scream. It'd been six weeks since I was in the woods; she knew as well as I did.

Inbox>Drafts>
To: NJ_Kat0222@gmail.com
From: BridgeWalker@riseup.net
(no subject)

A year ago I didn't even know there *were* tribes in New Jersey. I assumed they all had to be out west

The therapist thought the sludge had something to do with the encampment.

I talked about it, of course: hauling supplies with Brigit on my days off, learning to pray with tobacco and sage, sleeping out under the stars. How much I'd liked it. The therapist asked why.

"Because ... with the people there I could talk about the things I can't talk about with Kat."

"What things?"

I knew, but I didn't say. The Anishinaabe people call this the time of the Seventh Fire, when humanity has a choice: to walk a path of green and growing things, or a path that is blackened and burned. The Lakota people have a prophecy: that they will gather all the peoples of the world through a unique web, like the Internet, only this web will give us the message that will save the world.

My therapist wasn't Anishinaabe nor Lakota.

"I liked going because I could help them," I said instead. Sometimes they asked me to treat simple injuries or sort the medical supplies. At first, I didn't recognize what the different herbs were for, but I learned from Ruby, their medic.

I also called the mayor, my representatives in Trenton, and—because the pipeline would go across both states—Kat's boss in New York, and wondered if she'd answer the phone and I'd have to hang up. But she didn't answer, and if she took other calls about the pipeline, she didn't tell me anything about it.

Then, there was always someone to call, and I didn't mind. I could hide in the bedroom with the phone while Kat was vacuuming, and read polite, reasonable scripts about leaks in other pipelines, and how the Ramapough and others in the encampment were peacefully exercising their constitutional rights on their own land. It was tiny, anyway: just three teepees, a supply hut, and a vegetable garden. Nothing like the four big camps in North Dakota.

"It sounds like you were standing up for your principles," said the therapist. "What about that wouldn't your wife understand?"

"Well. She really believes in citizens petitioning their government."

He had to prompt me to get more. "It sounds like you've done a lot of that, and your efforts paid off. It sounds like she'd be proud of you."

I nodded, because I understood that this is what the injunction was supposed to mean. That the system worked.

Inbox>Drafts>
To: NJ_Kat0222@gmail.com
From: BridgeWalker@riseup.net
(no subject)

Broadly we agree about governance: it should be the will of the people, and consent of the governed. I just don't get why you think that's what we have.

There was a party at the encampment, the night we thought we'd won. Bonfires. Drums. The neighbors called the cops, and for once, the cops didn't hassle us. They drove up, they stood outside their squad cars while the blue flashers turned the grove into a dance club, and they watched us stepping in a wild round, yelling our victory to the moon. Brigit and I danced the circle with our friends, and then danced with each other. I never forgot for a moment that my sister-in-law wasn't my wife.

Even when I kissed her.

It was less than a second. Less than half a second. She blushed and shrugged away, shorter than Kat and harder to hold onto. No angles.

"I'm not," she started to say, and never finished.

No need.

It was a mistake. Caught up in the moment, the excitement, the victory (we thought) we shared, how alike she and Kat smiled when they really let go. Both very serious women, in their way.

The next weekend, Kat got us matinee tickets to *Hamilton*, and I asked

Brigit if she could find someone else to drive up to the Reserve with her.

"Yeah," she said. "Okay. Not so critical now." They were only weeding the garden.

Inbox>Drafts>
To: NJ_Kat0222@gmail.com
From: BridgeWalker@riseup.net
(no subject)

The will of the people only means something when the people have the power to enforce it.

Kat liked her bananas green-yellow; I liked mine just starting to freckle brown. Buy a whole bunch, so by the time they were too ripe for her, they were a day away from perfect for me. That was Kat's theory. We fit like jig-saw pieces.

Long before I saw the sludge, I'd asked her, "Do you remember the last time you slept outside?"

Wheel of Fortune was on the TV, muted. Waiting for *Jeopardy*, her favorite, while she sifted emails. "Never."

"It's amazing." I sat down at the end of the couch, one leg tucked up under me, facing her, so I could massage her feet. "If you lie on your back on the ground, you can feel it curving up against your spine. Like an exercise ball. But it's solid, heavy. All the way going down and down through the core out the other side, and in every direction north, south, east, and west."

Kat thought I was charming. "I would think the Earth's too big for you to feel the curvature of the planet."

"You can feel it! It's like all of Mother Earth is holding you up. Cradling you." I lifted her right foot between my palms and stroked the arch with my thumbs.

She put down her phone and bicycled her legs, exhaling. "Ah! That. Right there."

"Then, if you turn the image 180 degrees, you've got the whole planet on your back. *You're* carrying *her*."

"It's very poetic," she sighed. A few soft, deep kisses, and she'd be mine instead of Alex Trebek's. "But I'll leave the campout to you guys. I'd rather change the world indoors."

I caught her ankles, one in each hand. "That's why we're a good team." I wrapped her legs around me, knotting them at the base of my spine like apron strings, and leaned in.

We stopped a pipeline.

It was easy to forget, because like everyone else, Kat and I had gone back to normal. We put gas in the car (oil from Alberta, Canada), played on our phones (metals from the Democratic Republic of the Congo), opened our eight-ounce plastic containers that will ultimately join the eight million metric tons already floating in the oceans.

We watched the news while hurricanes hit Texas. Then Florida. Then Puerto Rico.

We slept in a bed.

Once, at the encampment, Ruby told me a story of the McMansion neighbor across the road, running out in the morning with an air horn, shaking his fist and blasting at the whitetail deer who were grazing on the lawn. "In our culture," said Ruby, shaking her head, "when the deer come on our land, it's a blessing."

Five hundred years, and the machine that can only build and build has been steamrolling every group of people who might give us a chance of survival now.

After the encampment, after kissing Brigit, after stopping one pipeline, I knew that. I *knew*. In that part of my brain that still can't figure out Slack and hates the little plastic stirrers they use in coffee shops, I wanted to tell others, to convince them. But I couldn't even convince myself. All while I was thinking about how the world was ending because we wouldn't change, I was also not changing. On my days off, I drove the Xterra for miles: into the city, to surprise Kat for lunch, maybe with new earrings or a pair of kitten heels; or the opposite direction, north and north, over the state line, playing showtunes and folk music, drinking macchiatos and eating canisters of potato chips. Some days the taste on my tongue—the balance of salt and sweet—was all that kept me from driving right through the guardrail.

"I'm for sustainability, too," said Kat. "But the stuff Bridge wants ... that isn't winning anybody over."

Kat had the master's in political science, so I couldn't argue.

Brigit didn't call me, and then she did. Almost four weeks to the day I'd kissed her. "They're still building it," she told my voicemail. "Ruby and Bear saw the bulldozers. Those bastards, I—we—I have to do something."

The third time the sludge came, I was at work, writing down a patient's blood pressure. (Good—110/60.) When I looked up from the clipboard, I saw it welling from the seams in the linoleum floor below the patient's stocking feet. The smell overwhelmed me. I dropped the clipboard to cover my nose and grabbed the patient by the right arm, trying to pull her away, trying to pull her somewhere safe. But her left arm was still in the blood pressure cuff, and she wasn't cooperating, either way. She screamed —not because of the sludge that was seeping toward her feet, but because of me. Three other nurses and the shift supervisor came running.

They put me in an empty exam room while they figured out how to handle the situation. It's funny, isn't it? A bunch of health professionals trying to decide what to do with one of their own, who was having a "psychotic episode" (on the one hand), but who'd "assaulted a patient" (on the other). They didn't know better than anybody else.

I crouched on top of the examination table, watching the floor. I knew I should have been worried about getting fired, but it's hard to care about things like that while you're seeing the world around you drown in poison. The floor was already covered, the filth was seeping up higher and higher. The thought occurred to me, *This time, it won't vanish. This time, I'm seeing it, and I'll keep seeing it.*

It was comforting. I didn't want to go through life *not* seeing it anymore.

Maybe I'll get strong, I thought. *Like Bridge or Ruby. This will be my life. Stop one pipeline, then another.*

Maybe I wouldn't drink overpriced espresso anymore, and waste whole afternoons on YouTube clips, and buy cheap shoes that wear out in a year.

When Dr. Brenner opened the door to check on me, he was wading through it, the bottom of his white coat destroyed. I stared into his face, wondering how he could stand it—having the sludge touch him, having the fumes in his face.

He didn't look any different than usual. Concerned and professional. Imagine if you saw someone put a hand in a flame, and just keep talking to you about the game last night or what you're doing for your birthday, like nothing else was going on. I wondered if he were really a mutant or an alien, because how could you be human and real and not feel something like that?

I heard him talking to me, but I couldn't tell you a word he said.

Kat came to get me. I hadn't left the examination table, and she almost had
to carry me to the car to get me out.

"Nonie," she said, very quietly, "if you don't put your feet on the floor
and come with me, I'll know: you don't love me anymore."

I jumped down from the table, crying. First, because I couldn't stand
to have her think that. Then, because I could feel the sludge eating
through my sneakers and the bottom of my scrubs, scalding hot.

She took my hand. If she was a mutant, she was a heroic one. Toxic
Avenger. Professor X.

I told myself to mirror her. To act like it was nothing. In high school,
I'd sprained an ankle mid-soccer game, and played through the pain because I was so shy, I didn't want the male trainer touching me. I could do
it.

Outside the clinic, the sludge was seeping from the storm drains into
the street, filling the gutters.

"I'm around the corner." Kat pulled me toward the crosswalk.

Until a car turned in front of us, I managed. When the spinning tires
churned the sludge into a fine spray, I felt it hit me in the face, then I pan-
icked, lunging for safety. Kat lost her grip on my hand, and I slipped, the
sludge squelching below me as I landed in the crosswalk. Fumes overwhelmed my mouth and nostrils. My lungs reacted, forcing out poison
and air, and I stood up, desperate, and started shedding my clothes. My
shoes were covered now, and there wasn't anything I could do about that,
but I shrugged out of the top of my scrubs and used the cleaner part to
wipe my right arm where I'd landed. It clung to my arm hair, sticky and
thick as molasses, and I wiped harder. I could feel it on the side of my face,
in my ear, in my hair.

"Winona, stop, stop!" Kat grabbed my arms, left and right alike, in her
clean palms.

I stared into her face. There were tears in her eyes, on her cheeks. A
breeze came up, and I shivered. Here I was standing in my bra, the middle
of the street in a canyon of high-rises. On the corner, people stared while
they waited for the light to change.

"Let's go home," I told Kat, slipping my shirt over my head.

I walked to the Xterra without waiting to see if she would follow.

Behind me, she beeped the keychain, and the door locks popped open. I got into the passenger side calmly and buckled my seatbelt. Kat didn't say anything on the drive, but a new tear rolled down her cheek every other minute. I could smell the sludge she'd tracked in on her sensible heels, but this wasn't what pained her.

She was crying while she changed out of her work clothes, and while she made dinner, and while we ate in front of the TV. She got every answer on *Jeopardy* perfect, in the form of a question. "What is ..." she said, always, even if the answer was a person. "What is Saturn?" "What is quantum mechanics?" "What is Jules Verne?"

I couldn't speak. I had to concentrate very hard on not screaming, not panicking, and not seeing the sludge that was burning holes in her bare feet.

When the plates were in the dishwasher, Kat finally turned to me. "I don't want to lose you, too." Her knees buckled, and she slumped onto the floor, landing in five inches of poison that she couldn't see.

I breathed deeply. My nostrils burned, but I could imagine the air was clean. I didn't want to lose her, either.

"Kat," I said, gathering her up. She was taller than I am, but I could hold her up, like a stake against a weak stalk. "I'm here," I said, because I couldn't make any other promises. "I'm not leaving," because the sludge was coming to choke and swallow us, and I was more afraid of what would happen to Kat if she did start feeling it, than of what would happen to the world if she didn't.

Some people have to be worth loving, don't you think? Or what good is a world.

Inbox>Drafts>
To: NJ_Kat0222@gmail.com
From: BridgeWalker@riseup.net
(no subject)

Kat,

I've started this message over and over, and I don't know how to make it easier, so I'm just going to say it: I'm going. I can't tell you where exactly, but you can probably guess why, and you probably understand that you're better off not knowing more. You and Winona.

Please try to explain to Mom and Dad. They didn't raise me to pretend everything is okay when it's not. Tell Winona she didn't do anything wrong. None of you did. It's just, this is the fight of our lives, and either you see it that way or you don't. But I can't sit and watch anymore.

Your sister,
Bridge

GULF COAST

Deborah Kelly

I wade in ankle foam,
                sand milk.
          Where sea oat and sea grape
basket their dunes,
and turtle eggs.

Where wide-grinned pelicans
          glide nautical miles with
their wrinkled sacks of fish.

On a beach pocked with radials,
of rain-dimples and my damn tears:
          See, I wade in surfactants,
the ocean breeze of benzene,
                  where trawlers scrape
          sunflower sea stars
while raking for shrimp.

And red algae bleeds
an estuary pinned by rigs.

LAST SNOW

Eric Shonkwiler

There were license plates from as far out as Missouri. Illinois was practically common. Tennessee and Kentucky, Georgia: these, she understood. Farther west than the Mississippi, and Janine didn't even know how they were already here. Colorado would be more crowded, if they had the same weather—days ahead of them, surely. The traffic was slow, but not awful; every manual car on the road made every other car on the road act like the next bridge would be ice. They drove unsteadily upward. Curves cut them low, avoiding sometimes a hill and sometimes an indestructible portion of rock. Or maybe the road only followed an older path, wound with rivers. Grooves in the mountainside, the teethmarks of some cartoonish and overlarge rock-saw or drill. Oil wells had drills with three rolling, knobby wheels. For all she knew, they did use teeth.

Emily was fast asleep beside her. Fast, from fasten, the opposite of speed. In her car seat, just the bump cushion now, her hair flattened where she had pressed it to the seat and stuck there, fast, in the pink hiragana of sleep written all down her face. Elsewhere, her hair was in true ringlets, of the sort Janine would have loved in school, the sort every girl with straight hair says she would love. The car corrected her veer toward the shoulder, wheel stiffening. The caravan of cars passed a sign for the park, next exit. She leaned to see the sky through the windshield and still doubted. When they rounded a curve, she saw the automatic zippering of lanes, merging for the exit. Still a crawl. Emily muttered, shook her head. They dropped down the exit ramp and all turned left, passing under the highway. The road became tight, hardly two lanes. A gas station, a small parking lot cut into a wedge in the hillside. Another gas station, smaller still. Miles yet ahead, there would be a third where she would have to stop, if only for a minute. The charge was low, would maybe get them to the park. The icon on the dash was a dark, threatening red.

Are we close? Emily said, rubbing her eyes.

We are.

It's not raining.

It will soon.

I'm thirsty.

Just a little while longer, sweetie. Hold tight. Janine smiled down at her.

Emily pursed her lips and made a practiced smacking sound, grinning.

I wish he hadn't taught you that.

Why?

She closed her eyes for a beat, two. Above them, a wide metal bridge, spanning only sixty or seventy feet across the gap, hilltop to hilltop.

What's that for? Did this used to be underwater?

Janine shook her head. I'm not sure. Maybe it's for trains.

Emily twisted in her seat to look behind them. I think it used to be underwater.

Well, maybe. But that's not what the bridge is for. There was water here a long time ago. Janine glanced around them. Houses ran along the right side of the road with small yards, old trees with their leaves still driven in pockets. Behind the houses, the empty crag where a creek had flowed, would flow. Can you see over there? There's a stream in those backyards.

So, it was underwater?

No. This valley was probably made with water. There was just one hill here. Maybe that's not right. Maybe the water came after.

They fell quiet, both peering through the windows. It was midafternoon, but every so often, the brakelights of the caravan came on, and the glow was high on the road and hollow. The cars wound, wended. Signs went by for unincorporated towns, one after the other without distinction. Houses got smaller and cheaper. They passed a spraypainted sign set at a curve: firewood.

I used to live near here, Janine said.

Where?

Just a little town. She glanced at the charge indicator on the dash.

Can we go see it?

Maybe someday. Today, we've got a special goal.

Ten minutes later, the cars were all stopped. They were at the top of a hill and the land sagged ahead of them, belled to one side, but the road went on straight, and there was no movement. Janine could see the sign for the gas station and the cars wrapped around the lot, waiting to get in. There were only two plugs—four pumps. The dash was blinking red.

Are we gonna run out of batteries?

She smiled thin, shook her head. Nope. We're fine. Just waiting on everyone else. She reached back behind the seat and came up with a tablet. Want to watch something while we wait?

Emily shrugged. Okay. She opened a movie player, started a cartoon.

Janine put her hands back on the wheel. Emily watched her, the screen. They moved ahead one car-length, and Janine sighed. The clouds overhead thickened, and the bare trees in their clusters along the road darkened. A call on her cell, and she set it on her thigh, let it buzz. It buzzed again, and then a text came through. The brief: *You need to pick up,* from Brandon. She opened the message, read on. *Mom wants to know where Emily is. The school said you have her.* Janine texted back: *I do.* There was a lag before his response: *You have got to tell me when you do this. Mom was supposed to pick her up, and she's freaking out. I haven't answered cuz I knew you had her.* Janine glanced over at Emily, started typing again: *Well I do. We're fine.*

She closed the message and pulled up a map to the park on the screen. Reception was bad, and it was slow loading. When she looked up, a shadow passed by the car on the passenger side, a man in a denim jacket rounding the hood and sliding to the road. He glanced through the windshield, and Janine gave a slight smile, checked the locks. The man walked down the left side of the road and stopped, waving. A truck pulled out of the line behind her and gunned past, cleared the next hill beyond the gas station and then went out of sight. A moment later, another car followed suit, rust along its bottom, bad muffler. The blinking on the dash grew.

Emily looked up. Mommy?

I know. We're fine.

Janine put a hand to her head and rubbed her temple. Her phone buzzed again. It was only a few hundred yards to the gas station. Four or five football fields, end to end. There was more than enough of a charge for it. However many dozens of car-lengths. She looked at the message: *They called the cops.* She replied, *On me?* A pause. The signal broke down on the phone, then perked back. She did the math on how far they'd gone since reaching the top of the hill, punched the button on the dash to see how much time it estimated was left. She looked at Emily, rapt attention to the cartoon, now. A police car was coming the other way, and Janine pushed their car ahead, almost to the bumper of the SUV in front of them. Another light flashed on the dash, a collision warning. She watched the policeman drive by, a sheriff's deputy, glancing at her. Emily's head was ducked to the tablet. Brandon's reply: *Where are you? I need to calm them down. I messed up my story, and now they think you kidnapped her.*

Janine pressed her head against the headrest, sighed, and pushed the car the meager distance they'd gained. *I kind of did*, she typed. *We're going to see the snow. I wanted her to get the chance.* She put the phone away. Just ahead, the shoulder was flattening, jutting out the rock face that formed the crest of the hill. The traffic moved a foot, two, and she pulled the car off onto the dead grass and put the car in park. She shut it off, and all the red lights vanished. Emily looked up.

We're going to walk from here, okay, babe?

Emily pushed pause on the tablet. Is it cold out?

A little.

She reached back and got Emily's coat, took the tablet, and hid it under the seat. She helped Emily into her coat, wiggling in the seat, and got out. It felt good to stand, and the air was cool and full of the smell of dry grass, leaves. She opened Emily's door and took her hand, and they walked down the shoulder. People watched. She thought they might point, but there was no reason to. They were just a mother and daughter.

The grass crackled under their feet. Going uphill was slow, and starting on the second one, Janine bent down and had Emily climb onto her shoulders. They neared the gas station, full of people, and she turned back long enough to see the row of cars some mile or two long. She expected localized fog, the exhaust from the cars and the breaths of the drivers. They followed the road right. She'd forgotten the food. Her cell phone again: *I knew it. Listen*, and a break before: *Em's got a phone. Mom insisted. It's got a tracking app.*

Janine cussed to herself.

Ten minutes down the road, it began to rain, lightly, but heavier than the mist she had expected to precede the snow. Emily looked back at Janine and grinned, ran ahead and returned to just in front of her on the side of the road. The park was a half-mile away, and the flow of traffic thickened coming back from it, people turning around to park along the shoulder, getting out to walk. There were intermittent packs of cars off the road where one driver had gone far enough and his neighbors schooled to follow, more cars now beside them on the road, waiting to get into the park. Every so often, someone honked, near and far, somewhere through the trees, up a switchback. She thought of that word, its etymology so literal. Oxbow was better; there was metaphor, there. Brandon: *I'm on my way. I told them to stay behind and play command center, but they did tell the cops about the app.* Janine beat back: *There are a million daughters here.*

Finally ahead, the grade easing, Janine saw the sign for the state park. Turning onto the entrance road, they found it steepening immediately, taking the hill at a hard ascent before sweeping to the left, brakelights glowing through the trees showing the way. She looked at Emily, stalwart, not a peep, going on. How far could Janine walk as a child? Disney World, the length of all the walks between rides? How far had school been?

The road was turning glossy from the rain. Between their footsteps, they could hear the gathered drops of water from tree branches pelting the dead leaves below, the constant simmer between that. Squeak of windshield wipers. Janine leaned and picked Emily up again, threw her to a seat on her crossed forearm, smiling.

I think you're due for a rest, right?

Emily shrugged a shoulder and put her arm around Janine's neck. Okay.

Janine carried her on, picking up speed. At the turn of the first switchback, she could see the next above them, cars still lined, unmoving. Children in the back seats, parents in the front. College students, high schoolers. Her legs burned. A car came down the other side of the road, then another. They rounded to the second switchback and an SUV descended, the driver glowering. Janine watched them go. Just ahead was a plaque commemorating some mining incident. Past it, a small hole, plugged with metal bars, fenced off. She carried Emily on. Rain had begun to seep down her neck, coat pulled to the side as it was. They crested the second switchback, and the hill leveled off for a space. There was the full parking lot, cars circling. She let Emily down, and they started walking toward the visitor center.

We're almost there. Just through that building, and then we'll park our buns and wait for it to snow.

But it's still raining.

It'll turn over soon. Just wait.

There were families walking in and out, people carrying heavy coats and sleeping bags, tents bound up in bags. They skirted around a cluster of stopped vehicles and made the sidewalk for the visitor center. A man in his mid-forties with a heavy camera around his neck was leaving as they got to the door, and he shook his head.

Don't bother.

Janine opened her mouth, but he went on. She pushed the door wide, and Emily went below her arm. There was a circuit of poles and green belt barriers meant to form a maze of a line, but it was empty, and a young man was dragging a sign across the polished stone floor, families ahead of him with arms crossed, hands on hips. A woman at the ticket counter was shaking her head to a family that pressed past him. The hall was too crowded for Janine to see the sign as the young man set it upright, but there was a ripple through the visitors, a momentary parting. The sign read: At capacity, park temporarily closed.

Oop, Emily said. We're in the wrong line.

Janine spun them back out the doors. In the minute they'd been inside, it seemed to have gotten cooler, and there was a little thrill down her back that they might really see snow, that she'd accomplished something. She was looking at the clouds when she noticed the police car, and an officer parked it at the curb and got out. No-Eyes sunglasses, though the light was dim. She gripped Emily's hand, and he walked on by. Janine was rooted. She looked at Emily, smiled, and waited for the sound of the doors before they moved on. She started them toward the parking lot, glancing back over her shoulder, and then they went between two cars, Janine pulling Emily behind her, and they hopped the median to get onto the path up the hill. At the top of a switchback, there was a park officer standing by an orange sawhorse, and a line of families on foot waiting to get by him. She stopped for a moment, reining Emily back. Burgundy jacket, fine. Emily's light turquoise, not fine.

We're gonna run up through these woods, okay?

Aren't we going to wait in line? Emily raised an eyebrow. We'll get in trouble.

It'll be worth it. Try to keep up.

Janine took her hand and pulled her along, across the road and into the ditch, then up the hillside. They scrambled along in the grass, grabbed thin trees, roots. Emily was on all fours almost immediately and navigating like a spider, gaining every time Janine tripped, had to shift weight. She stopped long enough to glance down at the road below, the people still in line, the park officer still behind the barrier. Above them was the path, recurved, and they crossed it and kept on in the brush, diving between two families, children exclaiming. Janine was breathless, desk-job-lunged. A rag of moss came unbound from a rock below Emily and she slid, and Janine was there, hooking her arm below her and heaving her back up. They could hear people above them, cars, music. Janine straightened, stretched, checked her hands, red and cold, and Emily's looked cold. As she thought it, Emily brought her hands to her mouth and blew, smiled at the vapor.

I can see my breath, Mommy!

Janine grinned, exhaled a stream. That's a good sign. I bet the rain will turn real soon.

She put her own hands on Emily's cheeks, held them there, and they continued upward until the hill leveled out for a time, broadened and peaked itself by a smaller hill. The park visitors were strewn about on blankets, tarps strung between trees over their heads. Thermoses of hot chocolate—she could smell it. She looked at Emily and pointed for a clear spot below a tree, and set her jacket down for them both to sit on.

You'll catch cold, Emily said.

Cold doesn't give you a cold. Don't believe everything your grandma says.

Grandpa.

Not him, either.

People were emerging from the slope behind them. Couples, young men and women, a few children. A man sat down a dozen yards from them and slipped a large bag from his back and, from it, removed a cooler. Beers emerged, were passed around to approaching friends. Tarps laid out.

Did you used to come up here for the snow? Emily said.

No. She smiled. When I was a little girl, we didn't have to travel anywhere to see it. It fell all over.

But now it's too warm.

That's right.

Daddy says it's because people didn't pay attention to scientists like you.

I'm not a scientist.

Daddy says you are.

Janine smiled. Well, that's nice of him. She looked away, up. The rain was cooler, maybe. Would it lighten, turn over to snow? Or mix first? She knew little about rain or snow. She hadn't had to think about it.

Down the treeline, the partiers were getting loud. Emily was watching them. Janine's phone buzzed. It was an AMBER Alert. Her blood chilled, ears rang. The alert described Emily, Janine, the car. Janine saw people reach into pockets, purses, all at once. Compared phones, glanced around. She stayed still, leaned Emily's head to her and kissed her hair. The sky was getting dim, the rain thinning, perhaps. Janine stood, locked her fingers and pretended to stretch. Coming through the trees was a gray-uniformed policeman. She watched him approach through her motions, arms out, back. He was holding a duty phone ahead of him, glancing up from the screen to the people and trees, spinning. Janine quit stretching and walked up to him, and he put the phone away.

Excuse me, officer? I hate to spoil their fun, but those kids down the way are getting a bit too loud. I've got my young daughter here, you see.

He looked their way. Looks like they're drinking, too. I'll speak to them.

Thank you.

She smiled, watching him go across the leaves and grass for the college students, now trying to pack away their beers. He stood over them. Janine turned to Emily.

Let's see if we can go a little higher, huh?

She reached out her hand and pulled Emily to her feet, tugging Emily's coat down, then slipping her hand in the pockets and dropping her daughter's phone to the ground. She covered the action with her own coat, whipping it out. It was almost wet through, chilly when she slipped it on. They started the way the officer had come.

There wasn't much of a slope left, but they exited the trees for a clearing where the last of the cars were parked, set off the path. The rain had turned to a heavy mist. Beyond the cars, they climbed a short grade. Fewer people were there, walking with them. A storm or fire had thinned out the trees, and the ground was covered in grass. Through the bare treetops below, Janine could see far west, the hills and other hills slope-on-slope until they faded back into a hazy sea. She had seen the ocean just once, miraculous flatness. She had wondered how there were no curve to it, none to be seen. The hills seemed truer for that.

Still looking west, she saw that the haze grew stronger, moved, and that it was snow. Emily was digging through the grass, and Janine touched her shoulder, and she looked up and saw Janine pointing. They could see it coming, feel the cold before it, and then the heavy flakes were nearly upon them, a wall so thick it seemed unaccountable. Emily was skipping ahead and spinning as the flakes reached them, and Janine was wondering how they were not missed, how the sky didn't fall to pieces, blue showing through, or black. Janine joined Emily and took her hands, sirens down below them.

SOME THINGS ONLY GOD CAN DO

Kim Harvey

As if the hills themselves were vermilion
waves, a liquid blaze. The things
they saved: cell phone and chargers, laptop,
wedding bands, handgun, three pairs
of underwear, a towel, their two dogs if
they were lucky. Left behind, everything
else: baby book, passports, family
heirlooms, guitar, photos on the wall.
Then the world disappeared
around them, the steering wheel
melted in her hands, the rubber soles
of his shoes dissolved into the asphalt. It started
with a spark, as all fires do, small brush ignited, maybe
a downed powerline, they say. Now we're naming
the dead: Carl, Ernest, Jesus. You want to
call your people, hold them close, even the ones
who are no longer there, or anywhere.
I mean, what would you do? All the neighbors'
houses are gone, Black Bear Diner, Safeway
gone, Jack in the Box, the kids' school, the hospital
where a baby boy was born just hours before, all gone,
horses and mules jumped into swimming pools
to escape the flames. Strange terrain, this
panorama of disaster, of total darkness, exploding
of propane tanks, car tires popping from the heat
of the canyon vortex, of the Jarbo devil wind,
of chaos, of choking black smoke hundreds of
miles away, the ash on our windshield
we recognize as human
remains, the grace of God or the lack of it,
the growing list of the missing, singed
cats in the grasses, of the waiting, of all
the not knowing, of sleeping in cars
and tents, prayers of thanksgiving
in a Walmart parking lot, of a place called
home that suddenly no longer exists.

AUTHOR
Biographies

ELLERY AKERS is the author of three books of poetry, most recently *Swerve: Environmentalism, Feminism, and Resistance* from Blue Light Press. She has won 13 national writing awards, including the Poetry International Prize and *Sierra* magazine's Nature Writing Award. She is a writer and naturalist living in California.

JOUMANA ALTALLAL was born in Baghdad to Iraqi and Lebanese parents. She is currently a second-year MFA candidate in poetry at the University of Michigan. Her work appears in *Poets Reading the News*, *Rusted Radishes*, *Mikrokosmos*, and other outlets.

LEAH ANGSTMAN serves as editor-in-chief for *The Coil* magazine, a reviewer for *Publishers Weekly*, and a culture writer and copyeditor for *Pacific Standard*. Her work has appeared in *Los Angeles Review of Books*, *The Rumpus*, *Nashville Review*, *Tupelo Quarterly*, *Maine Review*, *Electric Literature*, *Slice*, and elsewhere. Find her at leahangstman.com.

MARC BEAUDIN is a poet and theater artist based in Livingston, Montana. He is the author of the hitchhiking memoir *Vagabond Song: Neo-Haibun from the Peregrine Journals* and believes Brahms' "Violin Concerto in D" is more powerful than all the guns, smokestacks, and coal trains in the world.

HANNAH BLASER has degrees in Creative Writing and Communication from St. Ambrose University in Iowa. Her poems and creative nonfiction pieces have appeared in the 2015, 2016, 2017, and 2018 editions of *Quercus*. She spends her free time writing, hiking, and playing boardgames while drinking Moscow Mules.

LAVINA BLOSSOM is a visual artist and poet. Her poems have appeared in various journals, including *3Elements Review*, *Kansas Quarterly*, *The Literary Review*, *The Paris Review*, *The Innisfree Poetry Journal*, *Poemeleon*, and *Prompt and Circumstance*. She is an associate editor of poetry for *Inlandia: A Literary Journey*.

C. W. BUCKLEY lives and works in Seattle with his family. Graduating from Stanford University with a degree in Human Biology, he earned an MA in Religion after two years as a chaplain resident. His writing explores geek culture, conscience, faith, and fatherhood. He is the author of *Bluing*.

PINNY BULMAN is a Bronx Council on the Arts BRIO award-winning poet, who has been the recipient of several ADR Poetry Awards and a finalist for the Raynes Poetry Prize. His poems have appeared in a variety of literary publications, including *Muddy River Poetry Review*, *Artemis*, and *Pressenza International*.

JOSH DANIEL currently lives in southern Kentucky as he finishes up his MA in English Literature. In his spare time, he enjoys reading and writing poetry and hiking with his fiancé.

CARALYN DAVIS lives in Asheville, North Carolina, with her cat, Henry. Her work appears or is slated for publication in *Fiction International, The Normal School, Decomp, The Bitter Southerner, The Molotov Cocktail, Word Riot, Eclectica, Monkeybicycle, Flash Fiction Magazine, Superstition Review, Bull, Writers Resist*, and other journals.

ANN V. DeVILBISS has had work in *BOAAT, Crab Orchard Review, The Maine Review, Pangyrus*, and elsewhere. She is the recipient of the 2017 Betty Gabehart Prize in poetry and an Emerging Artist Award from the Kentucky Arts Council. She lives and works in Louisville, Kentucky.

STEPHANIE DEVINE's fiction and nonfiction have appeared in *Gone Lawn, Nano Fiction, Louisiana Literature, Columbia: A Journal of Literature and Art, The Austin Review, Joyland, Pembroke Magazine, Cheap Pop, Atticus Review, Fiction Southeast, Treehouse*, and *Glassworks Magazine*.

KEVIN DOYLE is a writer from Cork, Ireland. He is the author of the political crime thrillers *To Keep a Bird Singing* (2018) and *A River of Bodies* (2019)—both published by Blackstaff Press. He also cowrote with Spark Deeley the award-winning children's picture book, *The Worms That Saved the World*. More at kevindoyle.ie.

DIONNE CUSTER EDWARDS is a writer and arts educator at The Wexner Center for the Arts, and the creator of Pages, a writing program for high school students. She coedits an anthology of student writing and art. Her writing appears in *3Elements Review, The Seventh Wave, Grist, Tahoma Literary Review*, and elsewhere.

MARILYN J. EVANS lives in Kansas City, Missouri, with her husband and cats. She has retired from foxhunting and the world of pharmaceuticals and biologics, but still writes and gardens every day. Her first novel, *Beloved Lives*, is available from TCK Publishing. Visit her blog at marilynjevans.com/blog.

STACEY FORRESTER is a writer, educator, and misfit who can be found being towed by her dog through the alleys of East Vancouver/Coast Salish Territories. One day, she stepped on the class salamander on her first day at a new school, and she has been writing poetry ever since.

CYNTHIA GALLAHER is a Chicago-based poet and playwright, and author of four poetry collections, including *Epicurean Ecstasy: More Poems about Food, Drink, Herbs, and Spices* (The Poetry Box, 2019), and three chapbooks, including *Drenched* (Main Street Rag, 2018), poems about liquids.

ROBERT RENÉ GALVÁN was born in San Antonio and resides in New York City where he works as a professional musician and poet. His last collection of poems, *Meteors*, was published by Lux Nova Press. He was a shortlist winner nominee in the 2018 Adelaide Literary Award for Best Poem.

MICHAEL GARRIGAN writes and teaches along the banks of the Susquehanna River in southern Pennsylvania. He enjoys exploring the river's many tributaries with a flyrod and hiking the riverlands. You can find out more at mgarrigan.com.

MADELINE GRIGG is a second-year MFA candidate in Poetry at Bowling Green State University. Her work has previously been published in *Analecta, Hothouse*, and *Feminine Inquiry*.

KIM HARVEY is a San Francisco Bay Area poet and a reader for *Palette Poetry*. She is an alumna of the Squaw Valley Community of Writers. Her work has recently appeared in *Rattle*, *3Elements Review*, *Raw Art Review*, *Wraparound South*, *Poets Reading the News*, and *The Comstock Review*.

ANDREW M. HOWARD graduated from Texas Tech University and Georgia College & State University, where he earned an MFA in fiction while teaching GED students in the nation's oldest mental institution. Work has recently appeared in *Hobart*, *Miracle Monocle*, and *Bluestem Magazine*. He currently lives and teaches in Washington, D.C.

ANNA KAYE-ROGERS' previous work has been published in or by Illinois Valley Community College's *River Currents*, *The Feminine Collective*, *Eastern Iowa Review*, Zoetic Press' *Non-Binary Review*, *Cosmonauts Avenue*, Pen 2 Paper, and Zimbell House Publishing. She studies English, Creative Writing, and Professional Communications at Northern Illinois University.

DEBORAH KELLY is from Minneapolis and Chicago, but the high deserts and mountains of the West kept calling. She now lives in Boulder, Colorado, where she writes as a way of life and a practice. Her poems appear in *Thalia Magazine* (Montreal), Wundor Editions (London), *Stone Coast Review*, and *The Fourth River*.

CHRIS KETCHUM is a poet from northern Idaho. He is a current MFA candidate at Vanderbilt University in Nashville. His first chapbook, *Invasive Species*, was published by The Chrysalis (Willamette University) in 2015.

OLIVIA KINGERY is a farmer of plants and words in the Upper Peninsula of Michigan. She is an MFA candidate at Northern Michigan University, where she reads for *Passages North*. When not writing, she is in the woods with her Chihuahua and Saint Bernard.

LEAH KUENZI is pursuing an MFA at Georgia College in Milledgeville, Georgia. She previously spent several years in nonprofit fundraising before committing fulltime to the writing life. Other interests include step aerobics, cheese-intensive cooking, starting (but rarely finishing) home improvement projects, and listening to every podcast under the sun.

DORIE LaRUE teaches writing at Louisiana State University in Shreveport. She has published poems, short stories, book reviews, a novel, and a poetry collection.

HALEY LASCHÉ is a yoga teacher and writing professor. Her poems have appeared in such places as *Nasty Women & Bad Hombres*, *Hartskill Review*, and *Nice Cage*. She has two poetry chapbooks: *Where It Leads* (Red Bird Chapbooks, 2016) and *Blood and Survivor* (Locofo Chaps, 2017).

L. N. LEWIS lives in Detroit and has been writing since childhood in various genres: fiction, poetry, stage plays, screenplays, journalism, and essays. The online magazine, *RaceBaitr*, recently published her essay, "Three Arrests, One Strangulation, and $2."

TRACY K. LEWIS teaches at the State University of New York, Oswego, with the rank of Distinguished Teaching Professor of Spanish. His poems in English, Spanish, and Guaraní have been published in three books of poetry, and in various journals, including *Blueline*, *Qualitative Inquiry*, *Confluencia*, and *Discurso Literario*.

HELENA LIPSTADT was born in Berlin and lives in Los Angeles and Blue Hill, Maine. She mentors young writers at Hollywood High School in Los Angeles and designs native plant gardens.

TRAVIS MADDEN is a current student of Towson University's Professional Writing graduate program. He was born in Washington, D.C., and raised in Baltimore.

C. S. MALERICH grew up in northern New Jersey. Her fiction has appeared in *Ares Magazine* and *Among Animals* anthologies; a first novel, *Fire & Locket*, was published in 2019. *The Factory Witches of Lowell*, a historical fantasy about labor organizing and magic, is forthcoming from Tor.com in November 2020.

ALLIE MARINI is a cross-genre Southern writer. In addition to her work on the page, Allie was a 2017 Oakland Poetry Slam team member. She writes poetry, fiction, and essays, performing in the Bay Area, where, as a lifelong Floridian, she is always cold. Find her online at alliemarini.com or at @kiddeternity.

DEBORAH MARR writes from a tiny cabin in the hills of Los Angeles, which she shares with her husband, son, and little white terrier. She was once the lyricist and singer for local band Glen Iris, and today she works for the Huntington Library, spending ridiculous amounts of time writing Instagram captions.

V. C. McCABE is an Appalachian poet and the author of *Give the Bard a Tetanus Shot* (Vegetarian Alcoholic Press, 2019). Her Pushcart-nominated work has been featured in exhibits and journals worldwide, including the Kurt Vonnegut Museum & Library, *Poet Lore*, *Prairie Schooner*, *The Minnesota Review*, *Appalachian Heritage*, and *Tar River Poetry*. Her website is vcmccabe.com.

JASON MORPHEW lives in Laurel Canyon with his family.

RYAN NAPIER is the author of *Four Stories about the Human Face* (Bull City Press). His stories have appeared in *Queen Mob's Tea House*, *minor literature[s]*, and elsewhere. He lives in Massachusetts. Find more information at ryannapier.net and on Twitter at @ryanlnapier.

ROBBI NESTER is the author of four books of poems, the most recent being *Narrow Bridge* (Main Street Rag, 2019). She has also edited two anthologies. Her poetry, reviews, and essays have been widely published.

KUNJANA PARASHAR is a poet living in Mumbai. Her poems appear or are forthcoming in *SWWIM Every Day*, *Borderlands: Texas Poetry Review*, *The Indianapolis Review*, *UCity Review*, *Heavy Feather Review*, and elsewhere.

VIVIAN FAITH PRESCOTT was born and raised in Southeastern Alaska and lives at her fishcamp on the small island of Wrangell in the Alexander Archipelago. She holds an MFA from the University of Alaska. Her poetry has appeared in *Prairie Schooner*, *Yellow Medicine Review*, and elsewhere.

KATHLEEN ROONEY is a founding editor of Rose Metal Press, a nonprofit publisher of literary work in hybrid genres, as well as a founding member of Poems While You Wait. Her most recent books include the national bestseller, *Lillian Boxfish Takes a Walk* and *Cher Ami and Major Whittlesey*, forthcoming in August 2020.

ROTA is a member of the MMPR Collective and the Interfaith Poets, and an editor of *Knights' Library Magazine*. His work has been featured in *Button Poetry*, *Entropy*, and elsewhere. His chapbook, *Giveth and Taketh*, is forthcoming from Wild Pressed Books. By day, he supervises law students who provide legal services to veterans.

WLS is a poet. She earned her MFA in Creative Writing from Indiana University. Monster House Press published her chapbook, *Psychogynecology*, in 2015. Her work has appeared in print and online on Poets.org and in *The Portland Review*, among other outlets. She lives in Bloomington, Indiana.

KELLY R. SAMUELS is a Pushcart Prize and Best of the Net nominee. She is the author of *Words Some of Us Rarely Use* (Unsolicited Press) and *Zeena / Zenobia Speaks* (Finishing Line Press). Her poems have appeared in numerous journals including *Salt Hill*, *The Carolina Quarterly*, and *Heron Tree*.

ASHLEY SHELBY is the author of *Muri*, *South Pole Station*, and a work of narrative history about a catastrophic flood in North Dakota. Her fiction and nonfiction have been published in many literary journals, including the *Los Angeles Review* and the *Southeast Review*.

ERIC SHONKWILER is the author of *Above All Men, 8th Street Power & Light*, and *Moon Up, Past Full*. He was selected as a Coil Book Award winner, a Midwest Connections Pick by the Midwest Independent Booksellers Association, and a New River Gorge Winter Writer-in-Residence in West Virginia.

MATT TOMPKINS is the author of the novel *Odsburg* (Ooligan Press). His stories have appeared in *Puerto del Sol* and *Monkeybicycle*, among other outlets. He works as a copy editor and lives in Virginia with his wife and daughter.

DONNIE WELCH teaches creative writing at the Rebecca School for Autism and freelances as an environmental journalist specializing in the digital divide in Appalachia and rural America.

WENDI WHITE currently muses among the herons and egrets of Coastal Virginia's tidewater region where she cares for a small wetland, one spouse, two sons, and a naughty puppy named Rafiki.

SHANNA YETMAN's fiction has most recently appeared online in *Jellyfish Review*. Her story, "The Miracle Is to Walk This Earth," was the winner for the *New Millennium Writings* 39th Flash Fiction Competition. Shanna lives in Chicago with her husband, Peter, and her two children, Gabriel and Nora.

PUBLICATION

Acknowledgments

- "Planetarium" was previously published in *Fiction Southeast*.
- "Reconnaissance" was previously published by Barking Sycamore Press.
- "Chez Magnifique" was previously published in *The Carolina Quarterly* and in the chapbook *Topia*.
- "And in Barrow, Roses Will Bloom" was previously published in *Jet Fuel Review*.
- "Carbon" was previously published in *Ibis Head Review*.
- "Post-Katrina Mardi-Gras" and "Crossing Portages" were previously published in the chapbook *Drenched*.
- "LinkedIn Thought You Might Be Interested in This Post-Climate Impact Job: Environmental Migrant Management and Soil-Free Solutions" and "Ruination Day: What the Great Depression Told Us about Climate Change, and Why We Should've Listened" were previously published in *The Coil*.
- "Avalanche" was previously published in the book *dead boy*.
- "Southern Cryptozoology: Altamaha-ha" was previously published in the chapbook *Southern Cryptozoology*.
- "Color Blind" was previously published in *Eclectica Magazine* and in *Eclectica Magazine Speculative VI*.
- "Watching Sandy on the Weather Channel, October 2012" was previously published in *Broadsided*.
- "Ronald Reagan Was an Idiot (and other observations about my birth year)" was previously published on *Entropy*.
- "Watershed" was previously published in the book *Give the Bard a Tetanus Shot*.
- "The New World" was previously published in *L'Éphémère Review*.
- "No Firm Fortress: Reading and Mourning *Moby-Dick* on the Cusp of Climate Change" was previously published in *Los Angeles Review of Books*.
- "Honeymoon in Temporary Locations" was previously published in *Arcturus*.
- "rising" was previously published in *Muddy River Poetry Review*.
- "Shifting landscape" was previously published in *The Adirondack Review*.
- "First Light June" was previously published in *A Dangerous New World: Maine Voices on the Climate Crisis*.
- "Alive with the Others: Steller Sea Lions" was previously published in *Story Quarterly*.
- "Raptured in Kudzu" was previously published in *Sonora Review*.
- "Emergent Norm Theory and Post-Climate Change Impact: Appendix A" was previously published in *Enizagam Magazine*.
- "They Are Still Building It" was previously published in *Apparition Literary Magazine*.
- "Last Snow" was previously published in the book *Moon Up, Past Full*.
- "Some Things Only God Can Do" was previously published in *Poets Reading the News*.

COLOPHON

and Permissions

The edition you are holding is the First Edition of this publication.

The bold title font is DIN, created by Albert-Jan Pool. The cursive font is Dialova, created by Alde Design, with full commercial license. The electronic text font is Alcubierre, created by Matt Ellis. The Alternating Current Press logo is Portmanteau, created by JLH Fonts. All other text is Athelas, created by José Scaglione and Veronika Burian. All fonts are used with permission; all rights reserved.

The Alternating Current lightbulb logo was created by Leah Angstman, ©2013, 2020 Alternating Current. The globe divider was created by Ocal, courtesy of Clker.

The cover artwork was created by Leah Angstman, Susan Cipriano, and Gerd Altmann. Images used with permission; all rights reserved.

All other material was created, designed, modified, or edited by Leah Angstman. All material is used with permission; all rights reserved.

Other Works from
ALTERNATING CURRENT PRESS

All of these books (and more) are available at
Alternating Current's website: press.alternatingcurrentarts.com.

alternatingcurrentarts.com